EDITH AND KIM

CHARLOTTE PHILBY worked for the *Independent* for eight years as a columnist, editor and reporter, and was shortlisted for the Cudlipp Prize for her investigative journalism at the 2013 Press Awards. A former contributing editor and feature writer at *Marie Claire*, she has written for the *New Statesman*, *Elle*, *Telegraph*, *Guardian* and *Sunday Times*, been interviewed on BBC Radio 3's *Free Thinking*, BBC Radio 4's *Loose Ends* and presented documentaries for the BBC World Service and *The One Show*. Charlotte is the granddaughter of Kim Philby, Britain's most infamous communist double-agent, the elusive 'third man' in the notorious Cambridge spy ring. This is her fourth novel.

Praise for *Edith and Kim*

'Completely fascinating. A sophisticated and brilliantly constructed
fictional retelling of a crucial relationship in 20th century
espionage history. A tremendous achievement'
WILLIAM BOYD

'A tense and brilliantly structured story of power and intrigue . . .
I couldn't put it down'
JANE SHEMILT

'Philby's stunning fourth novel thrusts this former bit-player in the
Cambridge Spy scandal to the centre stage where she belongs.
Edith and Kim combines the authenticity of your favourite true
crime podcast, the intrigue of a spy novel and the page-turning
grip of a psychological thriller – all wrapped up in beautiful,
evocative prose that transports the reader to shady corners of
1930s London and Vienna. Her best book yet'
ERIN KELLY

'A dextrous writer who gives her tale a quickening,
thrillerish propulsion'
NEW STATESMAN

'In *Edith and Kim*, Charlotte Philby brings to life a dangerous
game of shadows that kept me reading late into the night. A
dark, atmospheric and addictive novel'
CHRIS POWER

'Wonderful. Beautiful writing, evocative setting, fascinating
story and so very moving'
LAURA SHEPHERD-ROBINSON

'A fine achievement'
THE TIMES

'Complex and powerfully written . . . a persuasive repurposing
of the lives of real-life figures'
i NEWSPAPER

'Impeccably researched and atmospheric'
DAILY MAIL

Also by Charlotte Philby

Part of the Family
A Double Life
The Second Woman

EDITH AND KIM

CHARLOTTE PHILBY

THE BOROUGH PRESS

The Borough Press
An imprint of HarperCollins*Publishers* Ltd
1 London Bridge Street
London SE1 9GF

www.harpercollins.co.uk

HarperCollins*Publishers*
Macken House,
39/40 Mayor Street Upper,
Dublin 1
D01 C9W8
Ireland

This paperback edition 2023
2

First published by HarperCollins*Publishers* 2022

A catalogue record for this book is available from the British Library

ISBN: 978-0-00-846641-1

This novel is entirely a work of fiction.
The names, characters and incidents portrayed in it are
the work of the author's imagination. Any resemblance to
actual persons, living or dead, events or localities is
entirely coincidental.

Excerpt from *Four Quartets* by T.S. Eliot reprinted with permission from Faber and Faber Ltd.

Set in Garamond by Palimpsest Book Production Limited, Falkirk, Stirlingshire
Printed and bound in the UK using 100% renewable electricity at CPI Group (UK) Ltd

MIX
Paper | Supporting
responsible forestry
FSC™ C007454
www.fsc.org

This book is produced from independently certified FSC™ paper
to ensure responsible forest management.

For more information visit: www.harpercollins.co.uk/green

In memory of John Philby, 1943–2009

Author's note

There have been countless books written about the double agent Kim Philby, often with conflicting views on the hows and the whys and, indeed, the whos. Far fewer have been written about Edith Tudor-Hart, the woman who recruited him, referred to in British intelligence files as 'the foreign woman'.

What follows is not meant as a comprehensive retelling of a highly contentious period, but a work of fiction based on the facts as I have variously found them, reimagining the lives of two people from starkly different backgrounds whose very existences transformed one another's, and changed the course of history.

While much of this story is true, *Edith and Kim* is a novel. In pulling together strands of the principal characters' lives into a work of fiction, I have chosen to exclude certain family members and friends on both sides, either because it didn't feel fair or right to include them, or simply because they didn't serve the version of events as I have reconstructed it. Some characters in the story are entirely invented.

For suggestions of non-fiction books I have leaned on and drawn from in my research, or simply been inspired by, please see the reading list at the end of this novel.

NOTE: The Secret Intelligence Service files used within are faithfully reproduced - including some inconsistencies, not least the interchangeable use of the names Litzi and Lizzy, and the conflicting dates on which Edith is believed to have joined the Communist cause. Where names have been redacted, this has been done in line with the documents found at the National Archives in Kew. In places, I have also removed sections of text where the names or events referenced are not part of the story I am telling. Where this happens, I have indicated so in the text.

'Every generation bears the ineluctable stamp of the strategic historical experiences to which it has been exposed. The history of Soviet youth, and indeed of Soviet society, has been a unique tale of turmoil in a turbulent age.'

Merle Fainsod, 'The Komsomols: A Study of Youth Under Dictatorship', *American Political Science Review*, 1951

'It was an idea. This kind of resonance [could not be] achieved through organisation, nor through propaganda. Only an idea has the power to disseminate itself so broadly.'

Ludwig Mies van der Rohe, third and final director of the Bauhaus

'In the hands of the person who uses it with feeling and imagination, the camera becomes very much more than the means of earning a living, it becomes a vital factor in recording and influencing the life of the people and in promoting human understanding.'

Edith Tudor-Hart, from the essay 'Photography as a profession', written for the magazine *Housewife*, 1945

'It is rarely the risky operation that brings most danger . . . The real risks can be assessed in advance and precaution taken to obviate them. It is the almost meaningless incident that often puts us in mortal hazard.'

Kim Philby, *My Silent War*, 1968

Time present and time past
Are both perhaps present in time future,
And time future contained in time past.
If all time is eternally present
All time is unredeemable.
What might have been is an abstraction
Remaining a perpetual possibility
Only in a world of speculation.
What might have been and what has been
Point to one end, which is always present.
Footfalls echo in the memory
Down the passage which we did not take
Towards the door we never opened
Into the rose-garden. My words echo
Thus, in your mind.
   But to what purpose
Disturbing the dust on a bowl of rose-leaves
I do not know.

               'Burnt Norton', *Four Quartets*, T.S. Eliot

All history is fiction

Dear Edith,

I've just received copies of various articles about yours truly, in the British press, sent via my children. The *Observer* pictures were a bit more flattering than the ones in the *Daily Mail*; thankfully I am much too old to worry about my looks. Much mention of Cambridge. It rather leads me to wonder what bothers them more: what I did, or the fact of who I was. The Third Man, apparently - poor buggers can't even count.

Old Guy is also getting rather a time of it on account of his taste in men, it seems to me. Hypocritical bastards. You should hear the stories he tells about his days at Eton . . . !

It's all rather strange, reading about oneself in the papers. For a moment, I find myself taking umbrage at something that is said, and which I know to be a total fiction, but then I am reminded that what others think of us is none of our business, and should be of little interest. It is not, after all, what they think of us so much as a reflection of what they think of themselves; of what they loathe and envy in others.

It was A.A. Milne who said it best: 'Every human being is a mystery and nobody knows the truth about anybody else.'

Yours,

Kim

Prologue

London, June 1934

The journey from Marble Arch to Regent's Park takes longer than it should.

Despite the morning sun, the woman wears a dark turtle-neck and long skirt, a beret pulled down over bobbed hair. She moves quickly, sticking to the shadows. The man, a few years her junior, keeps pace, his hands pushed deep into the pockets of his overcoat, the bit of his pipe clenched between his teeth.

There is a portentous quality to the silence as they turn into Hyde Park, the scuffling of horse-hooves closing in from behind causing him to clench his fists until the sound passes, the morning riders kicking up dust as they skirt the perimeter.

A bead of sweat forms on his forehead as they turn left, away from the grass, and cross Park Lane. The streets that slice through Mayfair are blessedly shaded as they continue their walk for an hour or so, along New Bond Street and Shaftesbury Avenue, the woman's eyes focused ahead but alert to every sound as the city comes to life: peals of laughter from a young couple bursting out from a doorway, the clatter of a rag-and-bone man fading into the echoes of a thousand muted voices, layered over one another across the city's streets.

Somewhere near Aldwych she hails a taxi, the man ducking in beside her, a ripple of electricity passing between them, along with unspoken questions, as his hand accidentally brushes hers.

London skids past on the other side of the glass, the two passengers facing away from one another, their attention fixed on the scenes playing out on their respective sides of the street as they head back the way they came: children skipping behind impatient parents; lovers walking arm-in-arm, locked in their own private world, faces tipped upwards like buttercups in the morning rays. A doorman outside the Ritz adjusts his cufflinks as they roll back along Piccadilly, stifling a yawn, his eyes flicking up, suddenly aware that he is being watched.

The couple inside the motor-car sit in silence until, after a while, the woman leans forward and asks the driver to stop. The response to her distinct Austrian lilt is an immediate slowing of wheels. She steps out and the man follows her, their footsteps weaving an invisible web. A while later still, she holds her arm out again, flagging down another passing cab; this time her companion pauses, raising his hand to his pipe, opening his mouth as if to speak.

But the words fall away as he steps in behind her, one of them the spider, the other the fly.

By the time they reach Maida Vale tube station more than two hours have passed.

The sound of their own footsteps follows as they take the stairs to the platform. It is cooler down here, below ground.

The man bristles with nervous energy as the train approaches; a rat scuttles across the tracks and disappears into the black. The woman boards first, her companion stepping in behind, his thoughts turning briefly to his mother and father far from home, somewhere on the other side of the world.

Home. The word comes to her as they stand side by side in the carriage, and she lets it roll a moment in her mind, her thoughts tilting this way and that, unable to find a flat surface on which to land.

'I do beg your pardon.' The passenger seems to appear from nowhere, catching her eye momentarily as he squeezes past, touching the brim of his hat. Without warning, as the doors start to close, the woman takes her companion's hand and pulls him out of the carriage, leading him across the empty concourse to the opposite platform where another train hurtles towards them, the sound of the brakes escalating into a scream.

It is only once they are on the path cutting through Regent's Park, some four hours after they set off, that the man finally speaks.

'He is expecting us?'

The woman says nothing in reply, only slowing slightly, allowing her charge to move ahead as they catch sight of a figure on the bench: short, stocky frame, boxer's ears partly obscured beneath a hat.

Alert to their footsteps, the man looks up.

Instinctively the younger man, out of breath from all the walking, takes the pipe from his lips, turning briefly towards his chaperone. But she has already gone.

The fact of who I was

One of Edith Suschitzky's most formative memories is her father's first arrest, though she wasn't there. It isn't possible, some would say, to recall an event one hasn't witnessed. But Edith Suschitzky lived with that day, on a loop, either regaled to her as a medal of defiance over family lunches, or whispered into her ear at night as she fell asleep, as a warning: *Never let them break you. They will never let you be free.* When you grow up with a story, the way she has grown up with this one, it becomes partly your own.

The story of that day in 1920, not long after her twelfth birthday, at the bookshop at Favoritenstrasse 57, refracts in Edith's memory, parts of it growing more or less vivid with every retelling. On some days, she focuses on the smell of diesel and yeast carried on the air from the bakers along the street as the shop door creaks open, her father looking up from the counter, his eyes instantly hardening. On others, she pictures the officer's shadow obliterating the doorway, homes in on the shine of his boot as he makes his way unhurriedly through the store, his fingers running over the spines.

Both Edith and her brother Wolf – now eight years old – have already headed to school. The fog had risen thick that morning, blanketing the city's streets, obscuring Wilhelm

Suschitzky's view as he made his way past the brickworks and the row of shops that led to Brüder Suschitzky: *the first Socialist bookshop in Vienna's tenth district of over 120,000 people.* These were the exact words he had used to his wife, Adele, the day he and his brother Philipp had first pulled back the doors in the autumn of 1901.

Already, those days felt like another lifetime. Post-war, the world had changed. *Life* had changed – though not as much as it would, not least for a business which extolled the virtues of enlightenment in one of city's largest working-class districts, first simply as a bookshop and then, for the past eight years, also as a publisher.

Wilhelm paused that morning, as he did every morning before opening up, to take in the shop and its evidence of a life's work: the original sign, BUCHHANDLUNG ANTIQUARIAT, now hanging alongside a second sign advertising Anzengruber-Verlag publishers.

From the moment the men had first opened the doors to Brüder Suschitzky almost two decades earlier – long before either of them could have envisaged what fate had in store – it was more than just a business. This was a manifesto for the world the Suschitzky brothers had wanted for the children they were yet to have. A middle-class family choosing to live amidst the poverty and the oppression of the working classes, dirt steeped in a growing sense of despair, the Suschitzky brothers – and their books – were consciously paraded as a bastion of hope.

It was this hope, Wilhelm would tell his daughter, soberly, as he stroked her hair at night, that the officials were trying to shut down when they came and seized the tomes and leaflets, novels and texts, from workers' poetry to tracts on the women's movement, pedagogical reform and sexual emancipation. That first time – the officers storming through their shop, trampling not just the carpet but the very fabric of their lives – was the ultimate act of aggression. And yet, Wilhelm would recall, repeating the events of that day as one might a lullaby, seeing those men there in their perfectly pressed clothes, their well-fed bellies moving self-righteously through the world he and his brother had created, he hadn't cowered. Rather, Edith's father had felt himself stand taller. A self-proclaimed pacifist, he hadn't lashed out. He had refused to fight in a way against which they could have immediately retaliated.

But he never stopped fighting in the years that followed, as the harassment escalated along with the confiscation of books, the court trials worsening as Austria's democratic government fell. Wilhelm Suschitzky fought quietly – he fought with his mind, he would tell Edith, proudly. And he never stopped fighting. Right up until the moment he held a gun to his own head.

When she was ten years old, Edith Suschitzky had pursued an argument with her father over supper as he condemned the attempted *coup d'état* by the newly formed KPÖ, the Communist Party of Austria, claiming that violence was not the answer, that it undermined the efforts that men like him had been making for years. (*Men*, she noted.) It wasn't simply that she disagreed, she replied – more horrifying was the fact that someone she loved so dearly could think so strangely. A man who had seen with his own eyes the bodies floating in the Danube.

'Books and ideas alone aren't enough,' she had chastised Wilhelm in no uncertain terms. 'You can't feed a dying man with thoughts.'

'Your voice,' he had snorted, marvelling at her passion. 'It teeters at the edge of some terrible catastrophe. You are just a child, you cannot understand.'

But she did understand, innately, and with a received wisdom gathered over the weekends spent in Grundlsee; she felt it, vibrating through the words of the scholars at the camp organised by Eugenie Schwarzwald, sorrow hovering over the brushstrokes of the artists she met there, resonating through the semi-quavers and crotchets of composer Arnold Schoenberg as he taught. She understood in a way that, once acknowledged, was impossible for her to ignore.

Change requires action.

'Father, for an atheist,' she replied, 'you do love to preach.'

'Preach on, St John.'

This is as much as the boy hears before the men's voices lower again so that Kim cannot decipher the rest of the conversation, beyond the odd snatched words: *Hashemites* and *Gertrude Bell.*

Not that it is of much interest anyway. The child's eavesdropping is little more than a way to pass the time until his father's attention is – if only briefly – his again.

Looking about him, Kim strains his eyes to adjust to the brightness of the sun, which burns as hot as tar, its harsh glare stretching across the sky and the endless dust beneath their feet, bouncing off the stone of the building's archway, where they now stand.

He has not long since stepped off the plane from London, and the Trans Jordan heat prickles at his skin – though he won't show his discomfort. Despite his weariness, and his thirst, and the increasing need for shade, he works hard to hold himself straight as his father talks to the other man, to whom the child has not been introduced.

'You know you shouldn't be listening.'

The voice startles him. When he turns, he is greeted by a plump young woman with blonde curls and an amused, precocious smile.

'I wasn't,' the boy replies, his cheeks colouring, the words *And you should not creep up on people* sticking to the back of his throat.

'That's my father, talking to yours. Your name's Kim, isn't it?'

Kim turns away from her, slightly, regarding the heavy black beard and white robes, his father's appearance growing more swarthy and unkempt with every moment that has passed since he was sent to the Emir Abdullah as chief British representative, two years earlier, following a short spell in Baghdad where – so the boy has gleaned – he made no secret of being in favour of a republic rather than a monarchy.

'Yes, St John is my father,' Kim says, pulling himself upright.

Something about this woman – the haughty voice and knowing eyes – makes him uncomfortable; and yet he finds himself keen to impress her, working hard to disguise the stutter that occasionally peppers his speech.

'Kim is a nickname, actually. After the character in my father's favourite novel—'

'Kim, the boy with two separate sides to his head . . . You look surprised – did you imagine I wouldn't have read Kipling?'

When the boy doesn't reply, she continues. 'My father says your father is a very difficult man. He says he is firmly against the policy of the British government.'

'Well, perhaps that's because your father lacks the imagination, or the vocabulary, to truly understand a man such as mine.'

She laughs. 'I like your spirit. My father also says St John is pugnacious. Do you know what that means?'

'Do you?'

'Yes. Although English isn't my first language.'

'What is?'

'Russian.'

Kim regards her, his eyes narrowing. 'Say something to me in Russian, then.'

'What would you like me to say?'

'I don't know. Introduce yourself.'

'Добрый день, меня зовут Флора Соломон – приятно познакомиться, наглое дитя.'

'What did you say?'

'Learn Russian and then you'll find out.'

'My father speaks ten languages,' Kim replies.

'And what about you?'

He shrugs. 'I spoke Hindi before I even spoke English. I was born in India – I nearly died when I was a boy. My ayah found a cobra in the bath; if my father hadn't come along and shot at it, I would be dead.'

'How very shocking.'

Kim struggles to hold himself upright, feeling the woman consider him, an amused look on her face.

'I have a son,' she says. 'He's only two years old. How old are you, Kim?'

'Eleven.'

'Small for your age, aren't you?'

'Not really.'

'My son is Peter; we live in London. You do, too, don't you?'

'18 Acol Road, Hampstead. My father lives here, and I stay in England with my mother and three sisters.'

'Well, in that case, young Kim, perhaps our paths will cross again.' The woman smiles, turning away from him.

'Hey, what's your name? You never said.'

The woman looks back at him briefly, her expression becoming serious. 'I did tell you – it's Flora Solomon – you just weren't listening.'

Listening a moment, her ear pressed against the wood, Edith Suschitzky turns and glances briefly over her shoulder before pushing open the door and stepping inside.

It is January 1926, six years after Wilhelm Suschitzky's first arrest and the same year that Adolf Hitler publishes the second volume of his autobiographical manifesto, *Mein Kampf*, in which he sets out his ambition to create a union between his birth country and Germany by any means possible.

Edith is not yet eighteen, though the men who wish to sleep with her and then discard her would say she could be taken for so much older. When she speaks, her words are urgent and melodic, demanding a response.

On the cusp of adulthood and tall for a girl, she knows how to hold herself – but she is also used to ducking and she does so now, pushing through the doorway into the darkened room where she is met with a sea of faces in profile, all fixed on a man at the front of the room. The smell inside is of smoke and hope and youthful indignation, the space cramped and energetic, the number of attendees seeming to swell with each week that passes. Usually she would smile at this thought but this evening she is distracted as she leans back against the wall, the man's voice floating in and out of range.

'To speak of democracy when working people are starving, exhausted, unable to clothe their children because of the bourgeois capitalist machine that seeks to keep them captive, is contemptuous. The state exists for the purpose of the oppression of one class by another.'

Running a finger over her coat, she feels a damp spot where the boy, Helmut, had clung to her and wept.

The speaker continues more intensely, the energy of the crowd turning febrile.

'There is only one response to such a threat, and that is to demolish it. The Red Army didn't claim victory by asking for it nicely. There was only one difference between the Bolsheviks and the Mensheviks, *one* reason why we prevailed – the simple reason that Bolsheviks are prepared to *fight*. We fought and we won. But, comrades, the revolution doesn't *end* with victory. Victory is only the beginning.'

There is no applause, the speech giving way to galvanised conversation, Litzi at the centre gathering leaflets.

'I know you, don't I?'

The voice belongs to a man: shorter than Edith, and stocky. His blue eyes remind her of the lakes in Sweden years before – a summer of physical recuperation for the children whose schools were commandeered. Children who, once the wounded piled in, spent their days digging vegetable patches, collecting smoking material for the soldiers maimed in the *war to end all wars*, which of course ended none.

'I don't think so. Perhaps you've seen me here,' she says.

He continues to stare. 'This isn't your first meeting?'

'No.'

'What did you think of the speaker?'

'I think he would have been more convincing if he hadn't gone barefoot.' Her dark eyes move to a pair of shoes discarded in the corner. 'There is enough to be angry about without cheap tricks to demonstrate solidarity.'

'What's your name?'

She pauses. There is something familiar about the man's face, or perhaps they have been staring at one another too long.

'Edith!' Litzi moves through the crowd towards her, thick waves of hair bouncing off her shoulders, as if struggling to keep up. 'You made it!'

Edith smiles, squeezing her friend's hand. 'I'm sorry I was late. There was a problem at kindergarten. The boy I told you about – there was no one to pick him up.'

Litzi frowns, reassuringly, before turning to their companion. 'I don't believe we have met.'

Edith takes the long route home, stopping to listen to the strains of an accordion, tossing the last of her Schillings into the beggar's cap, and slipping a leaflet underneath:

Einheitsfront Aktion: Gegen faschistische reaktion. United front against Fascist reaction.

'Where have you been?' Wilhelm asks, his tone reprimanding, in the doorway of the apartment.

'Helmut, the boy whose mother has TB . . . no one came for him. I had to wait.' Only a partial lie.

'You are a good girl, Edith. You have a good heart. Rudolf Serkin is waiting for you.'

In the living room he sits, long limbs wedged awkwardly under the piano, fingers spread wide on his knees, practising a silent arpeggio. The room is warm compared to the night air, a dim lamp perched on top of the piano illuminating the blush on Rudolf's cheeks as he watches her, his eyes bugging behind thick glasses as she takes off her coat.

Edith closes the door behind her. 'I lost track of time. I do apologise, Rudolf.'

'It's not so late,' he says, resting his thick fingers above the keys.

'Play something for me while I warm my hands,' she replies, slowly pulling off her gloves, enjoying his discomfort.

Rudolf shifts on the stool, his whole body preparing to yield. And then it does, the raw pain of his notes fracturing the silence.

When he stops, tears run down her cheeks.

'Have I upset you?'

'No.'

'You have been practising?'

'As much as I can, between work and—'

'Then not enough,' he says. 'Only after five hours am I sufficiently warmed up to start playing.'

'But Rudolf, you are a professional—'

'Because I practise. Because I have dedicated myself. It is one thing to want something – in order to have it you have to make it happen, Edith. No one else can do it for you.'

Enough time has passed since their first interaction that Edith would be forgiven for doing a double-take when she feels him fall into step beside her as she makes her way along Petzvalgasse, the early-morning air thick with the scent of industry and unemployment. But when she looks up and finds him there, regarding her with the same intensity that he had at the meeting, everyone and everything else falls away so that it is just them: two hearts throbbing amidst cobbles and brick.

Years later, it will be said that the first thing you notice about Arnold Deutsch is his eyes. He looks at you as if nothing more important in life, or more interesting than you and talking to you, exists at that moment.

'How did you know where I live?'

'I remembered where I've seen you. Your father owns the bookshop Brüder Suschitzky.'

'I'm on my way to work,' Edith replies.

'Ah, yes, you mustn't keep the infants waiting . . . It is

commendable, truly, to have made it through Lili Roubiczek's methods, at your age: living in the school during the week, theoretical training in the evenings, the study of psychology, architecture and the natural sciences. How long were you there, three months? And you were what – sixteen, seventeen years old?'

'Am I supposed to be impressed, or frightened?'

'I don't believe you are easily frightened, Edith Suschitzky. To make the journey to London alone to train under Maria Montessori, you must be brave. And you must have done well to have been chosen . . .'

'You know they say talking to yourself is the first sign of madness?'

The man smiles. 'I'll come and meet you when you have finished work.'

'I don't know when—'

'I'll find you.'

Inside, the nursery is cold. When they forget their hunger, the children play, their heavy coats too small or too big, or sometimes with no coat at all.

Helmut doesn't play. When the others are outside, Edith pulls out the scraps of food she had taken from breakfast and watches him chew, the movements of his mouth slow and deliberate.

'It will be OK,' Edith tells him, but it won't.

The hours pass slowly, but Edith's mind moves quickly, keeping her warm. Before leaving, she stops in front of the window. In the reflection of the glass she watches herself pull fingers through bobbed hair that looks dark in one light, pale in another, before turning away.

Her eyes search for him as she takes her usual route back towards Favoriten, but he is nowhere to be seen until suddenly he is there, moving alongside her.

They walk in silence a while, the wind tapping at their shoulders.

'Your father is an impressive man.'

Edith pictures Wilhelm behind the small wooden counter, his eyes fixed on the pages of a book – drinking in another man's plight, his own personal tipple.

Her stomach rumbles, and the man pulls out an apple bun from the bag he is carrying. Edith pauses then takes it, considering something before taking a bite, her hunger intensifying with every mouthful.

'If it's information on my father that you want, then it would be easier to go to him directly.'

'We both know that if I were after Wilhelm Suschitzky, I would not need to go via his daughter. Your parents are free-thinkers. Wilhelm is a loyal advocate of the SDAP. I respect his values, to a point. But his beliefs do not go far enough.'

Edith turns, watching his lips move as he speaks.

'The problem with Social Democratic parties is that they refuse to acknowledge the reality of the state – i.e. with the proletariat positioned as the ruling class, which is fundamentally at odds with the possibility of reformism. The *philistine illusions about the "peaceful development of democracy"*. You have read these words?'

Edith shakes her head.

'Vladimir Ilyich Lenin, founder and leader of the first socialist state. My dear Edith, a whole new world awaits.'

Their tête-a-têtes continue over the coming months, at first with an affected spontaneity – him turning up outside her work or home, appearing beside her in a crowd as if he had always been there – and then with a uniformity that brings new punctuation to Edith's days, transporting them beyond Vienna's streets to the unspoiled forest land that lies to the west and south of the city.

Work, home, piano, meetings. Him.

Some days they walk as they talk, drifting in their own bubble through the crowds. Other days, they go back to the apartment and make love in his bed, Edith working hard to ignore the woman's comb in the bathroom. He was born in Czechoslovakia and moved to Vienna as a child, he tells her. He studies psychology, philosophy and chemistry at the University of Vienna. He supports the theories of Wilhelm Reich and runs clinics designed to bring birth control and sexual enlightenment to the workers in his adopted homeland. He quotes Karl Marx: *a new world order which will free the human race from exploitation and alienation.* He strokes her hair and tells her it is possible to think of a world where there are no social differences, where there is no religious prejudice, where everyone will be paid the same.

When he touches her, she feels like both a woman and a child.

But today he is late. Edith holds the book inside her coat, relishing the pressure of the cover pressed up against her heart; her heart which slowly flips at the sight of him. He sits slightly away from her, distracted. She catches a trace of perfume and then it is gone, replaced by the smell of burning that still hangs over the city, days after they pulled the final bodies from the rubble; the smell of death drifting on the air far beyond the Palace of Justice, serving as a reminder. It hasn't been given its name yet – the July Revolt of 1927 as it will be remembered, once safely indexed away in the back pages of a history book, a neat memorial at the Wiener Zentralfriedhof to honour the dead. For now, it is still the footprints of angry people met with police truncheons; someone's child reduced to skin cells and body parts; flames flickering against a night sky.

She hands him a copy of Bruno Frei's *Das Elend Wiens* from inside her coat, adjusting her horn-rimmed spectacles. 'To congratulate you on obtaining your chemistry PhD. I heard Josefine telling one of the other teachers.'

He places his fingers closer to hers. 'Don't be jealous, Edith. You are not so bourgeois.'

'I'm not jealous, I just wonder at it, that's all. Two women both working at the Montessori school, both captive to your attentions. I wonder why you need us both – why you wouldn't choose me.'

'Your father would never allow it.' His voice is matter-of-fact.

A newspaper cartwheels in front of them, the headline: *Wiener Justizpalastbrand* and beneath it: *89 protestors and five policemen dead.*

He takes the book. 'Have you read it?'

'Yes.'

'What did you think?'

'I like the way he talks about commitment to revolutionary activism and change. But I prefer his photographs – there is a truth in a photograph.' She takes out a cigarette. 'In Montessori, we photograph the children at play as a means of pupil observation. Did Josefine tell you about that? If you ask a child a question, they will tell you an answer that they think you want to hear, but if you study them for yourself you will find the truth, not what they choose to tell you. It's not just about the lies we tell other people, but the lies we tell ourselves – a photo captures a person as they are, not as they choose to present themselves.'

The months roll past and Edith's circle at once widens and narrows. When he is not away performing, Rudolf Serkin comes to the house, his hands hovering above hers as they work the keys to Beethoven's sonatas, Mozart, Schubert. He impresses the importance of clean fingerwork, of discipline and rigour over feeling, making her thump out the same bars again and again until her fingers ache and blister. When she can bear no more, she sits beside him and massages the grooves of her hand while he plays for her: The 'Moonlight' sonata; Brahms' First Concerto; the fugue from Beethoven's *Hammerklavier* sonata. 'I am hard on you,' he tells her, 'because I know you can take it. You are strong. It's all in there, waiting to come out. You must study, Edith: find something you love and give it everything you have. I was talking to Schoenberg about you – he agrees you have great talent.'

While Rudolf plays, she closes her eyes and imagines someone else's breath on her neck.

Helmut's mother dies. In her nightmares Edith sees the body ravaging itself, the bacteria from the TB attacking the lungs. At meetings, men and women rally against the para-fascist movements already thriving in Austria. A chorus of voices: *These traitors to socialism – those who have supported the war of the predatory imperialists – the Scheidemanns and Eberts, Austerlitzes and Renners of this world – speak of 'pure democracy' in order to deceive and detract from the true nature of their purpose.* She meets academics and students, scientists and writers, all bound together by a common ideal. She meets a young woman by the name of Beatrix Tudor-Hart, a Cambridge graduate of classics with a mutual interest in progressive education, who speaks six languages and who introduces Edith to her brother, a medical student accompanying his sister on a research trip. He is taller than Edith, and thin, with a dimpled chin and an expression that suggests he is laughing at some private joke on matters too academic to be understood. He tells Edith his name is Alexander. He is married and has a child, though still he looks at her in a way that she recognises for what it is, and she likes it, although when she finally drifts to sleep at night the eyes that look back at her are not his, but those that remind her of the lakes in Sweden.

Dear Edith,

Another very silly piece in the papers by Miles Copeland, I noticed. I wonder whether he really believes all that Munchhausen stuff about Stephen Meade and the rest? The poor old CIA and FBI are taking a helluva beating over in the USA – press, Congress, academics, the lot. It couldn't happen here! Meanwhile, *The Times*, BBC, etc., are gleefully reporting the disastrous grain harvest, with much chortling about tightening of belts and new hardships facing the Soviet consumer. On their own showing, the drop to about five per cent is in the rate of growth – more like three per cent if confined to light industry. That, of course, is not so comfy as the ten p.c. we have become accustomed to each year, but I imagine that it is nevertheless a growth rate that Mr Wilson would be very happy to settle for. Of course, another drought or two in a row might be a little serious.

I recently caught wind of Copeland's new book. I think it was more than an ego trip. I have occasionally heard his golden voice on the wireless, and of course have been following his lively, one-way correspondence with Mr Rees-Mogg. He seems increasingly to be making himself a (probably self-appointed) apologist for the CIA. He is probably quite genuinely concerned to restore at least some of its reputation, which has been sadly eroded in recent times. That is no excuse for making wild claims about huge network operations in likely places, and it would be very easy to tear him to pieces in detail. In addition, the book seems to have been written very quickly – probably dictated at top speed; and Miles is very unfortunate in his proofreader; the book is full of slips, e.g. the Kassim-Aref coup in Iraq is put at 1947, two digits and eleven years wrong! He also ties himself up in knots when he denies the validity of the ideological motive. He says on p.147: 'I still have no firm ideas on what makes spies spy'. Precisely; if you deny the ideological motive, the question in many cases is unanswerable.

Ordinarily, I wouldn't deign to put words into your mouth, but on this I feel confident you would agree with me, dear Edith. However, Miles is a good fellow, and in denying me the ideological motive (on the grounds that he never spotted it in Beirut) he either underrated my intelligence or overrated his own. He claims that, unbeknownst to me, he was studying me; would it surprise him to learn that I was studying him – very warily! And finally, the remark about Miles attributed to me on the publishers' dust cover is obviously apocryphal; I just don't make that sort of remark, and I have never read *The Game of Nations*. Perhaps Miles would like to send me a copy of that, too? What nerve, he will remark; and he will be right. I have asked my son, via whom my copy was delivered, to thank him for this gift, and tell him that I much appreciate his good wishes and very sincerely reciprocate them. I have no objection to him retailing to Miles the above comments, with the reservation that a definitive judgment would take far too much time in what is proving to be a very busy period for me.

In other news, the ban in respect of my flat was lifted this summer. But that refers only to my immediate family, and the restrictions remain in force for anyone outside the family circle. This means that, if anyone other than family came, they would have to put up at a hotel. The bill for a ten-day stay, at three times the ordinary rate, would be truly formidable – say about three hundred roubles. Added to that, the necessity of eating every meal out would more than double the food and drink bill; they could scarcely get away with it on less than five hundred.

There is a seemingly arbitrary approach to the rules here, which change liberally. The latest change to regulations, as far as I can tell, is that my foreign currency coupons are no longer acceptable at hotel *beriozkas* or bars. By contrast, currency is not acceptable at *bori ozkas* outside hotels, only my coupons. I suppose there is some reason for these new arrangements, but it is difficult to guess what it can be.

Autumn was much as normal, with interchanging sunshine and rain, and quite a nip in the air. And now winter is upon us and we have had the first flurries of snow – always rather exciting. From my study, I have an uninterrupted view over the playground of the local school and there is always joy in watching the children in their knitted mittens, rolling snowballs with renewed wonder. It is hard to look at it and not compare it to the relative blandness of my own school days. So far the winter has been so-so; more snow than last year, but not as much as we hoped for, and with temperatures rather too near zero. Yesterday and today things have taken a turn for the better, minus ten to twelve by day, and a beautiful blue sky. We are keeping our thumbs crossed, in the hopes of skiing in the woods beyond Ma-in-law's flat next week.

As for today, I've just returned from a pleasing performance by the Royal Shakespeare Company of *All's Well That Ends Well*. And so it must be.

Yours,

Kim

New arrangements

In May 1928, a few months before Edith enrols on a foundation course at the Bauhaus, the German Federal elections are held. Only two parties make significant gains: the Social Democratic Party of Germany (SPD), which with 153 of the 491 seats remains the largest party in the Reichstag; and the Communist Party of Germany (KPD). The recently reformed Nazi Party, led by Adolf Hitler – now released from Landsberg prison, where he has been held for his involvement in a failed *coup d'état* – receives less than three per cent of the vote. Without a clear SDP majority, another coalition government is formed, led by Hermann Müller, comprising members of the SPD, the German Democratic Party, the Centre Party and the German People's Party. It is a union plagued by internal divisions from the outset, which will soon implode, with Müller quitting: a doomed coalition declared the last genuinely democratic government of the Weimar Republic.

The town of Dessau stands on the junction of the rivers Mulde and Elbe, an industrial city emerging amidst swaths of national park. A short walk over the footbridge she finds the hostel, the woman at the front desk looking up at the new arrival with weary contempt, checking her book, lifting a bundle of keys and swinging it like a jailer as they move through the hostel.

'Edith Suschitzky. You are studying at the Bauhaus, yes? There are more of you on the next floor up.'

The key rattles in the lock, revealing a single bed, a side table, a lamp, a wooden chair. 'The bathroom is there – third door on the right. Come with me: you will pay and then the room is yours.'

Edith is too wired to sleep. When it is finally time to get up for her first day of the *Vorkurs*, the foundation course in basic design, she stands and dresses in her usual uniform of dark skirt and beret, studying her skin as she brushes her teeth in the basin in the corner. Running a comb through her hair, she lifts her keys and closes the bedroom door carefully behind her, turning to find a young man around her own age in the hallway, clad in a heavily worn white linen shirt and braces, apparently waiting for her.

'You are joining the Bauhaus?' His smile is broad, and there is an openness and enthusiasm about his manner that demands reciprocation.

'Yes,' Edith says. 'I've signed up for the preliminary course.'

'Me too. I'm Maks. I just travelled overnight from Hamburg. Where are you from?'

'Vienna. I'm Edith.'

'Do you know anyone here, Edith?'

She shakes her head.

'Well, now you know me.'

Light refracts off the sculptural lines of the university buildings as they approach: an assembly of metal, glass and light rising from the grass. Nothing to give away the disquiet that rattles beneath the surface: the internal divisions that threaten to crack the foundations of the Bauhaus, as both an ideal and an institution.

'For three Marks fifty you can get two breakfasts, lunch, coffee, and dinner,' Maks says as they line up for food.

Once they are seated, he reels off their new professor's credentials between mouthfuls of potato cake, the clatter of the canteen echoing around them. 'The Royal Art School in Berlin, the School of Applied Arts in Essen, the Royal Bavarian Academy of Fine Arts in Munich . . .'

'You are his official biographer, then?'

Maks laughs. 'My cousin Stefan is one year ahead of us here; I made him tell me everything . . . My father works for the banks – he does not believe in art as an education. Stefan helped persuade him for me, otherwise I would be back in Hamburg right now. Not that Stefan cares much for the concept of art for art's sake. But we all have our own reasons, wouldn't you agree?'

The studio stands on the ground floor of the Prellerhaus, a white cubed building with four windows across and five down: twenty-eight studios within, available for use by students and junior masters, including Josef Albers, who bustles into the room in a three-piece suit, hair brushed to one side, a pile of newspapers stuffed under his arm.

As he walks, he launches into his welcome speech as if resuming an ongoing conversation with old friends.

'Ladies and gentleman, we are poor, not rich. We can't afford to waste materials or time. We have to make the most out of the least.'

Moving around the room, at pace, he hands a newspaper to each of the twenty-something men and women scattered around the room on chairs. Outside the window, a group of students gather on the grass, deep in conversation. Among them, a young woman with blonde curls, wearing a red shirt and black culottes, settles herself against a tree. At the sight of her, Edith's mind retreats back to Vienna, to the bench beneath the maple, Arnold Deutsch by her side. The lessons he taught her again and again until the words started to bleed and lose their meaning. *The colour of the shirt you wear can convey a message, be it the success or failure of a mission; or simply signalling the need for a meeting.* He had looked at her, once, and frowned. 'Of course, for you we will need to think of something more discreet. The sight of you in anything other than dark clothing would surely arouse suspicions.'

'I like to wear dark colours,' she had replied, and he'd smiled.

'I know. You know who you are, Edith. It's one of the things that I admire about you, my very own dark horse . . .'

The sensation of Josef Albers' eyes fixed on her draws Edith back into the present, dust dancing in the shafts of sunlight that fall across the studio as he talks.

'Under my watch, you will learn that experimenting is more important than studying.' He holds her eye before moving on. 'You will learn by discovering. All art starts with a material, and therefore we have to investigate what our material can do. I am not *teaching* you – my job is simply to enable you to discover for yourselves. So, at the beginning we will experiment without aiming at making a product. Economy of form depends on the material we are working with. Notice that often you will have more by doing less. Our studies should lead to constructive thinking.'

Albers dusts off his hands as he talks, moving to the doorway and leaning back in to finish his instructions. 'I want you now to take the newspapers you've got and try to make something out of them that is more than you have now. I want you to respect the material and use it in a way that makes sense – preserve its inherent characteristics. If you can do without tools like knives and scissors, and without glue, the better. Good luck.'

And with that, he is gone.

They work in silence for hours, the sun skirting the trees scattered across the lawn outside. By the time the professor returns, with the same zeal with which he left, the floor is a sea of paper creations: a penguin, a chair, a boat.

'You see! The simplicity and efficiency of using one material to create something else.' He picks up a castle, its turrets stiff, attempting to bend its rigid sides. 'With the right manipulation, even the weakest material can be made strong.'

Back in the canteen, they fill their trays with coffee and cake.

'I think I'm in love,' Maks says, taking a bite.

'Albers, or the canteen?'

'Both.'

'You know he's married?' Edith replies, her thoughts returning to Litzi's sudden wedding to Karl Friedmann, earlier in the summer.

'I thought you knew nothing about him?' Maks laughs as they move through the throng, his grin widening as they approach a group of students seated in the courtyard, slightly away from the rest. 'Over there, that's my cousin Stefan . . .

There is a family resemblance in the thin face, and the wide-set eyes that acknowledge Edith before moving to Maks, briefly.

'This is Edith,' Maks says. 'Edith is from Vienna; she's staying in our hostel.'

'Join us.' Stefan moves up, making space for the pair to sit beside him. 'This is Lydia.'

His companion nods by way of greeting, blowing smoke rings with a barely visible flick of the tongue. She is slim and pale, with copper hair cut just below the jawline.

'Lydia and I were just having a debate about Meyer's approach to Bauhaus and society. What do you think, Maks? Would you agree that as designers our activity is determined by society – that our duty above all else is to act as servants of the community? Or do you still see Bauhaus as a style or a fashion? Or are you just here for the sex?'

There is a pause and Maks laughs. 'That's a lot of questions – and to think I was just here to enjoy my lunch. Stefan, you know what I think. I am interested in the original concept of Bauhaus – a unified art school, bringing together art and technology.'

'Of course.' Stefan absent-mindedly taps a finger on the table. 'I forget, sometimes, why you are here. To become an *artist*.'

'Don't be like that,' Lydia says, a lock of hair falling across her face as she leans in and gives Stefan an affectionate prod, her amber eyes studying Edith, before extinguishing her cigarette.

Maks chews his meat without looking up. 'I want to study under Wassily Kandinsky, yes. I am not ashamed, Stefan, and you know it. If that makes me simplistic or self-serving, then perhaps that's what I am.'

'You know I am joking. You are always so sensitive – a born artist. And what about you, Edith?' When Stefan turns to face her, she notices a tiny pool of black polluting the blue of his right eye.

'What about me?'

'Why are you here?' He holds her gaze, pointedly. 'What do you think about Meyer's appointment?'

'I don't know much about him. I've just arrived,' she replies.

'But if you're asking which I consider to be my first duty – to create beautiful objects or to provide for my fellow workers – then I would hope the answer would be obvious.'

The day Arnold Deutsch is recalled to Moscow, sunlight strains through the sky, slivers of light cutting through shadow across Vienna's 4th district.

'What do you mean, leaving Austria?' Edith feels her throat constrict, the words hanging between them.

'The Comintern have asked me to go to Moscow. Things are heating up. They need me—'

'Why didn't you say?'

'I am saying—'

'I could come. I have finished the foundation course. I don't want to go back to Dessau, anyway. It's full of phonies: people pretending to care about the cause while doing nothing. What is the use of all this *talking*? They're no better than my father.' She falters at the sound of her own disloyalty.

'You can't come, not yet,' Deutsch replies.

'I'm not a child any more,' she snaps, catching sight of the parcel by his feet.

He leans into her, speaking more quietly. 'This is not about you, Edith, or *us*. Have you learnt nothing?'

Swiping at the tears with her wrist, she looks away so that he won't see her cry. 'You know how committed I am, Arnold. But things are happening *here* – the new constitution, the increased powers of the President . . . We need you.'

'I am needed where I am told I am needed.'

'Is she going with you?'

'Josefine is my fiancée.' He reaches for Edith's arm as she stands. 'Sit down. You need to control yourself. You are no good to us if you can't.' He waits, and when he speaks again his voice is kinder. 'I am needed in Moscow. But you are needed here. We need you. Your commitment to the workers, to revolution . . .'

'But what if I need to contact you?'

'There are ways. Signals.'

He leans down and picks up the package at his feet, passing it to Edith. The weight of it is unexpected and she holds it in her lap, peeling back the brown paper.

'It's a prototype – a Rolleiflex. You mentioned that they're opening a photography department. You should go back, finish studying.' He reaches out to steady her, his grip firm. 'This isn't the end, Edith. It's just the beginning.'

The heatwave in Vienna that summer is relentless, the heat closing in like fingers around Edith's neck. She wears the camera given to her by the man she loves in a leather case held diagonally across her chest, like a soldier's rifle. Her fingers close around the strap as she thinks of him in a country she cannot picture, Josefine alongside.

She waits for the call, and, when it comes, she is ready. The money in her pocket is just enough for the train ticket from Vienna to Paris, and from there to London. Her instructions are simple. A small package, contents unknown, wrapped in an old glove. A lamp-post, a stone's throw from the Arc de Triomphe, marked in lipstick with a small 'x'.

She doesn't ask what is inside; to do so would be to imply a hint of doubt, and she feels none. She will return the same day, as soon as her mission is complete.

Her name is Betty Gray.

Edith's twenty-first birthday, 28th August 1929, falls in the days before she is due to return to the Bauhaus.

She meets Litzi at her parents' house on Latschkagasse, and they walk arm-in-arm towards the city centre, the dirty narrow streets of Favoriten giving way to wide-open boulevards that echo with the calls of the street-hawkers and hungry mouths; the roar of the early 1920s having risen to a howl.

In Leopoldstadt, the Ferris wheel stands against a bright blue sky.

'Let's go on it – I'll pay,' Edith says, and they sit side by side, knees touching, their gondola swaying slightly as they rise above the Prater: the light catching the white circles of the tablecloths, which appear like blank faces staring up at them from the courtyard of a café below; the empty ghost-train rattling over rusty tracks, and then, beyond, the city opening up like a mouth: Kahlenberg, Leopoldsberg, St Stephen's Cathedral.

'I don't want you to go back,' Litzi says.

'You don't mean that.'

'I do.'

Edith takes out her camera, holding it at chest height, peering down through the lens, angling it so that the metal lines of the gondola cage cuts the frame into several parts. 'I've met so many people, Litzi, committed people. There's a whole movement—'

'I thought you said it was full of people debating their ideas without *doing* anything for the cause?'

'There are those, too.' Edith takes the shot. 'But this term a new department is opening: I get to study photography. Arnold says if I learn to be a photographer, and with my connections in London, I will be of great use to the party. Otherwise, life goes on much as before. I can't bear that thought. This way, I can be so much more than just a courier.'

As she adjusts the frame, Edith's mind slips back to Paris,

the thrill of stepping out at Gare de l'Est, the city enveloping her as she winds her way along the Rue La Fayette, turning left on to the Rue du Faubourg Montmartre, ducking into the Musée Grévin and pausing in front of the hall of mirrors, watching several versions of herself slip one way and another, distorting in shape and size until she doesn't know which is her original form; moving on, making up time as she walks to the allocated spot, not far from the Jardin d'Acclimatation, the site of the old zoo where, during the Siege of Paris, the chef Alexandre Étienne Choron was ordered to cook many of the animals for a feast.

'I know you will,' Litzi says, smiling sadly.

'Stay strong, Litzi. You are the strongest person I know. Now, how is Karl?'

'I don't want to talk about Karl.'

'Then we shan't. Lean in,' Edith says. 'I want a picture of you.'

While Vienna cracks and bows under new political strain, back in Dessau the Bauhaus appears to burst with life, the green curves that surround the town yielding to an illusory vision of the future. Conversation butterflies through the dining hall and across the auditorium. Students sprawl, catlike, across every surface, gathering on the roof terrace of the Prellerhaus, soaking up the end of the summer sun.

Edith sleeps well that first night back at the hostel, waking early, leaving her bag on the bed, lighting a cigarette before heading upstairs to find Maks.

'Edith?' Stefan is walking out of his room. His face brightens at the sight of her.

'How was your summer?' she asks – then, without waiting for his reply, 'I was looking for your cousin . . .'

Stefan shakes his head. 'Maks isn't coming back.'

'What do you mean?'

His expression darkens. 'His father – my uncle – lost his job. Maks has to work, there's no other option.'

'But that's not right—'

'Of course,' Stefan says, his voice cutting. 'None of this is right. Are you coming across now? We need to talk about how we are going to fight.'

There are six of them seated along the benches that line the garden area outside the canteen. The sky is overcast and Lydia, seated to Edith's right, reaches for another cigarette.

'So the protest is set for tomorrow,' Stefan concludes, claiming an authority that no one contests.

'What if we are arrested?' asks Lydia, striking a match.

'Then you tell the truth,' Edith says, and feels the attention of the group turn towards her. 'You keep to the truth until you are forced to lie, and then you stay as close to the truth as you can. We should create a code so that if one of us is detained we can transmit messages in hidden ink in any letters sent to the outside world.'

Edith repeats the words exactly as she first heard them, lying side by side with Deutsch in the apartment he borrowed for their meetings once Josefine had caught wind, and then again while seated opposite one another at one of the safe houses in the Jewish quarter of the city. 'For example,' she says, '*I hope to be released soon* might mean *I have been forced to give up names*; or *it is cold at night* might mean *I have managed to withhold information*. If you don't have a code for something because it is too specific, you can write in secret ink.'

'Secret ink?' Lydia replies.

Edith raises an eyebrow. 'Urine.'

Stefan smiles approvingly. 'Well, I would never have guessed. Is there anything else we should know?'

'I'm interested in your work,' Walter Peterhans tells her one afternoon as they pore over negatives in the darkroom.

The director of the newly formed photography department, Peterhans has a receding hairline and a reputation for the avant-garde.

'Take this picture, for example – there is an energy to it,' he says, holding a pair of tweezers in one hand, which he uses to adjust one of the images hanging from a line of string above their heads. 'And a sadness, but perhaps also an anger. The way you use light and shadow to illuminate and restrict, to control the viewer's gaze.'

Edith looks away, embarrassed by the directness of his praise.

'Tell me, what do you think of what you have learnt over the past few months?'

She considers the question. 'I'm not so sure about the philosophical side – the idea of pure beauty. If I am honest, I find it a little élitist.'

He raises his eyebrows in amused contention.

'I enjoyed what you said about the capability of photography going far beyond the purely reproductive; that, used properly – consciously – the camera holds within it unlimited possibilities.' She shifts from one foot to another. 'I find this aspect of it interesting, and the practical lessons,' she says. 'I want to be a journalist one day, to use photography to show what is happening in the world.'

He considers her for a moment. 'Well, in that case you're going to need to learn how to spot a print. You see these white marks here, caused by dust on the negative? If we use

a very fine brush coated with dye, we can disguise them
. . . Creating the perfect image is all about manipulation,
about what we choose to reveal and what we choose to
hide.'

A ragged wooden fence runs through Vienna, separating two
worlds: the slums on one side, newly erected public housing
on the other.

At the apartment, Edith's mother cooks in silence, her
movements mechanical as she lays out the plates. She looks
up as Edith walks through the kitchen, filling a glass of water
from the tap.

'Where have you been?'

'I was with Litzi. She and Karl are divorcing.'

'That's a shame, though I suppose she hardly had time to
become attached,' Adele says, plainly, taking the *Eingebrannte
Erdäpfel* from the oven and placing it on the table.

'Fourteen months,' Edith replies, leaning back against the
counter, sipping her glass of water, as her mother moves back to
the stove. 'But just because something only happens for a brief
period of time, that doesn't diminish the significance of its impact.'

'You're right, of course.' Adele concedes, picking up a
wooden spoon. 'Though I can't say I'm surprised it was so
brief; she may be smart and headstrong but dear Litzi is even
younger than you. Sometimes in youth we believe we know
what we want – and Litzi more than most – when we don't
yet know ourselves.'

'I know myself,' Edith replies, sharply, her jaw tensing.

Removing the lid from the pot, Adele releases a sudden
plume of steam, waiting a moment for it to settle before
placing the ladle in the pot and stirring methodically. 'Yes,
but do you know what you are doing? What danger—'

They are halted by the sound of the door opening. Wilhelm and Wolf stop short at the sight of them.

'Are we interrupting something?' Wilhelm looks between his daughter and his wife, the weight of what has not yet been said hanging between them.

'I was about to call for you; dinner's ready,' Adele says, resuming her preparations, dishing the potatoes into the bowls.

'Mother was about to explain why she thinks I'm incapable of making decent choices.'

'Edith, I am not criticising your spirit.' Adele lets the ladle drop to the counter, her eyes shining with something worse than tears. 'I am saying you need to be careful. The Heimwehr is gaining influence—'

'Exactly,' Edith interrupts.

'—and now is not the time to be drawing attention to yourself, or to the family!'

'So our family is more important than the welfare and future of our country?' Edith turns her attention to her younger brother. 'Wolf, what do you think? Say something. You must have an opinion?'

'Edith—'

'He doesn't need your protection, Mother. Come on, Wolf, speak your mind for once.'

'What I think is not relevant,' her younger brother says, taking a seat at the far side of the table.

'Not relevant? You can do better than that.' Edith slams her cutlery on the table. 'Speak up!'

'Enough!' Wilhelm raises his hand but it is Wolf who replies, his voice level.

'I think you've forgotten what it is to hope, but I certainly haven't.'

'Hope? We don't need your *hope*, Wolf, we need your action, your commitment—'

Wolf shakes his head. 'You cannot speak for everyone, Edith. You can't claim to believe in equality and at the same time stifle another person's view.'

She stands, pushing back her chair. 'Can't you see what is happening? Any of you?' She turns to her father. 'You have dedicated your life to *ideas* and *theories* that you claim will change the world. But you're a hypocrite! Just out there, beyond the bookshop, Europe is imploding, and you do nothing. You think teetotalism and pacifism will save us from *them?*'

Her voice cracks and she looks at Wilhelm, willing him to answer, to fight back. For a moment he looks as though he is about to speak, but instead he simply turns and walks out.

Dear Edith,

We have a dacha now, just outside Moscow, 30–40 minutes, according to traffic density, from door to door. It is where the main road ends abruptly in the forest, so that there is no through traffic of any kind – a real blessing these days! It has three rooms and a big glass-enclosed veranda, with all mod cons, including central heating. The latter served us well through a cool and appallingly rainy summer. This morning I got a whiff of pine as I was lighting my morning cigarette and for a moment I was back in the Vienna woods, the old Daimler chugging beneath me. It is peculiar to think that I have arrived at my final destination, that time has stopped for me, in a way. Not that there isn't plenty to keep me occupied, even without the reading of international news, which I seem unable to avoid even out here in the sticks.

I need have no anxiety in the matter of reading material. It was towards the end of January when we gave a big office party to celebrate the 13th anniversary of my arrival in the USSR. In the course of it, the subject turned to my book supply, and I mentioned that I could only manage the odd paperback because my foreign currency reserves were at a very low ebb. Whereat the

senior general present told me to shed my bourgeois prej-
udices, forget about money, and order whatever I wanted
through them. I promptly placed a large order, which they
took without turning a hair. He also asked me if I liked
Czech beer, and I gave him the obvious answer. Since
then, once a week, Panatlon (the fat one who speaks no
English) has turned up panting with a case of Pilsener
in close embrace. I am allowed to pay for it!

Back in the city our new Metro line has opened, so
now we have a station only four minutes' walk from the
flat, as against eight minutes hitherto. Best of all, that
ugly and inconvenient hoarding has been removed from
Gorky Street. Here in the sticks, our bi-weekly delivery
of spring chicken, eggs, milk, smetana, etc. has just
arrived, and I must help with gathering it in. We hope
to stay in the dacha until the end of September, but our
spirits are being sorely tried by apparently endless rain.
Otherwise life goes on much as before, with steaks in
the freezer and our winter store of pickled cabbage and
cucumbers nicely chilled on the balcony. The supply of
zhoog, zoog, zhug, or чжог is holding up very well, so we
face the New Year in merry mood. Sixty-four, God; I think
I've made it.

Yours,
Kim

PS. Writing on an ancient typewriter is rather like a
team going into the Cup Final with an unreliable goal-
keeper. Jitters in the last line of defence can upset the
whole team. In just the same way, my fingers expect the
keys to jam, the ribbon to jump, etc. So morale is low.
High time for a good lunch! Peace be upon your house.

The last line of defence

Alexander waits for her after the meeting, his lecture having overrun. They walk side by side through the rain, their fingers touching, shadows merging into one another along grey Vienna streets, Edith only half-listening as he continues on from his news on the latest of the exams and studies that keep him occupied for most of the day and night. He asks questions that demand no answers: *You have heard of Arbeiter unfallversicherungsanstalt, what in Britain we would call the labourer's accident insurance?* – regaling her with details of his time at Cambridge and the intricacies of macroeconomics, with an assumption of both knowledge and interest on the part of the listener that amuses Edith as acutely as it had irked Litzi on the occasions when they had all been together.

There is a dourness about the young British medical student, a fundamental absence of frivolity that her friend finds fundamentally repellent. Not that Litzi is in a position – or of a disposition – to comment on who another woman chooses to make love to. They have both read the books Wilhelm publishes on themes of the New Woman and the New Man. They understand that in order to break society's shackles, you have to escape pre-existing definitions.

'How long will you stay in Vienna, this time?' Edith asks.

'As long as the course lasts.'

As they make their way towards the city centre, away from Favoriten, Edith's eyes automatically search for Arnold, though he is far away.

'I start my medical studies on Monday,' Alexander says, rearranging his glasses. 'Lorenz Böhler is an excellent teacher. We are learning about accident treatment and surgery, but I also admire him greatly for his political approach.'

As he talks, Edith watches his body language – those occasional, restrained gesticulations – trying to picture his limbs under all those clothes. He is taller than Arnold, and thinner. She wonders, briefly, about the woman and the son and daughter he occasionally pays reference to.

'How is your sister?' Edith asks, lighting a cigarette, distracting herself.

'Beatrix is well. She's had a baby, Jennifer, and has been working at a new school, Beacon Hill, outside of London, which certainly gives a relative blandness to my own school days. It has come to the attention of the press as a place where, and I quote: *no classes are held, no punishment inflicted and clothes are barred in warmer weather.*'

Edith smiles. 'It sounds wonderful.'

'I thought you'd approve. It was founded by Dora and Bertrand Russell – I don't suppose you've heard of him? He worked with my old professor, Maynard Keynes, and the writer H.G. Wells, to found the Workers' Birth Control Group.'

'So once you've finished your studies here in Vienna you will work as a doctor?'

'Wherever I'm needed.'

Edith laces her fingers through his thin surgeon's hands. 'I admire that.'

'You should come with me to London; there is a rally. You could stay at my place.'

'Really?' She grins.

'For as long as you like.'

'I would like that, very much. You live alone?'

'I share with two others – one of whom, Rosa Shar, is from Vienna, too. My children and their mother live elsewhere, but you will meet them.' He studies her a moment, pushing a lock of hair from in front of her eye. 'We are alike, you and me. We understand each other. We are both drawn to defend the damned.'

When she is questioned, days later, Edith will say she has no idea whose flat they piled back to after the march, which had continued until nightfall, the crowd dispersing to various corners of the city, eight or ten of them heading back to someone's apartment and drinking into the small hours. She will claim she was distracted on the journey back by the thrum of London: commissioners buckling under the weight of other people's Christmas shopping; headlights casting pools of light across rain-sodden streets; beggars with placards reading *No Home, No Dole*.

She never caught their names, she will say. She had no way of knowing they were leading members of the Communist Party of Great Britain. Just as she had no idea that the party was even illegal in Britain until the morning she was rudely awoken, she and Alexander entangled in a single sheet in the flat at 5c Westbourne Gardens, by the sound of fists on the door.

But that comes after.

Trafalgar Square is already ablaze with life by the time Edith and Alexander arrive at the march, the rallying cries rising above them as she makes her way through the crowd gathered in front of Nelson's Column. *Workers of London support the Communist candidates! The Communist Party is the vanguard of the working class, leading the way to the ultimate conquest of power. Our candidates are tried and true fighters in the revolutionary struggle. Show that you back them in their fight!*

'It's so good to see you here!' Beatrix says, pushing her long straight hair away from pronounced cheekbones, hugging Edith and then her brother.

'Congratulations: Alex tells me you have a daughter now.' Edith smiles, her voice raised above the fray.

'Yes, Jennifer.' Beatrix grins. 'This is her father, Jack Pritchard. Molly, his wife, is looking after the children today. They have two boys, a few years older than Jennifer.'

'Good to see you, Jack,' Alexander says, leaning across them towards the man with a strong jaw and warm eyes. 'How is the building coming along?'

'Oh, just fine.' Smiling, Jack turns to Edith. 'My wife Molly and I are planning a new complex founded on rational principles, you see. Some might call us mad; I prefer to quote from an old illustrated book of the alphabet: *O is for optimist glad, Who doesn't know how to be sad. If he woke up one day, in Hades he'd say, Well really it isn't so bad.* But then, *sad* and *mad* do rhyme, don't they, so perhaps that's no coincidence?'

'Pay no attention,' Beatrix says, moving around to stand next to Edith. 'Though I must say, Lawn Road Flats is shaping up to be quite something. Actually, Jack works closely with Walter Gropius and László Moholy-Nagy . . . don't you, darling? Edith attended the Bauhaus – you may well know some of the same people . . .'

'They had both left by the time I arrived,' Edith replies.

'Edith was also trained by Maria Montessori,' Beatrix continues. 'My plan is to enlist her to work with Molly and me at the Children's Group nursery.'

'You see, you can't stand around here for long before you're signed up to something, I'm afraid,' Jack says. 'You're from Vienna, yes? Wonderful city. Beatrix mentioned that she had met you there, on one of her many research trips. You seem to have made quite an impression on both her and her brother. How long do you plan to stay—'

'Jack Pritchard?'

The voice that interrupts them belongs to a stout, sincere-faced man with a sober moustache and a heavy accent that Edith cannot place. Beside him stand two other men, one shorter with a wide girth and heavy eyebrows, the final man with a side parting accentuating a receding hairline.

'Bob Stewart,' Jack replies, holding out a hand. 'Excellent to see you. Fine turnout.'

'You remember Harry and Percy?' the Scot asks.

'Of course,' Jack says. 'And I'd like to introduce you to someone. Harry Pollitt, Percy Glading . . . this is Edith Suschitzky.'

In hindsight, when she trawls back through the cast that day, Edith won't be able to recall which of them saw each other first, she or Maks, through the gathering of Englishmen crying out for better social conditions at the foot of Nelson's Column. But she will remember that it was she who spoke first. '*Maks, bist du das?*'

'Edith?' His whole face seems to transform into a smile as he moves away from Stefan and Lydia, who follow him with their eyes.

'But I thought you were in Hamburg!' Edith hugs him tightly.

'I was, I mean I am . . . but I am visiting Stefan and Lydia, and here we are.'

'I knew we'd win you over eventually,' Edith says, signalling at the banners held aloft around them.

'I never said I was at the march by choice. But we both know how persuasive my cousin can be.'

'Stefan.' Edith smiles as he and Lydia approach, unchanged since she had last seen them on the grass outside the Prellerhaus, a few months earlier. 'It's so good to see you. Come with us. We are going on somewhere now, back to a flat not far from here.'

Maks looks over Edith's shoulders towards the group, pausing before shaking his head. 'We were only passing through on our way to have lunch with Lydia's father. It's remarkable that we even found each other.'

'How long are you in London for?' Edith asks.

'Only a few more days,' Maks replies, his expression shifting. 'Perhaps we could meet? Where are you staying?'

Edith waits under the clock tower, Caledonian Market heaving with the heckling of the traders, the smell of fish and meat and shoe polish.

Through the heads in the crowd, there is a streak of copper as they come into view, Lydia first, followed by Stefan and then Maks, who follows at a slight distance, resigned to always walk in his cousin's shadow.

'I'm sorry if we were late – it's Lydia's fault.'

Lydia, beside him, rolls her eyes. 'I was simply admiring a ring; I said you could go ahead.'

'Not at all.' Edith kisses them each in turn, on the cheek. 'I came early – I wanted to take a few pictures. I've heard about this place, but I never managed to see it for myself.'

'Until today,' Lydia says, smiling, beckoning the others to follow as she leads off through the stalls.

Looping her arm through Maks's, Edith shivers, her free hand instinctively touching her Rolleiflex, her eyes searching for subjects.

'I wondered if you'd lost interest in photography when they told me you'd left the Bauhaus,' Maks says.

'Never. But after Hannes Meyer was forced to leave in order to appease the Dessau authorities, it didn't feel right to stay on.'

'You gave it all up as an act of protest?' There is a hint of revulsion in Maks's voice and Edith looks away.

'Meyer was pushed out for his political views – views that I share. How could I not support him?'

She recognises that he is upset, that to him she has sacrificed the very education he craves and is denied for reasons he deems beyond his control. But if he cannot see that the system that oppresses him, the system that caused his father's job loss which prevents him from returning to the Bauhaus, is the very same enemy that she and Meyer are fighting against – making every sacrifice necessary to overturn – then he doesn't deserve her pity.

Maks looks ahead, saying nothing. Edith's attention turns to a stall filled with rows of clocks, each giving a slightly different version of the time.

'I was sorry you had to go back to Hamburg. You deserved to be there, more than I did – certainly more than Stefan.'

Maks looks straight ahead, keeping his expression bright. 'We don't always get what we deserve in life, Edith.'

They stop, beside a pair of green and orange love-birds, their necks hooked around one another.

'So you and the Englishman are really in love, then?'

'I respect him very much.'

Maks laughs. 'I never knew you to be so diplomatic. And you plan to stay in London?'

She nods. 'Yes. What about you?'

'As I said, I'm just visiting. I'll be going back to Hamburg in a couple of days.' His smile fades as he squeezes her arm. 'So we had better make the most of the time we have left.'

Secret Intelligence Service file on Edith Suschitzky

CONFIDENTIAL:

31st October 1930

Dear V.V.,

A woman named Edith SUSCHITZKY, an Austrian, born 28th August 1908 in Vienna, took part in the demonstration in support of the Workers' Charter in Trafalgar Square on the 26th October. She was noticed to be in conversation with a number of prominent Communists. This woman is the holder of Austrian passport issued in Vienna on 21st December 1928, No.656336. Her address in Vienna is given as No.4 Petzvalg. She appears to have paid several visits to this country, the first occasion being in April 1925, when she came as a governess and schoolteacher.

```
She is said to be a daughter of the head of
the firm of publishers, Gerbrüder (Brothers)
Suschitzky, Anzengruber Verlag, Vienna 10. Her
description is as follows:—

  Height: 5'6"
  Slim build.
  Pale complexion.
  Eyes blue-grey.
  Blond bobbed hair.
  Wears almost colourless horn-rimmed spec-
    tacles.


We should be grateful for any enquiries which
you could make about this woman abroad.
  Yours sincerely,
  S M L
```

The officers batter at the door of 5c Westbourne Gardens with their fists, waiting impatiently in the corridor while Edith dresses. 'Why are they here?' she whispers to Alexander, her tone fearful. Her eyes are wide and alert despite the rude awakening, her fingers fumbling as she pulls on the long, dark skirt and turtleneck sweater that hangs over a chair, where she had discarded them the previous evening.

His voice is low, matching hers. 'They were monitoring the march. They say they saw you there – they want to expel you from the country. It will be fine. I will make some calls.'

'I'm scared, Alexander.'

'Don't be,' he says. 'Everything is going to be fine.'

Fine weather marked his arrival at the University of Cambridge the year Kim Philby turned seventeen, the recipient of a history scholarship, having made up for lost time following the illness that had threatened to mar his education, after all those months off school.

Shimmering with possibility, Trinity College appeared to bask beneath its own golden halo, those first weeks flying past, the clinking of champagne flutes along the banks of the River Cam fast becoming the rustle of leaves, then the patter of nascent snow, flurries which thawed almost as soon as they landed, never quite settling before spring swiftly reached in and warmed the city once more.

It is now a year since his arrival, the winter of 1930 closing in around him, as Kim heads out early one morning, making sure not to wake his friend, Guy Burgess, who remains comatose on the sofa where Kim returns an hour later with a letter from his father in hand, the postmark an indeterminate Arabic.

'Guy?' He kicks his friend's foot affectionately as he passes, the bottle of whisky tucked under Burgess's arm like a teddy bear dropping to the floor as the horizontal figure groans in indignation.

'What?' His voice is sharp and begrudging, his eyes kept firmly closed. 'Can't get a bloke get a blow-job or a bloody kip around here?'

'I'm due to see Dobb in half an hour,' Kim replies, in every sense un-aroused.

'Good. Fuck off, then. Where's Maclean?'

'Presumably he went back to his own place.' Kim's eyes move once more over the letter. 'Imagine that.'

Picking up a stack of papers from the table and tucking them under his arm, Kim looks over as Burgess reaches for the bottle of whisky, noticing the fingernails bitten down to the quick as his friend unscrews the cap and takes a gulp, before once more closing his eyes.

Eyes fixed on the view through the passenger-side window, Edith takes a sip of coffee, feeling the thermos warm her fingers, the taste bitter on her lips.

Through the glass, London gives way to the Cambridgeshire countryside, rolled out like a threadbare carpet, hemmed in by rows of lifeless trees. Compared with the forests and hills that envelop Vienna, there is something coy about the scene, the gentle folds of the land so English in their restraint.

She keeps her attention focused on the sharp November sky as they enter the city, Cambridge itself a picture postcard of dons in scarves and students on bicycles carrying paper parcels wrapped in string, the sound of a choir rippling through the shadows as they approach Jesus Green.

Glancing at Alexander, so at home within the setting's structures, negotiating the roads towards the Red House without the need of an *A to Z*, she holds up a hand as they circle the green. 'Stop the car for a minute. Just here.'

Unquestioningly, Alexander pulls over at the corner of the park and opens the door, leaning his long body awkwardly against the bonnet, sipping, cautiously, from Edith's thermos.

Pausing in her seat, Edith glances in the wing mirror before pulling herself from the car. She walks a few steps, and turns, appearing to stretch her legs, alert to any vehicles that may be slowing down around them. Across the green, her attention is briefly caught by the figure of a young man, his hurried gait and the papers tucked under his arm marking him out as a student. Otherwise the street is empty, no sign that they are being followed.

Turning her attention to Alexander, she considers the lines of his face in profile, the slight flaring of his nostrils as he looks up at her above the opening of the flask.

'Are you all right?' he asks. 'You look as if someone just walked over your grave.'

'What if he can't help?' Edith says.

Alexander opens the car door. 'Come on, we mustn't keep him waiting.'

On Chesterton Lane, the door to the Red House is unlocked, Maurice Dobb appearing, unperturbed, in the hallway, leading them into a living room inhabited by weary furniture and rows of books: Rosa Luxemburg, Friedrich Engels, John Maynard Keynes.

The professor is younger than Edith had imagined, his pale, watery eyes soft and engaging – everything about him designed to deflect and reassure.

'How is dear Beatrix?' Dobb asks, shaking Alexander's hand vigorously before turning his attention to Edith, not waiting for an answer. 'I'm sorry you're facing this,' he says, pointing his guest towards an upholstered chair. 'It shows the scale of the resistance we're up against – but what else can we expect from Clyne's little army?'

'The Communist Party of Great Britain is not even illegal. I thought this was a democracy,' she replies.

The fire crackles in the grate as Dobb moves to the other side of the room, taking three tumblers from a silver tray beside a decanter on a side table, pouring each measure with a generous precision, the amber-coloured liquid swaying slightly as he passes Edith a glass.

'From what Alexander tells me, you are here on a temporary visa; you do not have the same rights as a citizen. I'm sorry, it's monstrous, but it's the way they see it.'

'I'm a woman and a Jew, I have no rights anywhere,' she replies, taking a swig and enjoying the gentle burn against the back of her throat. 'But you're a man of social standing, an economics professor. If you spoke to the authorities on my behalf, they would listen.'

'Perhaps.' Dobb refills their glasses. 'Of course I will try, though this might be beyond my sphere of influence. Alexander mentioned that your father has contacted the mayor, in Austria?'

'He has written to Karl Seitz and to the Burgermeister's office, but they say if my proposed expulsion is for political reasons then there is little they can do.'

'Then I'm sorry if this is not what you want to hear, but I am not sure how much help I can be. Although, perhaps . . .' He considers her for a moment. 'I have it on good authority that the Marx-Engels Institute is wanting a new translator from German into English—'

There is a knock at the door and Dobb stands. 'I'm sorry to cut you short, but I'm expecting one of my second-years and I believe that's him. If you wait here, I'll ask him to go through and wait in the other room.' He goes out into the hallway. 'Kim, good to see you,' he says, the voices fading as another door closes, on the other side of the hallway.

When Maurice Dobb re-enters the room, Alexander stands, ever the dutiful student. 'Well, thank you anyway for your time.'

My dearest Alexander,

It is hard to believe a month has passed since I left you in London.

In a way I am pleased to be back in Vienna. The Party here is making good progress and there is the chance of a small demonstration on 25th February. But, with reference to what happened in London, please will you get me at once from the Centre a statement saying that I, E. Suschitzky – as E. White – worked in the Party, in London, and was deported for that reason? Otherwise I will not be accepted into the Party here without three months' probation. It has become very strict here now because of the splits in the Party. Please do this for me, Alexander – and send it to me registered and sealed so that the English police do not come across it. I will otherwise not be able to work here, and at the moment it is extremely important. There are some fine people in the cell, and nearly all are workers. They were very friendly to me.

There has been a very interesting children's exhibition here, and the papers have been full of praise. I met a professor at one of the meetings who told me that in Moscow they have a children's museum where children can carry out their active pursuits, with books, and materials available relating to printing, and theatre, and general advancement of children's psychological interests. We talked about how important it is for children to have colour. Apparently the museum was a great success as far as propaganda is concerned. It was such an enriching conversation. The professor knows all about English and American children's literature. She said that the Social Democrat schools have instructions to take the children there. I hope it might be possible for me to go too, one day. I have started learning Russian in anticipation.

Have you spoken to the lawyer about us marrying in order to go, together, to Moscow? If necessary, I could certainly get in via France, but it would mean having to go into hiding. It is, of course, without doubt that if we married the situation would become very complicated. Even now we are a marriage à trois: you, me, and the long-suffering mother of your children, whom you see each week. (I would have killed you long ago if I were her.) It is true that we shall just have to wait – you would be very unhappy, and if you and I had six little children together in Russia, and your existing chil-dren were not there too – what can one do? For me it is quite simple but not for you, and only you can handle it.

I am sorry that my letters are not more cheerful. The days go well enough but, with all that is happening, at night my mind struggles to rest.

Today I am sending some photographs to the Russian news agency TASS to see if they might give me some employ-ment. Thank you for the cheque. I am sending back the pound I have left over from my time in England.

Yours,

Edith

PS. After finishing my letter to you, I went to see the TASS and I am now the official photo reporter of Austria – for the 'Press Cliché' Moscow. They said they liked my work very much, and what pleases me most is that it all came without recommendations, and I can now see what endless possibilities I would have had in London had I said more.

The man also told me that he knows one or two people who have allowed themselves to be adopted in London. But perhaps you are no longer interested in that possibility.

As Vienna emerges from the rubble of a collapsed stock market, Edith keeps her hands on the strap of her camera, occasionally stopping to pull the Rolleiflex from its case. She dresses plainly, in dark colours, her hairstyle nondescript, engaging with her subjects and then disappearing into the backdrop.

The city becomes her muse: queues of unemployed men in heavy coats and hats, shoulders hunched against the cold; toddlers asleep in old vegetable crates; flags pointed to the sky outside City Hall at the May Day gathering.

She shoots sparingly, never wasting a shot, a behaviour that is as much about economics as instinct, given that each Rolleiflex film provides just twelve square-format images. The setting up of each photo takes time, her camera providing a sense of invisibility: a shield behind which to hide as she moves from point to point, delivering and collecting.

The camera: the perfect tool for a photographer, and a spy.

Secret Intelligence Service file on Edith Suschitzky

Letter to S.I.S. re Edith Suschitzky
SZ/3193

20th March 1931

Dear V.V.,

Please refer to your CX dated 11.12.30, regarding Edith SUSCHITZKY. It might be of interest to your representative in Vienna to know that this woman, who is still in Vienna, has now been appointed the official photographic reporter of the "Press Cliché" in Moscow for Austria. Her appointment has been obtained through the Director of Tass in Vienna, and INGULOV, the agent of that organisation here,

is to send a recommendation of her to Herr
Ebel, Vienna 1, Bauernmarkt 24.
  Yours sincerely
  [UNKNOWN]

Dear Alexander,

I write with a heavy heart, wondering not only when you will return next to Vienna but what you will think when you do. It is several months since I left you, that bleak January day. As the ink brushes this paper, spring is officially taking hold across the few pockets of the city where nature still thrives, as if the world is moving forward just as it always has. Yet all I see is a world closing in on itself. Things have become so much worse since you were last here; the misery is horrifying. Just this month, the Creditanstalt declared bankruptcy. Father is subjected to almost weekly raids on the bookshop. Despite the longer days, there is a darkness that seems never to lift.

Personally, life has been made almost bearable by my work. TASS has taken me on as their official correspondent to Moscow after seeing some of my reportages in Die Bühne. *(Did I tell you that already? Sometimes I think I am going quite mad.) So you see, I am now a polymath, like you. I give what money I can to the Party, and, despite what I see around me, I remain hopeful. With the banks collapsing in the USA and now here, it is plain that capitalism is imploding. I await the final epoch with impatience, and I continue to practise my Russian in anticipation – ha.*

Send news from London, and please make it be that you are coming here.

I await your reply, and your return.
Yours,
Edith

In the upper windows of an apartment block near Edith's home, a row of swastikas looms over passers-by, a growing sense of disquiet taking hold on the streets of Vienna, families gathering to beg on the Stubenbrücke bridge that runs over the Wienfluss; elderly women selling single pieces of fruit; crippled veterans touting yo-yos on street corners.

Edith photographs them all, her images making it on to the covers of magazines stocked at Inveresk House, on the Strand, where Alexander collects them, keeping them in his room in Paddington along with the letters she sends telling him that she will be going to Sweden on holiday; that she has returned home and that home has become quite intolerable, her mother and father crying the whole day long. Letters explaining that congress is to be soon, that life is slow in Vienna, that the 25th February was tremendous with eight thousand people turning out for the demonstration, that twelve thousand foreigners have been kicked out of Paris, that there is no work in the city; that a lot depends on him. *I realise you are afraid to get involved in anything but I know what I am about and I am willing to take entire responsibility for whatever follows,* she writes. And she reads – Engels Bauernkrieg and Ludwig Feuerbach – books recommended to her by the scientists and professors she befriends at meetings, giving away the money she earns, learning Russian, always preparing for a call that never comes. Until it does, just when she least expects it.

Edith moves briskly through the 3rd district, sensing foot-steps catching up with her as she takes the corner, a hand landing on her arm from behind, squeezing firmly so that she cries out before noticing the fingers, stocky and firm. When she turns, the eyes that meet hers are those that recall the lakes she equates with replenished health and a first consciousness of the Russian revolution.

'You're back?'

'I'm sorry,' Arnold says. 'I wanted to surprise you.'

He indicates for her to move and walk alongside, their feet falling into a natural rhythm.

'I arrived from Moscow this morning.'

He glances back over his shoulder as they turn the corner on to the bridge, pulling out a copy of *Der Jugendliche Arbeiter*, April edition, 1931, the cover line '*Das Foto im Dienste des Sozialismus*' – the photo in the service of journalism – printed over one of Edith's photographs, a man focusing an image through a Leica lens.

'There is concern in Moscow that you are drawing attention to yourself, in the wrong way.' He speaks under his breath.

'Have you read the article?' she asks.

'Of course I have.'

'Well, then. It's an important point that Siegfried Weyr makes. The seductions of the bourgeois illustrated press are truly problematic, it's a threat to our cause – he is reminding members to take photos so as to manifest a new proletariat consciousness.'

'It's indiscreet,' Arnold replies.

'It's part of the fight.'

'But it is not your part.'

'How would you know? You haven't been here. You haven't seen what has been happening.' She looks away, putting her hands against her cheeks to soothe them. 'Photography is my job. You encouraged it. How do you think I can afford to eat, to live, to work for Moscow for free?'

'I understand that—'

'If I don't have an income, I can't afford to give my time to the Party. Besides, you told me you wanted me to make connections with England.'

He looks at her sidelong.

She smiles at him, knowingly. 'And now I am.'

The sun shines brightly over Vienna train station, shafts of light cutting through latticed windows, casting shadows along the platform. Edith spots Alexander the moment he steps off the train, his suitcase by his side.

She smiles. 'You're here.'

'Here, this way . . .'

'Thank you for seeing me.' Kim smiles, shaking Maurice Dobb's hand before following his professor into the sitting room. It is warm, a thin vase of daffodils stands above the fireplace, the fire unlit. Kim takes a seat while Dobb pours the drinks.

'It's always a pleasure, Philby. It sounded urgent – what did you want to talk about?'

'I want to know how best to devote my life to the Communist cause,' the younger man replies.

Dobb nods, considering the question as if any other in this moment would have come as a shock. 'You never did join the Party, did you?'

'Not officially—'

'Good.'

'My father has sent me some money, to go travelling. I have a motorcycle. I want to go where I might be most useful.'

Dobb holds his eye. 'In what capacity?'

'In whatever capacity I'm needed. I can go wherever I like: the world is my oyster.'

Dobb is true to his word, putting his former student in touch with Louis Gibarti, an Italian-born Paris agent of the Comintern.

By the time Kim arrives in Vienna, via France, wearing a double-breasted leather jacket, goggles hanging from his neck, the city is already at crisis point. Since the German federal election of the previous year, where the Nazi party won thirty-seven per cent of the vote, the KPÖ has moved underground. They were forced to resort to increasingly illegal and violent means; a recent battle in Silesia has led to the dispatch of the army, culminating with the assassination of the leader of the paramilitary organisation Sturmabteilung – and Austria teetering on the brink of civil war.

Vienna is cold, the austere grandeur of the buildings that surround the train station at odds with the cripples and beggars doubled up in their dark rags. Kim walks briskly, holding his nerve as he flashes his British passport, and finds himself waved through by the militia who stand guard at the checkpoints that punctuate the city.

Following the Italian's instruction, he stops only occasionally to buy a box of matches from a beggar; to toss a coin for a man with no legs selling yo-yos. Nothing too flash, nothing to draw attention to himself.

Absent-mindedly, he touches his back pocket for confirmation of the second-class degree, and the letter of recommendation to the head of the Austrian Committee for Relief of the Victims of German Fascism, the pianist and composer George Neller. Dobb's words replay in his mind: *the Party is illegal in Austria, the Communist leadership is in hiding . . .'* Instinctively, he pictures the £100 his father St John had given him for his birthday along with the note: *Go out and see the world – it's the only decent education* – and a few quid more that Kim had received as payment for assistance in typing up the manuscript of St John's book about his forty-four days charting the Arabian desert from the Persian Gulf to the Red Sea. The money that is now stuffed inside his left hiking boot.

'I'm ready to do whatever you need,' Kim announces as he hands over the letter at the relief headquarters, which is housed up three flights of stairs at Lerchengasse 13.

Holding his breath against the smell, he follows his guide through a series of rooms, men, women and children scattered across mattresses which lie at various points across the floor.

'As you can see, we need a lot. But first you will need somewhere to live, somewhere the landlord won't be keeping an eye on you.'

'Do you have any suggestions?'

'We have a close ally, Litzi Friedmann – a marvellous woman. She has previously let her spare room out to friends in need, including Josip Broz when he was wanted by half the Balkans. Last year she spent two weeks in jail for her activist work. You will find her at Latschkagasse 9. Her parents are excellent people: Israel and Gisella Kohlmann . . .'

He gives the self-confident young Englishman a final assessment, and nods in satisfaction. 'Yes, I'm sure we can make good use of you in Vienna.'

Vienna Police report, 16 May 1933

25-27 years old, one metre 72 tall, thin, pretty face, curly blonde hair, wears brown spectacles, always dressed in a dark coat and beret.

The men are waiting as Edith walks briskly through the 9th district, the sun grazing the tops of the buildings. As she turns left on to Lichtensteinstrasse, her fingers close more tightly around the bundle, as if in anticipation of what is to come.

She doesn't so much see as feel them as she finally steps into their line of sight, instantly changing course, away from Goethe Bookshop towards the taxi stand. It is a matter of seconds before their footsteps move in behind, their heavy coats throwing the world around her into shadow.

'What is your name?'

'Fräulein Braun.' Her voice doesn't falter.

'Please hand me those papers.'

As she does so, around her pedestrians scurry past, and the second man takes a step forward and prises the letters from her hand.

'Under the command of Chancellor Engelbert Dollfuss, you are under arrest. Please come with us.'

Neither man speaks until they reach the station. Inside, the first officer peels off into another room, the second leading Edith through to the back of the building. The sweat under her armpits has turned cold.

Lifting her chin, she steps inside, pulling her coat more tightly, not so much for warmth as for protection.

Closing the door, the policeman moves towards the corner of the room and hovers, his gaze focused straight ahead.

When no instruction is given, Edith moves forward and sits on the only chair in the room. In front of it is a table, a single bulb hanging from the ceiling.

They sit in silence, the policeman giving nothing away; Edith works hard to keep her heartbeat steady, trying not to think about the letters, about what their contents might reveal.

When the door opens again, the arresting officer enters, followed by a third man, short and squat.

'What is your real name?'

'I told your friend. I am Fräulein Braun.'

The man ignores her answer, standing straight and pulling the papers from the inside of his coat. The envelopes are no longer sealed.

'You were at the rally,' he says.

'What rally?'

'On May Day.' He slips one of the envelopes on to the table in front of her. 'What is this?'

She takes a moment, pulling out one of the papers and studying it vaguely. 'It looks like a mimeograph . . . I don't know what else you want me to say.'

'You don't know? But these are your letters.'

She shakes her head. 'I was delivering them; they are not mine.'

'Very well.' He sweeps the contents of the table into his lap and indicates for the other officer to take her down.

The days pass, Edith on the floor of her cell, or on the chair in the interrogation room, where she sits straight, leaning in despite the sourness of the officer's breath.

Blinking against the glare of the naked bulb, she pictures Albers, that first day at the Bauhaus, the walls of the studio bathed in light. *Notice that often you will have more by doing less.*

'You were delivering the letters to the Goethe Bookshop?' he asks her.

'Yes.'

'You are a Communist sympathiser and you were using this shop as a base for receiving and delivering—'

'No.'

Days bleed into weeks, punctuated by variations in her interrogator's breath, the growing crack in the plaster at the corner of the room. When they allow her to send a letter, her fingers grasp the pencil as she writes Litzi's name, telling her she doesn't know how long she will be here, that it is cold at night.

She hums to herself to keep track of time, to hold the minutes in her grasp. The 'Moonlight' sonata, her fingers working the keys, Serkin's voice coming to her through the delirium of sleep-deprivation. *I am hard on you, because I know you can take it. You are strong. It's all in there, waiting to come out . . . I have dedicated myself. It is one thing to want something – in order to have it, you have to make it happen.*

'This letter, Fräulein Braun, is a piece of anti-Government propaganda calling for – and I quote – *a "united front" in support of political prisoners in Austria and Germany*. It also calls for a campaign to send delegates to the International Anti-Fascist Workers' Congress in Copenhagen.'

'Sir, these are not my letters. I had no idea what they contained. I was delivering them for someone.'

'But you didn't, did you? When you saw my men, you walked away. You were guilty, and you tried to hide your activity.'

Her fingers move, under the table, working the keys. *Find something you love and give it everything you have.*

G sharp, C sharp, E. One, three, five.

Arnold's voice, now. *My dear Edith, a whole new world awaits.*

'I was delivering them for someone else.'

In the darkness of the cell, Walter Peterhans' face stares back at her, in the photography studio. *This picture . . . there is an energy to it, and a sadness . . . an anger. The way you use light and shadow to illuminate and restrict, to control the viewer's gaze.*

Her own voice, as his eyes shine through the dark. *It's not just about the lies we tell other people, but the lies we tell ourselves.*

Her whole body pulsates when she awakes to the clatter of the cell door being pulled open. Fumbling to stand, she pulls her body straight. How long has she been here? She will not ask. She needs to get out. *There is only one response to such a threat, and that is to demolish it.* She cannot demolish anything from inside these walls.

It is nearly nightfall when she concedes to give her name. 'You're right, I have not been honest with you. My name is not Braun. My name is Edith Suschitzky. I shouldn't have lied. But I was scared – that's why I walked away.'

'You are a Jew.'

'I am not practising.'

'And you are a Communist.'

Change requires action.

She shakes her head, allowing a tear to run down her cheek.

'Fräulein Suschitzky, if indeed that is your name, you are lying once again. You were seen at the rally.'

'We have searched your parents' home,' he announces one morning, and Edith's stomach knots. 'Among your things, we found leaflets – an appeal from the KPÖ for financial contributions—'

'Someone left them in my father's shop. He had thrown them away and I took them because sometimes I needed materials to make things with the children at kindergarten.'

'To make things?'

'Yes.'

'What sorts of things?'

'Animals, boats . . . It doesn't really matter what. It's about play, experimentation.' Her voice is a whisper.

'Speak up. There were a number of prints, including a photograph of a recent KPÖ demonstration, and also a photographic portrait of a man called Harry Pollitt, the General Secretary of the Communist Party of Great Britain. You took this photograph.'

Nelson's column, Maks's eyes meeting hers through the crowd. *To speak of democracy when working people are starving, exhausted, unable to clothe their children because of the bourgeois capitalist machine that seeks to keep them captive, is contemptuous. The state exists for the purpose of the oppression of one class by another.*

Which one of them spotted the other first?

'I was in England, visiting educationalist friends I had made while I was studying there, years ago, and the man Pollitt you mention asked if he could pay me to take his portrait. He was the one who gave me the Marx book – I took it out of courtesy but I haven't read it. And yes, I was at the rally. I am a photographer – a member of the press. I was there to record the event – an illegal event; I was not there in support of it. I was only delivering the letters as a favour to someone. I had no idea what they contained. If I had . . .'

'Who were you delivering them for?'

'A man I met in a café. I didn't ask his name. He was interested in my camera, we started talking. He said he was delivering letters to the bookshop in aid of a charitable refugee organisation, the Rote Hilfe. He was on crutches – I offered to deliver the letters for him . . .

'What did the man look like?'

It is cold at night.

'He had a crutch. I don't remember much else. He was a few years older than me, maybe, so in his late twenties . . . I wasn't thinking . . . Please, my parents will be worried.'

'Your parents have been informed.'

You are strong. You can take it.

The release, when it arrives, comes with no fanfare, no explanation, the ground seeming to sway from side to side as she exits the police station, unsure of how she made it out.

Outside, the city is louder than she remembers, the movements of the men who pass her too quick. She keeps her pace even, crossing the road, her breath held high in her chest, walking a while longer before turning into an alley and breaking into a run.

By the time she arrives at Litzi's house it is dusk.

The man who answers the door speaks in heavily accented German. 'Are you all right?'

Edith replies in English, her eyes darting inside, over his shoulder. 'Where is Litzi?'

'Who are you?' He runs a hand through his hair to neaten it, speaking with a slight hesitation that will later reveal itself as a full-blown stutter that comes and goes in waves.

She has no more lies left in her. 'I'm Edith, who are you?'

'Edith. Of course . . .' His face visibly brightens as he pulls back the door, revealing a well-cut shirt, his blue-grey eyes following her inside with a look of wary concern that he works hard to realign into something more self-assured.

'I think I'm going to be sick.' She puts an arm on the wall so that she won't fall, controlling her breath, unable to move to the bathroom.

He reaches for her. 'It's all right . . .'

'Who are you?' She says again.

She hears the rain begin to thunder on the roof.

'I'm the lodger. I'm Kim Philby.'

Dear Edith,

We have had a fairly strenuous year, and I, at least, am feeling rather tired. In April, we spent a week in Leningrad, partly business, partly pleasure; the pleasure was the more exhausting part. Then May in the Crimea, which was restful but rather spoilt by unseasonably cold weather. No fooling around in the sea! Then back to Moscow, and a lot of extra work in connection with the 60th anniversary celebrations, which coincided with more celebrations of the 100th anniversary of the birth of Felix Dzerzhinsky, our founder. I seem to be developing into a popular public speaker – believe it or not! Then July hit us with a real heatwave. I enjoyed it but Nina nearly collapsed. So our friends insisted on us going to a place in the countryside not far from here: classic Russian countryside, river, open fields, forest, the lot. But the heatwave broke the day we got there, so we shivered from start to finish. Then early September, off to Hungary for a month, divided between Budapest, Lake Balaton and the northern mountains. Here again the weather fooled us; a few warm days, but mostly too cool to get the full benefits. Also pretty tiring with people, old friends and new acquaintances, bobbing up at all times, expected and unexpected. Nina and I had breakfast alone just three times throughout the month. All the other ninety-seven meals involved company. Very sweet of them, and of course gratifying, but exhausting in the long run.

Back to Moscow, and two more public appearances; after all which, not very surprisingly, I succumbed to a nasty attack of bronchitis, which laid me low for ten days. However, I am now back to work again, about 90 per cent fit, and will doubtless be 100 per cent in a day or two. We had a filthy November, the mildest since 1926; no snow to speak of, and an awful lot of rain.

But four days ago the snow began to fall in earnest and it shows signs of lying, temperatures staying at between minus five and eight. That is still high for December, but the long-range forecast is that it will get colder in the second half of the month. I have just been listening to a BBC sports programme, in which many announcers complained of the bitter cold, plus four!! And here we are complaining of it being too mild at minus five!

Nina is taking her physical training very seriously, and goes off to bathe regularly at the open-air swimming pool opposite the Pushkin Museum. The water is heated, of course, and gives off clouds of steam; I am afraid I excuse myself the same indulgence, pleading too much work to waste myself in such fashion.

Yours,

Kim

PS. I have just read a report in the *New York Herald Tribune* to the effect that there are no matches in

Moscow. I suppose I keep up my two or three packets of cigarettes a day by rubbing twigs together. All very peculiar!

A fairly strenuous year

'Edith, thank God!' Litzi appears in the hallway, doing up the top button of her shirt. 'You're out. It is a nightmare. These bastards! Come, you must be starving. Kim, go and get food. There is soup on the stove. What did they do to you?'

'Nothing,' Edith says. 'Just questions.'

'What did you tell them?'

'Just as I told you in my letter. Nothing.' She lowers her voice, trying to clear her mind. 'Who is the Englishman?'

'He is one of us. He knows people in England. Rich, connected people.' Litzi's voice is excited as she takes her friend's arm. 'You are freezing. Come through to the kitchen, there is much to discuss. Have something to eat.'

'I can't.'

'Here,' Kim says. 'Have a drink. It will steady your nerves.'

They talk for hours, making plans to smuggle activists out of Vienna through the sewer system and on to France, listing people they can go to for money and assistance on behalf of the Relief Committee; adding to their code system for communicating. *May I have a cigarette?* indicates *The coast is clear.* *Thank you for the match* for *You are in danger.*

Edith tunes in and out, her mind unable to settle after nearly a month of sleep-deprivation. *C sharp, G sharp, E.*

'But I came here to serve the International Organisation for Aid to Fighters of the Revolution.' Kim's voice cuts through the mental whirring.

Litzi sighs. 'The most useful thing you can do is to keep a low profile, to play the part of a naïve young idealist here to assist the plight of refugees. Everything else is illegal.'

Edith closes her eyes. *You are strong, you can take it.*

When Litzi's mother Gisella gets home, hours later, she holds Edith like a daughter. 'We were so worried about you.'

'I should go,' Edith says. Kim was right, the drink has taken the edge off and now, more than anything, she feels drained.

Kim stands. 'I'll walk you.'

'There's no need.'

'Don't be ridiculous.' Gisella chastises. 'The boy will walk you. Be safe, Edith. For the love of God, be safe.'

Edith keeps her beret pulled low, her eyes fixed downwards. She walks briskly, holding her nerve as they turn, without speaking, to avoid a checkpoint that has appeared near the flat; the militia-man who stands guard has his back turned to them and does not see.

Kim lights his pipe, once they pass. 'You're shivering – would you like my coat?'

'I'm fine,' she says, without averting her gaze. 'What brings you to Austria?'

When he doesn't immediately answer, Edith turns to look at him. 'This is not a formal interrogation,' she says, drily.

'Just as well,' he replies, and they walk on in silence, the sound of the rain pattering around them.

'I'm sorry for what you've been through,' he says. 'It must have been hellish.'

'Well, I'm not the first. Did Litzi tell you that last year she spent two weeks in jail for her activist work?'

'Yes.'

'And you would be prepared to go to jail too?'

'This still isn't an interrogation?' He laughs, but, when Edith doesn't smile, he continues. 'I have no intention of doing so, but, if it came to it, I'd do whatever it takes.'

'You never told me what brought you here.'

'I want to help.' He shrugs. 'I've been to Austria before. Some old schoolfriends and I travelled together in the holidays, over the past few years. My first motorcycle took a real beating from the unpaved roads, on our way to Hungary – the main structure and the sidecar started leaning in a remarkably precarious manner; more worrying still to my passenger and his luggage – and we stopped to patch it up at a garage, before pushing across the border. In the end it took several more stops, and finally the expertise of a blacksmith, to get it into sufficient order to make it back to England.'

Edith smiles, for the first time in weeks. 'It sounds like quite a trip.'

'It was. I had my camera and money stolen by a youth I gave a lift to, which will teach me a lesson for trying to do the right thing. We came through Vienna on our way back—'

They move along the road towards the apartment, the windows coming into focus, when a sudden silhouette moving towards them makes them slow.

'Alexander!' The relief in Edith's voice is palpable.

'I got your letter, from jail,' he says as he reaches them.

She kisses him on the mouth before pulling away. 'Alexander, this is a friend of Litzi's. Kim is their new lodger, he walked me home.'

'How do you do? I'm Kim Philby.'

Alexander hesitates before taking the extended hand. 'Alexander Tudor-Hart. You're English?'

'I'm afraid so.'

The men study each other for a moment and then Alexander turns back to Edith. 'I was so worried.'

'Well, then, I'll leave you,' Kim says, tipping his hat and receding into the shadows.

Prisoners march two abreast through silent streets as they are led towards the camps that will become their graves, Europe dithering in the months following Chancellor Engelbert Dollfuss's disbanding of parliament. Across the city of Vienna, a fire takes hold.

At home in her parents' apartment, morale is low. With Alexander deep in his studies, Edith spends her evenings with Litzi and Kim, seated around the kitchen table at 9 Latschkagasse. By day, they take turns to ride on the back of Kim's Daimler, the exhaust pipe jolting as they weave through the city, evading the gaze of the guards who line the checkpoints, occasionally stopping for tea on the terrace of the Café Herrenhof: *a trough for our Anglo Trojan horse*, Litzi observes.

In years to come, the barricades assembled in front of the tenements will appear in their nightmares: fortresses comprised of old furniture and car parts, defended by the armed Schutzbund militia; the sound of machine guns and fireworks and futile resistance filling the air as the bulldozers arrived to tear them down. But for now, this isn't a dream but reality, and there is no waking up.

The contents of their deliveries mutate from leaflets collected at an underground printing press and deposited at the workers' militia headquarters in the housing projects, to disassembled pistols and rifles, which they have dismantled into their component parts, in silence at the kitchen table, and placed, concealed in old bits of clothing, for collection across the city.

And at every turn they get away with it, just as every man in history has got away with everything. Until suddenly he hasn't.

Alexander's first full day off following Edith's release is a day that stands out in her memory as brightly as the ball of sun that blazes above them. It is the kind of day when it is possible to close your eyes and tip your head back to the sky and hear the ripples of the river, and, for just a second, forget the tyranny of the world beyond the banks of the Danube where they laze, passing a bottle between them, a constant curl of cigarette smoke twisting above their heads.

Litzi rests her cheek on Kim's arm as he scans the newspaper, reapplying her lipstick using her reflection in his silver cigarette lighter, while he works through the headlines: *Feminicide in Favoriten.*

Edith inhales, taking in the warm summer air, the smell of grass and smoke and beer. When she opens her eyes, the world is blank, the Lobau slowly bleeding into focus.

'*Knockout victory Carneras over Sharkey*,' Kim says, reading aloud the title of the article, his eyebrows furrowed with concentration.

'Didn't have you down as a man interested in boxing,' Alexander says with a hint of disdain.

'I think you understand more than you let on,' Edith interjects, catching Kim breezing through the paper with relative ease as she looks around, her fingers moving instinctively to her camera as her eyes scour the shore. Mentally she frames the scene: topless, bronzed men on the benches outside the refreshment kiosk, sharing a packet of cigarettes; families gathered on blankets on the grass behind, playing a game of cards. As if, just the other side of the bridge, their lives weren't under attack.

'I should be more fluent than I am,' Kim replies, glancing up.

'Nonsense,' Litzi retorts. 'He was at the rally in Stuttgart when Alfred Hugenberg was speaking, and he watched Hitler address a torchlit rally in Munich. He regaled me practically verbatim with what was said.'

'What were you doing at Fascist rallies?' Alexander asks, his question pointed.

'Listening,' Kim says, evenly. 'Actually I was a keen boxer at school, to answer your previous question. Might have had a chance of winning occasionally if I weren't handicapped by a shorter reach than most of my opponents. Besides, I was usually on the defensive. Never does one much good,' he adds, glancing up at Alexander before returning to his paper.

'Well. There's rather a lot we don't know about you,' Alexander continues, the sharpness of his tone causing the women to listen more intently. 'I know you arrived in Cambridge the year I left.'

'We must have overlapped by a few months. I arrived at Trinity in the autumn of 1929, but our paths appear never to have crossed – shame.' Kim lifts the bottle to his lips.

Litzi looks away, suppressing a laugh.

'How is Maurice Dobb?' Alexander continues, sitting up a little straighter. 'He is the one who put you in touch with Litzi's family, I hear.'

Edith shivers, pulling the towel up over her legs, a vision forming of the Red House on Chesterton Lane, a few years earlier.

'Inadvertently.' Kim's lip curls. 'What is this, old chap, the Spanish inquisition?'

'We don't know much about you, that's all. I'm curious, how an English gent ends up here, among all this.'

'Well, I could say the same of you.' Kim shrugs, relighting his pipe.

'Actually Edith and I have known each other for years, from my research trips. She knows my sister, Beatrix. She knows where I come from.'

'Oh, of course. And she has met your wife and child, I hear?' There is a pause, Alexander's cheeks flushing an angry shade of red as Kim continues. 'Well, pray tell, what would you like to know? To start with, I'm afraid you might have misinterpreted the purity of my roots. You see, my father, St John Philby – known to his friends as Jack, and later as Sheikh Abdullah, on account of his converting to Islam – was, as you may or may not be aware, the first self-proclaimed socialist in the Indian British Civil Service. I was born in India, but when I was young – my mother considering Punjab too noisy and dirty a place to raise children – my sisters and I were brought back to London. I studied at Aldro preparatory school in Surrey and then at Westminster before following in my father's footsteps over the River Cam, for university.'

Kim pauses and Litzi leans in, entertained. 'Please carry on, I'm enjoying it.'

'Right. Well, at school, I was neither traumatised by regular canings nor bullied – even despite my stammer and preference for spending time alone. I wasn't particularly good at, nor enthusiastic towards, any sport – other than a predilection for boxing, aforementioned, and a vague interest in cricket – and no one seemed to care two hoots. While my contemporaries spent their summers holidaying in the Côte d'Azur, when I visited my father we spent time with the Bedouin in the desert of Saudi Arabia, and in Nazareth and Damascus, Beirut and Sidon. Other boys' fathers worked in banks and law firms, but mine was an adventurer. While those men passed their time working for a system designed to keep them as slaves, Jack Philby was a free man. So much so that when King Ibn Saud, to whom my father was a key advisor, gave him two slave-girls as a gift for his birthday, my father responded by freeing them both and marrying one of them.'

'While still married to your mother?' Litzi interjects, with a look of wry amusement.

Kim shrugs, taking a puff of his pipe. '*For with whatever judgment you judge, you will be judged; and with whatever measure you measure, it will be measured to you.* The Book of Matthew,' he adds after a beat.

'I hadn't taken you for a holy man either,' Alexander chides, finding his voice finally, though it is less self-assured now.

'Funnily enough, I'm not, but it was one of the few lines that actually stuck when we were forced to read the Bible at school – no time for the rest of it, with the possible exception of Sodom and Gomorrah. Plenty there to bring a blush to the cheek of a lady. Personally, I have no time for the Qu'ran either, what little I've read of it.'

'But you weren't upset?' Edith asks, taking out a cigarette.

'About what?'

'Your father marrying another woman in such a way.'

Kim half-smiles. 'I'm not sure. I've never really considered it. My point is, I suppose, that it's none of my business, and to assume to fathom someone else's motivation for the decisions they make is nothing short of arrogant. That isn't to say one shouldn't spend time *considering* the inner workings of the mind – but considering and *seeking to know* are quite different things. One can analyse without casting judgement. So no, Edith, in answer to your question, I don't resent my father at all. What I did come to resent, as the years passed, was the privilege that a certain kind of man wears as a second skin – a padding against the perils of the world. That, I confess, has started to itch a little.' Kim's eyes linger on Alexander, his expression hardening. 'Which leads me to answer your real question: how such an apparently upper-class creature such as myself might betray his roots by coming here to slum it in the process of helping others? In order to understand that, you must understand one other thing. To betray, you must first belong. And believe me, Alexander, I never belonged.'

'I don't see why you dislike him so much,' Edith says as they cool themselves in the river. She lies back, feeling the water pull at her hair. 'He's charming, and he is dedicated.'

Alexander snorts. 'Charm is not necessarily an asset.'

'You think I'm attracted to him, don't you? Oh, don't be jealous.' Edith laughs. 'Anyway, he and Litzi are inseparable. She tells me he really has given away all his money; he spends his days devoted to action—'

'Litzi would say that.'

Edith's expression hardens, defensively. 'I've seen it for myself. And you would have, too, if you'd been there.' She stops herself. 'If you are suggesting that Litzi would put a boy she has just met above the cause, then you don't know her at all.' Softening, Edith leans in to kiss him, reaching for his body below the surface of the water. 'Besides, he's totally inexperienced in bed, apparently. At least he was until Litzi got her hands on him.'

Without his glasses, Alexander's features seem more pinched

as he looks over her shoulder towards the bank. Staring at Kim, he shakes his head. 'There's something about him I just don't trust.'

It is getting dark by the time they leave, Litzi and Kim walking ahead, she giggling into his arm as she takes the helmet he hands to her.

'Come on, let's all go back to mine,' Litzi says as Edith and Alexander catch up. 'My parents won't mind.'

Alexander leans in, putting a hand on Edith's waist, talking quietly. 'Why don't you and I go back to my place?'

Edith frowns, pouting her lips. 'It's been such a nice day, I'm not ready for it to end.'

Back at the house in the 9th district, Alexander fixes Kim with his sharp gaze, a bottle of schnapps on the table between them.

'So how long do you plan to stay in Austria, Kim?'

Keeping his attention on the pipe he is packing with tobacco, Kim doesn't respond immediately, striking a match and inhaling deeply before replying, his words curling with smoke.

'As long as I am needed.'

'Take my photo, Edith.' Litzi stands, leading towards the living room, clearly bored with Alexander's posturing, and slightly tipsy from the liquor.

'Now?'

'Why not? We can immortalise today. It feels like one of those moments that lives on forever.'

'Or possibly it feels like you have drunk too much schnapps.' Edith laughs, standing and arranging the camera.

The men stop talking as Litzi positions herself on the chair, her eyes set on Edith, who looks down through the viewing lens, smiling slightly as she clicks, capturing Litzi's eyes and the thick dark curls that fall over her shoulder.

Glancing at Kim, Edith sees him watching Litzi too, his expression full of wonder. He wears a checked shirt and tie below a thick jacket, a pipe firmly held in his mouth. When she looks away again, she senses Alexander's eyes on her, from where he stands in the corner.

'Got it?' Litzi asks, standing and walking to the door. 'I'll get more drinks. Put on some music, Alexander.'

As Alexander moves to the gramophone, Kim looks down, his expression pensive. Working reflexively, Edith adjusts the image, peering through the viewing lens of the Rolleiflex, which she holds at chest height. Taking the shot, only she hears the low vibration signalling the image being immortalised. When a sudden burst of noise drifts in from somewhere outside the room, they all look up.

Recognising a sudden commotion in the hallway, Edith stands. It's Litzi's father Israel's voice, followed by those of men she doesn't recognise. Jumping up, Kim picks up two of the wine glasses and beckons to Edith and Alexander to follow him into his bedroom. 'Quick, through here.'

'But what about Litzi—'

She and Alexander are barely inside the spare room when she hears the guards moving into the living room behind them, inches from where she and Alexander stand, their backs pressed against the wall. Her heart swells and contracts in her chest, its motion mimicking the harpsichord played by the blind beggar on the bridge near the train station. Her mind rests there, at the arches of Wien Südbahnof: their escape route to another life.

'Who else is in the house?' the guards say on the other side of the wall.

The voice that answers them is Kim's, his accented German growing muffled as he pulls the door to behind him, obscuring the chords that warp and convulse from the record player. 'Only me. I'm the lodger, sir.'

The following morning Edith hovers on the corner of Litzi's street before making her way towards the front door, her movements skittish from nerves and excitement.

It is Kim who answers, his eyes brightening at the sight of her.

'Where's Litzi?' Edith says, removing her hat and following him into the kitchen. Moving to the window, she scans the street but it's empty.

'She will be back soon. Don't worry, she hasn't been arrested.'

Moving to the cupboard, Kim pulls out a glass and indicates to the bottle of whisky on the table.

'It's a little early for me,' she says, and Kim shrugs. 'No Alexander?'

'He's studying,' Edith replies, evenly, butterflies fluttering in her stomach at the mention of him, of the decision they have made. 'I've been at a piano lesson.'

'What were you practising?' Kim says, the mundanity of his question taking her by surprise.

'Bach's Capriccio in E major. You look disgusted. You know it?'

'No, but I know enough of Bach to know that he's not to my taste – he never developed. It's impossible to tell a piece he wrote when he was ten from one that he wrote when he was sixty.'

'What does it matter if a person fails to develop, if what they are capable of at the age of ten is truly brilliant? I can't quite believe we're talking about this. . .' Her eyebrows arch with incredulity. 'You're remarkably sure of yourself. Do you even play?'

'Not a note. Tried my hand at the French horn for a while, but let's say it's no great loss to humanity that I decided to focus on other matters.'

Her eyes move to the clock. If she doesn't tell Litzi her news soon she thinks she will burst.

'Actually, I will have one,' Edith says, pointing to the whisky. Kim smiles slightly, pouring a glass, which she takes from him and downs in a single appreciative gulp. Leaning back against the counter, she pulls a packet of cigarettes from her pocket.

'Is everything alright, you seem. . .' Kim regards her with curiosity.

She blinks up at him, and then back down at her cigarette as she strikes a match and inhales. 'Last night we were nearly arrested again, had you forgotten? Do you have any idea what will happen to me and Litzi if that should happen.'

'I know, I didn't mean. . .' Kim tips his head back and empties his glass. 'I'm writing to my father, asking him for more money.'

Something about way he says it causes her to smart. 'You think we can buy our way out of this?' She shakes her head, feeling strangely calm. 'It's too late for that. We can't do anything more from here.'

'Don't say that.' Kim's voice is quiet.

'It's true. Unless we can get out of Austria, to somewhere we can make a difference, somewhere we can live, freely. . .' Pausing, she looks up. 'I've spoken to Alexander. Last night, after what happened, he agreed to marry me. We're moving to England. You should do the same for Litzi, if you really want to help. Right now it's the greatest contribution you could make.'

The release at having told someone makes her stand taller.

'You're running away – what about your family?' The moment he says it, Kim backtracks. 'I didn't mean. . . But you can't go. You're needed here, for the fight. Things are just heating—'

Edith's cheeks burn. 'How dare you. What do you know about anything? What do you know about what it is to suffer, to watch your family and your country torn apart? Alexander was right about you. You, with your money and your power and your remarkable sense of entitlement; you who can leave at any time. What is this to you anyway, a game? A way to prove to yourself that you're as brave as your father; a way to get his attention? Or is it just a way to prove to yourself that your life means anything at all?'

In the silence that follows Edith hears Litzi walk into the room. 'What's going on?'

Edith holds Kim's eye for another moment before she replies, looking away from him, her expression one of disgust. 'Ask your boyfriend.'

Turning, she touches Litzi's arm with her hand. 'I have to pack.'

She pauses for a split second before accepting the pen from the registrar and signing her name next to Alexander's. A moment of doubt, if that's what it is, and then it is done – the two of them now officially side by side: Mr and Mrs Tudor-Hart. August 1933, the beginning of another life.

When she thinks back on the day of the wedding, in the months after they have come to London, she pictures a tender sun casting barrels of light along the Jaurèsgasse. She has the impression of peering back through a long tunnel, past the perfunctory ceremony and the walk home along wide-open streets to the apartment where Wilhelm raises his glass in cautious celebration, his eyes shining with love and fear and other emotions that it will never again be the time or the place to convey.

'Play us a tune,' Wilhelm repeats, in her memory, and Edith sits at the piano, feeling her father's hand on her shoulder, silence falling across the room as she holds her fingers above the keys before Liszt's Transcendental Étude No.12, 'Snowstorm', envelops them in its melancholic refrain.

Once again, she hears her father's voice on the stairs as he slipped off to bed that night. 'I'm proud of you. My beautiful daughter.'

Though the memory is growing weaker now, the sound fading, a hand around her heart, twisting, she pictures Wilhelm's eyes milky with a distant concentration as if memorising the shape of her.

It is February the following year when she receives the letter from Litzi, in the days after the Dollfuss revolt.

One thousand, five hundred people arrested in four days. Executions—

Edith's eyes skim over the words, blurred through tears as she pictures those she has left behind. Her mother and father. Wolf. Regardless of what she had told Kim, she does feel guilty. She does believe, somewhere in her gut, that she was wrong to leave.

And then, through the fog, an invisible hand reaches out from the page and wipes her eyes.

Kim has asked me to marry him. Edie, I'm coming to London.

London. The idea of it had been taking root at the back of Kim's mind for months, along with the other words Edith had used the last time he had seen her – her eyes boring into his as she spoke. She was right on some of it, not all. He wanted to do the right thing, he did truly care. But how could he accept that his biggest contribution would be to simply go home?

Like a flurry of snowflakes, the thought had gathered pace, almost imperceptible at first, taking hold over the weeks and months following Edith and Alexander's departure until the decision was settled, as firm and absolute as the snow that blanketed Vienna the day he made his way to the safe house where Litzi had been staying since going underground.

She was seated at the kitchen table, her expression grave, jumping to her feet when she saw him, her eyes moving over the blood-stains on his shirt.

'Kim! What happened – I heard the Karl Marx Hof and the Goethe Hof were shelled – were you there? Are you hurt?' She searches his body for signs of injury.

Kim shook his head. 'The blood's not mine. I swapped clothing with one of a group of workers we helped escape from the flats to the sewers. They should be on their way out to Czechoslovakia as we speak.'

'It's a disaster.'

'Yes.'

'I don't know what to do.'

'Marry me.' The words came out before he could stop them. And so it is: February 1934, the month Kim Philby and Litzi Friedmann are wed and move together to the homeland he had worked so hard to escape.

Dear Edith,

I have been meaning to write ever since the New Year, but something always seems to turn up to divert me. I suppose it would be more honest to confess that I now habitually grasp any excuse for postponing an assault on my typewriter.

In my defence, my eldest son, John, has just left. There was a real snowstorm, but they got off all right in the end. As we poured him on to the Air France plane at Sheremetyevo airport, it crossed my mind that he might either leave the furs and caviar we sent him off with aboard or give them to some attractive girl guerrilla at Orly. He was in one of his most generous moods.

He lives in north London, and it is therefore odd to think of him and his girlfriend attracting the notice of the Soviet trade delegation on Hampstead Heath with their furs of a certain origin.

I wonder if you ever think of those early London days?
Yours,
Kim

Those early London days

In the beginning, Edith lives between Alexander's house at 68 Acre Lane, in Brixton, and a studio she rents on Haverstock Hill, on the north side of the city, obtained through a friend of a friend.

'Half of Vienna seems to be in Hampstead nowadays,' the woman says, noting the single suitcase as she hands over the keys to the dingy basement flat Edith plans to sub-let to help cover the bills. 'Do you plan to live in it too?'

Edith smiles, evasively. 'I haven't decided yet.'

The day of the demonstration she travels from Alexander's place in south London, taking the Morden – Edgware line from Clapham North and changing trains before disembarking at Sloane Square, passing Oswald Mosley's barracks as she moves along the King's Road towards their allocated meeting place.

In the few months since Litzi had arrived in London, her appearance has changed so many times that Edith is unsure what to expect as she approaches the Markham Arms. Her friend waits at a table in the corner, her thumb nervously working the filter of her cigarette. The only woman in the bar, her hair is dyed unnaturally dark, and she chews a fingernail between agitated puffs. A copy of the *Daily Worker* lies on the table in front of her, the headline crying out: *Workers! Demonstrate Today!*

When Litzi looks up and sees Edith, she smiles weakly and stubs out her cigarette. 'Edie, I can't stand it here,' she says once Edith is settled on the stool opposite. 'In Vienna, we had roles – In London, I am so useless.'

'Well, today we march. That's something.' Edith places a hand on Litzi's. 'How did you get a table on your own?'

'Kim came with me.' Litzi pulls back her hand and lights another cigarette. At the mention of his name, Edith fidgets in her chair. 'He's gone to have a meeting around the corner – trying to convince someone to give him a job, as always. But it's true what he said about connections; you should hear the names of the people his family knows.'

'And how is his mother's apartment?'

Litzi shrugs, her manner sulky. 'Better than our previous room in that grotty boarding house, sharing a kitchen and a bathroom with people we don't know, surrounded by all my furniture from home to remind me of everything we've left behind . . .' She sighs. 'Sometimes I wish someone had tried to stop us leaving Vienna—'

'And who would you have chosen to do so – Dollfuss, or Hitler?' Edith asks under her breath, holding her friend's eyes. Her voice returns to a more natural volume as she changes the subject. 'I had a letter from Wolf; he met a girl on his course at the school of graphic art, they're coming to London.'

'And what about Wilhelm and Adele, will they come later?'

'They will have to pull my father from that bookshop in a body-bag. I like it in London, though.' Taking a sip of Litzi's gin, Edith pushes a lock of hair behind her ear, letting it fall back in front of her face as she surveys the room, the men in the bar each deep in thought or conversation or drink, or all three. 'I think I might have some paid photographic work,' she says. 'You remember Alexander's sister, Beatrix? Through her I've met a man who has promised to introduce me to someone who edits a weekly magazine established by the BBC.'

'I'm glad to hear it. You deserve happiness, Edith.'

Standing, she tucks the newspaper under her arm, and picks up her gloves. 'Yes, though I would be here whether it made me happy or not. We should go – the demonstration has already started.'

It is a week later, on a rare day off from his shifts at St Mary Abbott's Hospital in Kensington, when Alexander visits her at the basement flat at 158 Haverstock Hill.

'This is where I get to dissect life and put it back together as I see fit,' Edith says, holding her head high as she gives him the guided tour of the studio, which is divided into two sections. On one side there are large bottles of chemical developer and the silver gelatin paper Edith buys from Wallace Heaton Ltd in Mayfair, stored above the drying chest she purchased with money that was a wedding present from Wilhelm and Adele. On the other, the darkroom is defined by a heavy curtain, a light-box set up outside.

'Before the photographer enters the darkroom, this is where she, or he, checks the images for the first time, choosing which to develop.'

'Sounds rather like playing God,' Alexander replies, and Edith smiles.

'I suppose it is rather – not unlike medicine. A new photographer friend helped me with the set-up.'

'A friend?' Alexander's voice sharpens.

'A friend, yes. I have lots of friends in London already, through various societies. And my cousins, of course. You might meet them if you ever stopped working.'

Pulling back the long dark brown curtain, which is pinned to the ceiling and again along one wall, she exposes the space inside, the light a dank yellow. The smell of the chemicals, which sit in three separate trays along a wooden bench, seeps through the air.

'Speaking of which, I won't be able to come to the party tomorrow,' Alexander says, matter-of-fact.

'But Alexander, it's important—'

'I have to catch up on things before we head off to Wales.' His voice is short, non-negotiable.

'Right. Well, let's fuck now, shall we, and then you won't be held up any longer?'

She expects the slightest show from her husband that he isn't just here for the sex, before he heads back across the river to the house they nominally share. But once it is over he makes no attempt to protest or challenge her when she tells him she will stay at the studio again tonight. Instead, they arrange to meet the day after next, in order to travel together to Rhondda – and once again, less than six months after her wedding, Edith spends the evening alone.

Thinking of Arnold Deutsch in another land, her mind eventually drifts into an almost meditative state as she dips the paper between the various dishes – developing solution, water, ammonium thiosulphate – watching parts of the image emerge, still shadowy, at first, and, then startlingly clear.

She sleeps in the chair that sits in the corner, waking to sunlight drifting across the top of the drying chest. Pulling on a pair of cotton gloves, she takes a moment to consider the prints she hopes will demonstrate to Jack Pritchard's BBC contact the breadth of both her skill and style. The first is slightly out of focus, a family in the slums, dynamic as if with perpetual motion; then officers making an arrest in Vienna, the accused, flanked by armed police, just visible behind the torso of a businessman dressed in suit and tie.

The most recent was taken at the march a week earlier: two protestors, the first holding a placard demanding the release of the Comintern leader Georgi Dimitrov, arrested on Hitler's orders after the Reichstag fire; the second man with an illustrated face of the KPD leader Ernst Thälmann, held in solitary confinement after his arrest by the Gestapo.

Placing the prints side by side on top of the drying cabinet, Edith removes the gloves and opens the drawer, pulling out the photograph she has promised to Beatrix: herself and Alexander, the day of their wedding. The shot had been taken by Wolf, at the apartment in the hours after the officialdom was complete, each looking over the other's shoulder, as if searching for someone just out of view.

A wind grips her as she steps outside the studio that evening, as if bracing her for what is to come.

Glancing behind, she picks up pace, pulling her long, dark coat against herself as she turns on to Upper Park Road, the prints carefully stored between sheets of brown paper inside her bag. Despite the layers she has the sensation of sudden exposure, a creeping feeling, unmistakable as the hypothalamus part of her brain sends a message via the nervous system to the arrector pili muscles, causing the skin along the tops of her arms to tighten, the tips of the hairs standing on end, brushing against the insides of her clothes. A feeling that tells her she is being watched.

Keeping her eyes fixed ahead, she tells herself that she has nothing to fear, reminding herself that she is safe now. It is as she reaches the bottom of Lawn Road that he steps out in front of her, and she gasps as he moves forward, fixing her eyes in a way that tells her not to scream.

'Keep walking,' he says, and then, once they are in motion, 'I thought you would be pleased to see me.'

'What are you doing here? How long are you in London? I haven't heard a word from you.' Edith berates him as they continue along the pavement, keeping a brisk pace. Above the beat of her heart, which pounds in her chest, her cheeks are hot with excitement, her fingers curling in on themselves, nails pressing into her palms. 'You can't just appear and disappear—'

'I'll stay as long as I'm needed,' Arnold says, ignoring her rebuke. 'Officially I'm here taking a postgraduate course. My cousin Oscar owns a chain of cinemas in London; he is sponsoring me.' Arnold Deutsch moves straight to the point. 'Moscow is keen to find new ears and eyes on the ground – people who can be genuinely useful to the party.'

Edith keeps her eyes fixed ahead. 'Am I no longer useful to you?'

'I thought it was I who was no longer useful to you.'

'What do you mean?' She turns to him then.

'I heard about the work you have been doing for the South London Hospital for Women and Children, the so-called "Adamless Eden". It is an interesting experiment you have been cataloguing. Ultraviolet light treatment . . .'

'So you sought me out to discuss innovative hospital treatments and my views on the patriarchy?'

He ignores the question. 'You would be infinitely more useful if you would keep a lower profile, Edith. Moscow is not happy about you accompanying thousands of people on public demonstrations. Then there is the matter of your joining of the Artists' International Association and the Workers'

Camera Club, not to mention your part in the exhibition *Artists against Fascism and Against War.*'

'I am a photographer, Arnold. I have to work.'

'You are literally making an exhibition of yourself and your views. Many of the people at the heads of these organisations are openly sympathisers.'

'How could I not support my brothers and—'

'Edith, how many times? Your contribution is bigger than that. To support us in ways that really count, above all we need your discretion.'

They turn into an alley, streaks of ivy hanging down a high wall, and she steps towards him, her heartbeat rising at his touch. 'Arnold . . . Vienna, it's a nightmare.'

'Yes. But in Moscow there is much to be hopeful for.'

She says nothing, letting her cheek rest against his until he gently pushes her away. 'How is Alexander?'

'Busy.' She speaks roughly, unable to meet his eye, changing the subject. 'I saw Litzi a few days ago. She feels neglected.'

Arnold laughs, bitterly. 'It is not our job to entertain her.'

'I don't mean it like that. You know how important it is to her to serve the party. But she feels impotent, as though she has no role here. Her Englishman is busy all the time . . .'

'It was a bold thing for him to do, marrying Litzi to bring her to England.'

'Yes.'

'What else do you know about him?'

Edith pauses. 'I know that I like him very much. Alexander thinks he is too bourgeois to be trusted, but, from everything I have seen, he is committed.'

'What is his background?'

'Public school, Cambridge. His father is something of a celebrity, a famous Arabist. Kim could get a job anywhere, with his connections, but he is different; I believe that he cares. He wants to do something where he will be helping the Party.'

'And you trust him?'

'Absolutely.'

She watches him go, leaning back against the wall, letting her pulse return to normal before circling back towards Lawn Road, a light April breeze licking at her heels.

It is some time around six when she hears the bang – she will realise later the significance of the timing – the shock of it causing her to touch the side of her head. At the time she tells herself it is nothing more than the backfiring of the exhaust pipe of a motor-car. Yet she feels a sudden inexplicable nervousness as she approaches the flats. The shadow of a single tree contorts against a series of white walkways that run along the length of the Isokon building, which rises from the old-world salubriousness of Belsize Park like a portal into another universe.

Edith's hands are pale, trembling slightly as she rings the bell. Jack's wife answers the door, her smile fading. 'My dear, are you OK?'

'I'm fine,' Edith replies, kissing Molly Pritchard on the cheek, fixing her mouth in an unconvincing smile as she follows her into the living room, where metal windows frame an evening sky, the promise of spring still visible in the tips of the high branches and the chimney-stacks.

Despite the deceptively calm appearance of the building from the street outside, inside, the flat is ablaze with music and conversation. Across the living room and outdoor terrace there are faces she recognises from her time in London, and back in Vienna, and those she doesn't.

'It's beautiful,' Edith says, taking in the space with its curved honey-coloured plywood lines, Jack reclining on one of several long chairs that protrude from the right-hand corner of the room, under a pendant lamp.

'We love it, our little community.' Molly beams. Everything about her seems bright and hopeful. 'You've met Wells Coates, surely? No? Well, you will tonight. He is very clear on the concept of the Isokon: "a place which every actor in this drama can call his own". Isn't that grand? And Marcel Breuer designed all the furniture, with Jack. Could Alex not join us?'

'He's working.' Edith strains to be heard above the music and the shrieking of the young children on the adjoining roof garden.

'Beatrix says you're living in Brixton. Good God, what are you doing down there? You should come and rent one of our places. You'll know everyone coming through these doors – and those you don't know from Austria, you'll surely remember from the Bauhaus.'

'I also rent a studio around the corner from here; I stay there a lot. Is Beatrix here? I brought her the photograph of the wedding she asked for.'

'She'll be along later.' Molly takes the print and holds it under one of the lamps. 'Oh, but look how brooding and beautiful you are.'

'My brother took it. He has a good eye.'

'I know how sorry Beatrix was not to be there, but she will appreciate this. That brother of hers makes rather a handsome bridegroom. It's a shame he couldn't be here this evening, but no matter. You must know Lázló Moholy-Nagy and his ex-wife Lucia? They're both here. Lucia just arrived in London – she's a portrait photographer, you'll get on famously. And Brigitte Kuczynski, who was introduced to us by Gertrude Sirnis – I feel you'll have many people in common. Brigitte – I believe she now goes by her married name, Lewis – is moving in with her husband. You really should consider it.'

'I'm not sure I could afford the rent, Molly,' Edith says, scanning the room, her vision blurring at the edges.

'Are you sure you're OK, darling?' Molly's expression changes. 'You look terrible.'

'I just feel—'

She is interrupted by Jack, his amiable grin stretching from ear to ear. 'Edith! Excellent to see you. But you don't have a drink. Here, take one from the trolley – nothing says *I've made it* like a portable bar, am I right? And you've brought your camera, I see. Excellent, excellent. Now follow me: there are people I must introduce you to. You remember Percy Glading?'

'I'll leave you to it.' Molly pats Edith on the arm before slipping away.

The man beside Jack has a full mouth, his hair worn swept to one side.

'Of course I remember,' Edith says, trying her best to smile, her hand reaching to relieve the shooting pain at her temple. 'We first met at the rally in Trafalgar Square, years ago.'

Percy Glading is older than she is, perhaps by some fifteen years. When he smiles, it exposes a wide gap between the teeth on the top left of his mouth. 'You took the portraits of Harry Pollitt at our offices, I seem to remember,' he replies in a London accent that is starkly different from those around him. 'Good they were, too.' He watches her over the top of his glass as he takes a sip of his drink. 'And how is Alexander?'

'Very well, thank you. We are heading to Wales in the morning, to support the miners.'

'Too bloody right,' Percy says, raising his pint of ale.

'Hear, hear,' Jack agrees, addressing Edith. 'And this is R.S.

Lambert, editor of the BBC magazine *The Listener*. Richard is also a soon-to-be author. He's just been telling me he's writing a book with an expert on the paranormal, about a talking mongoose said to be haunting an isolated farmhouse on the Isle of Man, no less. Intriguing, wouldn't you agree? Speaking of intrigue, Richard, Edith is an incredibly talented and committed photographer, and the sister-in-law of Beatrix Tudor-Hart, whom you've met. Edith is taking the photographs of the Lawn Road Flats to use in our official literature. I was just explaining to Lambert here our vision of a rational, brave new approach to all problems, so as to make for a better world. Not too much to ask, is it?'

Edith is packing for Wales when the doorbell rings early the following morning.

Alexander's face, on the doorstep, is pale.

'I thought I was meeting you in—'

'Edith, a telegram arrived – it's your father.'

19 April 1934

The 56-year-old bookseller Wilhelm Suschitzky was found dead in the bathtub by his wife after she returned home yesterday at around 7pm. Suschitzky owned the bookstore and publishers Brüder Suschitzky on Petzvalgasse with his brother, Philipp. He was discovered in the apartment at Petzvalgasse 4 with a bullet in his right temple. Wilhelm and Philipp founded the bookstore 33 years ago after a number of difficulties in securing a licence, and an interpellation in the House of Representatives. The brothers later opened the Anzengruber-Verlag, Vienna-Leipzig, which published socialist and monist works. He is succeeded by his children, Edith and Wolf, and his wife Adele.

The day of Wilhelm's funeral, the sky above the Rhondda Valley is grey and wool-like. When she thinks of him, she pictures him in the bookshop in Petzvalgasse, seated behind the small wooden counter: the site of a battle he chose to fight in his own head, a place where the only victor and loser were bound to live side by side, fighting for air, until there was none.

Dear Edith,

I have been thinking, again, of our shared past – this nostalgia of mine is becoming something of an affliction. Perhaps it is the onset of spring that brings to mind that day. June 1934, Regent's Park.

I've been speaking to a journalist, here in Moscow. He keeps asking whether I was told, then, who 'we' were. I told him the truth, in part: that I didn't ask any questions, that I never learnt who our Hungarian friend represented. I didn't say that it wouldn't have mattered either way, were it the Soviet Union or the Comintern. But it is frustrating – these questions are so beside the point. The point, I told him, is that, after seeing how Austria was drenched with the blood of the workers, I understood which side of the barricades was my place. Besides that, I was being offered a very interesting future, a very interesting life. I had a life goal, and I was able to offer the Communists and anti-Fascists information that they couldn't get from anyone else. If I'm honest, the romance of it appealed to me. Also true is that I would have been susceptible to our mutual friend, in any case. The way he looked at you as if nothing more important in life, or more interesting

117

than you, existed at that moment. Do you ever think
of it, Edith?

I'm afraid modern life is always just round the corner,
to shatter the memories. If you were to visit, you might
have found Moscow a bit of a shambles. They seem to
be telescoping a twenty-year reconstruction programme
into five years, doing the place up pretty for the 1980
Olympics. At the age of seventy or so, I shall be living
in a posh city, though I doubt whether I will prefer it to
the one I know. That reminds me of that chump,
Copeland, who wrote that, if I had played my cards right,
I could be living now in retirement in Jersey. As to fact,
he is certainly right. But who the hell wants to retire to
Jersey?

I have just sent a telegram to my son, John, who has
had a terrible introduction to his new flat in London,
which has been broken into: 13 Anson Road. It shouldn't
have been altogether surprising, I told him, since Anson
was a notorious pirate in the Pacific before becoming
First Lord of the Admiralty. I did also have to ask what
on earth he was doing with two TV sets and three radios?
I suggested he spend the insurance money on one of
each, and keep the balance for the inner man. Too much
food for the soul is apt to make one sick and, like
Hermann Göring, reach for the revolver when one hears
the word 'culture'. The real problem seems to be how to
stop it happening again, as improved security locks seem
to make no difference. Steel doors and bars on the
windows? As I said, he might as well move straight into
the zoo – or Holloway Gaol for that matter. My other
suggestion was that he might rename his flat 12A, or
something. Even here, a while back in 1976 I was

attacked for a party celebrating the 13th anniversary of my arrival. But I pointed out – quick as a flash – that the 13th anniv. meant that my 13th year was over; that it was actually the first day of my 14th year!

I recently received the latest copy of *Private Eye*. Apart from its value as entertainment and gossip (I did not know, for example, that Princess Margaret was Horsey Llewellyn's paramour), I find it positively useful. It seems to be astonishingly well informed on the subject of financial skulduggery, and I wonder where they get the stuff? As they can't have a very big staff, I suppose it comes from city slickers who are disgruntled about other more successful slickers getting still deeper into the gravy. If his finances still run to it round about August next, I have asked John if he would renew my subscription.

Otherwise, no news in particular to report. Nina is having her English lesson in the next room, and soon thereafter we leave to have a cheerful dinner with a great friend from Bulgaria who is here for a week or so. Which reminds me that there is one item of news to give you: Nina has discovered a secret source of Scottish whisky. It says much for the marvels of Soviet economy that a bottle (approximately 700 grams) sells for 6.50; whereas Soviet vodka and brandy (500g) are four and eight, respectively. So you can say of Scottish that it's good and it's cheap!

Yours,

Kim

P.S. The funny world-wide weather is afflicting us. The last three winters have been barely colder than in

England. On the morning of Christmas, I looked out of my window and saw no snow whatever. We had one heavyish fall in mid-December, but it didn't lie more than a week. So no skiing; all very disappointing, but still no tornadoes or earthquakes.

June 1934, Regent's Park

The sky is as sharp as the one above Grundlsee, as blue as the lakes in Sweden, as cold as the metal that had grazed her father's temple, the day she makes the introduction. No tornadoes or earthquakes, nothing to indicate the magnitude of what is about to take place.

Despite the morning sun, Edith wears a dark turtleneck and long skirt, a beret pulled down over her hair. It is the first time they have seen each other since that day last year in Vienna, but neither mentions it, barely exchanging a word as they set off, each buried in his and her own thoughts. She moves quickly, sticking to the shadows, Kim keeping pace, his hands pushed deep into the pockets of his overcoat, the bit of his pipe clenched between his teeth.

The journey from Marble Arch to Regent's Park takes longer than it should. There is a portentous quality to the silence as they turn into Hyde Park, and then the scuffling of horse-hooves. He had mentioned it to her once, his fear of horses, and Edith watches him out of the corner of her eye, waiting for him to flinch. When he doesn't, she leads away from the park, a single bead of sweat visible on his forehead as they cut through Mayfair.

Keeping her training in mind, she leads them back and forth for an hour or so, focusing ahead, remaining alert to every sound as the city comes to life. Some time later she hails a taxi, Kim ducking in beside her, a ripple of electricity passing between them, along with unspoken questions, as his hand accidentally brushes hers.

London skids past on the other side of the glass: children skipping behind impatient parents, lovers walking arm-in-arm, faces tipped towards one another, locked in their own private world.

When she thinks of the figure awaiting them, she feels a flutter, a moth trapped in her ribcage, its wings catching on each of the bones, strumming out a sorrowful tune.

By the time they reach the tube station more than two hours have passed. It is cooler down here, below ground. Her companion bristles with nervous energy, shivering as the train approaches, a rat scuttling across the track and disappearing into the darkness.

Edith boards first and they stand side by side, backs to the wall, making way for another passenger who appears from nowhere – *I do beg your pardon* – as he squeezes past, holding on to the brim of his hat. Without warning, as the doors start to close, Edith takes Kim's hand and pulls him out of the carriage, leading him across the empty concourse to the opposite platform where another train hurtles towards them.

It is only once they are on the path that follows the perimeter of Regent's Park that Kim finally speaks. 'He is expecting us?'

Edith says nothing, only slowing slightly, allowing her charge to move ahead as they catch sight of a figure on the bench: short, stocky frame, boxer's ears partially obscured beneath a hat.

Still winded by the sight of him, after all these years, she turns before either man sees her face, the single tear inexplicably running down her cheek.

As she walks away from the men on the bench, her heartbeat finally slows. Letting her mind drift as she crosses Regent's Park, she feels as though she is looking down on herself from above, watching the solitary figure walking around the boating lake towards the newly opened Queen Mary's Gardens, where her brother awaits.

'Wolfi, it's good to see you. I wasn't sure if you would come.'

She hugs him tightly, feeling him taken aback by this uncharacteristic display of affection.

He carries a Rolleiflex in a leather case that matches her own. 'You know where you lead, I follow,' he says when he notices her looking.

'I think we both know that's not true.'

Edith takes his arm as they walk through the garden, the smell of the roses at odds with the ghost that hangs between them, his name as yet unspoken.

'In any case, there is no future for me in Austria,' Wolf says. 'Red Vienna has all but disappeared, Parliament is dissolved, trade unions have been forbidden, unionists imprisoned. But I don't have to remind you of that.'

'You never seemed to notice,' Edith replies, and feels him flinch beside her.

'There was an article about Father.' Wolf pulls a newspaper from under his arm.

Edith takes it and puts it into her bag without looking, breathing deep. 'I'll read it later.'

He looks straight ahead. 'We couldn't even go to the funeral.'

'How is your girlfriend – Helena Voûte, you said her name was?' Edith asks, changing the subject.

'We call her Puck. You will like her.'

Edith lights a cigarette, indicating towards his camera. 'So you're not tempted to pursue a career in zoology, after all?'

'Photography is more practical. Besides, I take photos of the animals in my spare time.'

Edith smiles, sadly. 'If only you had as much dedication to your people as you do to the animals. You know, if you need to develop your films, I have a studio . . .'

There is silence as they walk on, their feet slightly out of sync.

'You are still working for your same friends?' Wolf asks, after a while.

'I would have thought you knew me better than to have to ask.' She looks over his shoulder. 'You know we could always do with more friends.'

He considers her a while, before looking away. 'And you never even question it – giving everything for a place you have never visited. How can you be so sure, about your choices?'

She looks up at him. 'Because for me it is not a choice.'

That evening, new tenants arrive at Edith's flat, friends of friends seeking refuge while they await work and permanent residence permits. After a while they find somewhere else and others take their place, summer rolling on, the shadows of the trees on Hampstead Heath leaning out, Edith's silhouette growing long in front of her.

She spots Arnold as she reaches the point where the main path outside Kenwood House meets another, less distinguished track. The earth is dry beneath her feet as she follows the slight incline down towards the lake, the longer grass brushing her ankles as she veers off, meandering a little, out of habit, careful not to trample the occasional wildflowers that peek through a delicate blanket of green.

She doesn't look up, wary of anything that might draw attention – not that a young woman wandering through the meadows of Hampstead Heath on a fine midsummer's morning should rouse the suspicions of either the family picnicking under the tree on the other side of the water or the dog-walker making his way across towards the Spaniards Inn. Were they to be noticed now – the woman in the long dark skirt and jumper settling on the fallen log beside the man with the stocky frame – they might be taken for tentative lovers, the sun bleaching out their features through a broken canopy of trees.

Inhaling silently, she thinks of their nights together in Vienna. But when Arnold looks at her now, she sees it is with a different type of lust.

'You were right,' he says, smiling his approval. 'I believe the Englishman will be of great use to us. And he is providing a list of others, people he went to Cambridge with—'

Edith interrupts, switching to English, commenting on the bumblebee that moves between the yellow hawkbits and red poppies that line either side of a narrow stream, as a couple of children skip past in pursuit of a golden spaniel. Arnold waits until they are out of sight, glancing almost imperceptibly over his shoulder and in front again before continuing in a lowered voice.

'One of the men seems promising . . . the other appealing in some respects but also a homosexual and a drunk—' He cuts himself off. 'We shall see.'

They sit a while, and then Edith says, 'Have you found a permanent flat yet?'

'Not yet, but my cousin is arranging things—'

Slipping her hand into her pocket, she pulls out the advert she has kept folded inside. 'I believe this would be perfect for you. Lawn Road Flats – the Isokon building as the press are calling it – it was built by friends of mine, and now it's open for tenants.'

Arnold Deutsch reads aloud from the notice, his eyebrows cocking with disdain. 'Each flat has full domestic service including shoe-cleaning, and meals in the club . . . Chicken kebabs, crayfish, olives . . . How very bourgeois.'

'They call it *functional living*,' Edith says. 'I was there when they were being interviewed about it. The idea is that young professionals can move in and have life made as simple as possible, without the need to own many belongings; unburdening themselves of permanent tangible possessions, and creating instead the possessions of freedom, travel and new experience. I like the idea. It's beyond my means but I think you would find like-minded friends there. The building is not far from here; I could take you there.'

Arnold smiles and nods. 'I don't doubt it.'

Secret Intelligence Service file on
Edith Suschitzky

P.F.40997
CROSS-REFERENCE

Subject:— E. TUDOR-HART.
23.4.35
S.B. report No. 301/MP/3905 states that Mrs.
Edith TUDOR-HART occupies one the 3 flats at

158 Haverstock Hill, N.W.3, where she carries on a photography business and is known to S.B. (refs. 301/MP/2186 and 300/NM/199). She has staying with her H. KORTE and his wife Erna R. KORTE.

411/Austria/DS9.

26th April 1935

Dear Major Vivian,

Very many thanks for the most interesting report on Communist activities in Austria, forwarded under your CX/1387/V, dated 10.4.35.

[SECTION REMOVED]

In thinking of possible persons who might remit money from this country to Austria, A.E. TUDOR-HART and his Viennese wife Edith SUSCHITZKY strike us as likely candidates. Edith SUSCHITZKY was the daughter of a Viennese bookseller and used to live at 4 Petzvalgasse, Vienna. She came here as a student in 1925 and subsequently paid periodical visits to this country. In 1930, she was living with TUDOR-HART at an address in Westbourne Gardens. Both were associated at that time with Communist activity. After repeated warnings SUSCHITZKY left here in January 1931, but in August 1933 HART went to Vienna and married her. We cannot find, however, that Edith

SUSCHITZKY - TUDOR-HART - or her husband
stayed at Belsize Park.

Miss TUDOR-HART, sister of A.E. TUDOR-HART,
has an account at the Moscow Marodny Bank.
She recently paid in a sum of £300 and receives
cheques on the bank signed by H. POLLITT
and E. BURNS. In October last she sent a
cheque for £100 to the "Daily Worker". In
the same month, she applied for bonds worth
£1,200 of the "Second Five-Year-Plan Loan".
  Yours sincerely,
  K.M.M.S.

[To: Major V.Vivian, C.B.E., S.I.S.]

                              Personal M/F
                              31st May 1935

The Tudor-Harts:

The sister-in-law of Miss H.B. Tudor-Hart
recently cabled £25 to a Hungarian (?) Arpad
Haas [P.F.68990] at the Stadthof Posthotel,
Zurich. Haas is probably quite O.K., but the
sender seemed excited and urgent, it seems
worthwhile reporting.

Miss Tudor-Hart gives fairly large subscrip-
tions (£10) at regular intervals to the King
Alfred School, Golders Green. The Head of
the school (V.A. Hyvett) [P.F.41138] is a

member of the World League for Sexual Reform (Norman Haire) [P.F.49764] and the Federation of Progressive Societies and Individuals (7 New Square, Lincolns Inn, W.C.1).

P.F.40997
CROSS-REFERENCE

Subject:— Edith TUDOR-HART.

From 1.7.35 Elfriede NEUHAUS has been residing at 158a Haverstock Hill, N.W.3, the residence of Mrs. Edith TUDOR-HART, whom she assists in the house and also with photographic work. The object of her visit however is to study English, and Mrs. TUDOR-HART and Miss Beatrix TUDOR-HART assist her in her studies. Miss Neuhaus stated that she was not paying for her board and lodging and was not receiving any payment from Mrs. TUDOR-HART; she anticipates staying until February 1936.

Mrs. Edith TUDOR-HART née SUSCHITZKY is a freelance photographer; she has been known to S.B. as an extremist and an associate of leading members of the C.P.G.B. since October 1930 when she came under notice as Edith SUSCHITZKY, an Austrian, born 28.8.1908 in Vienna. She is the subject of H.O. file No. 577727 and S.B. file 301/MP/2186. On 4.12.1930 in accordance with H.O. instructions she was instructed to leave the U.K. After repeated warnings, she left for Vienna on 15.1.1931. Prior to her departure she co-habited with Dr. Alexander Ethan TUDOR-HART (S.B. 301/ MP/2270), a person actively engaged in Communist propaganda. About August 1933 Dr. TUDOR-HART went to Vienna and was there married to Edith SUSCHITZKY who subsequently returned to England with him. He is not now living with his wife.

The flat is rented for £150 per annum and part of it is sub-let to Miss M.G. SEWARD (S.B. 301/MP/3905). Another resident at 158 Haverstock Hill is Johanna BARUCH SB301/CSC/303, previously employed by Mrs. TUDOR-HART.

S.B. report no. 79/N/151 dated 16.8.35. Original in R. List 451(201) 1a.

The same day that Arnold and his wife, Josefine, move into the fully furnished flat No.7 on the ground floor of Lawn Road, North London, one hundred and sixty-eight miles away, in the hard-hit coal-mining area of Rhondda Valley, South Wales, Edith Tudor-Hart – who has recently rejoined Alexander, lodging in a room on a terrace of workers' cottages, supporting those struck by mass unemployment – tucks a map into her pocket and ducks into the car she has told her husband she needs to borrow in order to buy supplies.

She leaves at the crack of dawn, the roads still dark as she sets off north, light lifting slowly as she weaves through the Brecon Beacons, revealing lush green fields as far as the eye can see. Driving with half an eye on the curves and bends of road ahead, she checks the rear-view mirror for signs she might have been followed.

It is past lunchtime when she reaches Blaenau Ffestiniog, consulting the map before following the road towards Portmadoc, turning off some ten minutes later and following the track a mile and a half into the countryside.

The cottage stands directly facing the narrow-gauge railway line, but Edith arrives at the back, parking in front of a door that opens as she steps out of the car, the face that greets her breaking into a smile.

'Edith.'

'Kim.'

They sit at a wooden picnic table laden with pickled eggs and ham and bread in the garden, which leads down towards the train-track. 'I wasn't sure you'd find me, but now I can't believe I ever doubted it,' Kim says, handing her a sherry glass which he fills with wine. 'I'm sorry, I can't seem to find any decent-sized glasses. It's a pretty spot, isn't it? My mother rents it. We used to come here when I was a boy. My father, too. It's very peaceful.'

He pauses briefly, taking a sip of his drink.

'I had some of my favourite holidays here, and in Brighton. Have you ever been? Oh, you must, one day. Besides the sea, and the fact that every street seems designed for the purpose of pleasure, to me it always felt like a place one could get lost in.'

'So you brought me out here to give me a rundown of British holiday destinations?' She takes a sip of her drink.

'I brought you here to say thank you.' He pauses again. 'And to say goodbye.'

'You don't have to thank me.'

Kim takes an egg and slices it in half. 'I know. But I haven't seen you since you made the introduction and I wanted you to know how grateful I am to you for that.' He pauses. 'For having faith in me.'

Edith smiles, wryly. 'I didn't know you were such a sentimentalist.'

'Alexander did always say I was a dark horse, didn't he?'

'I don't worry about him, so you shouldn't.'

'Believe me, I don't. But you were right, what you said in Vienna, the last time we saw each other there. I was too eager to play the part of the hero. But you were wrong, too.'

She shakes her head. 'I wasn't wrong because I didn't really believe what I said. I knew you would do the right thing, eventually.'

Kim raises his eyebrows and laughs. 'Liar.' His expression turns serious. 'I worry about Litzi, though. I have been told to break off all contact with her, as well as with anyone else who might indicate my past.'

Edith holds his eye before looking away, her finger accidentally brushing his as she reaches for her glass. 'Litzi will survive – you are not irreplaceable. Besides, she has the same priorities – we all do.'

'How is life in London, for you, Edith?'

She thinks for a moment.

'I am keeping busy. As well as my photography, I have a new lodger.' Smiling knowingly, she continues. 'She will stay with us for a few months, during which time Beatrix and I are teaching her English, and helping set her up. One day, perhaps, she will be as well-trained as you.'

Kim raises his drink. 'Did you hear that I'm going to Arras soon, to report the war from Franco's side, for *The Times*, no less? I just got the telegram.'

Edith takes a sip of wine.

'I don't know when I'll be back.' He continues, wryly. 'You never know, Edith – perhaps by then I will have been approached by the British Secret Service.'

In Rhondda Valley, the weeks pass, Alexander heading out first thing, while Edith walks the streets speaking to subjects for her photographs, returning home to find her husband already asleep, exhausted from another day of working without pay.

The night she learns the news that will change everything forever, she sits at the table, making her way through piles of notes, writing captions to accompany a roll of film she will send back to the editor of *Geographical* magazine, in London, the following day: men in flat-caps and waistcoats, their backs resting against a wall, expressions listless. She reads over her own words. *Unemployed. Near the labour exchanges on Wednesdays and Fridays one may see this, but Rhondda has known unemployment too long to be content with idle contemplation.*

Setting down her pen, she surveys the room, which is dark apart from the faint glow from the fading wick of the candle on her desk.

Her eyes rest briefly on Alexander. In another time, the sight of him like this might have elicited some emotional response, but for now the only registrable effect is to remind her that she, too, needs sleep. She wonders, as semi-consciousness finally takes hold, whether the sight of Alexander had ever really moved her at all.

In the misty hinterland between wakefulness and slumber, her mind leads her back through the tunnel of the past year, away from the screams of the protesting miners, from the fighting with Alexander over unpaid bills; the sound of the gunshot that lodged in her own mind, as well as her father's, that evening last year.

It is dark when the cramps draw her from sleep. She moves quietly, cautious not to wake her husband. In the bathroom she lights another candle and pulls up her nightdress, holding it to her thigh and seeing the blood. Just a little, but enough to know, at the wrong time of the month, what it must mean.

When she calls out to him across the dark room, Alexander opens his eyes and is instantly awake, the capable medic coming into his own. She dabs at the blood with a cloth at the sink, but the spot will not budge.

It might not be a miscarriage, he tells her. It might just be the cells bedding in. She thinks of an animal using its claws to make its home, in a strange land.

That was how she first found out about Tommy – the baby who, from the first instant, she thought she had lost.

She watches him sleep in the cot in the days after he is born, chest imperceptibly rising and falling. A perfect infant with golden curls framing a cherubic face; Tommy has plump lips and a dimpled chin. Following his birth, Edith is also, in a way, reborn. An awareness previously reserved for the outside world turns in part inwards towards this new life, illuminating every fold and stretch as she gazes down at her baby in the pram.

London looms over them with its mackerel sky in the weeks that follow. Edith photographs the city, images that she either sells on to printed publications, or simply records in her scrapbook: images of banners outside shops offering to send tinned foods to Spain; families she meets through like-minded photographers and fellow workers, bundled into single rooms in slum housing across London.

The morning the wireless reports the abdication of King Edward VIII, in December 1936, Alexander is already at work at the surgery. Edith and Tommy leave the house early, and she imagines the world through his eyes as she walks from the studio at Haverstock Hill through Camden Town and Regent's Park, the sun rising above the water against a winter sky.

By the time they approach Hyde Park, a group has gathered on the bank to watch men in waders release a miniature steamboat across the Serpentine. Jack Russells yelp as they lurch in and out of the water, above the gentle hiss of the vessel as puffs of smoke dissolve into an English winter sky.

Edith is cold, but then she is always cold. She will not think of how cold she is but of how much warmer she is than those who do not have what she has; how much colder she was before Tommy.

When she looks down at her son she understands what it is to feel a love that is whole and unconstrained. Even the pang of guilt she feels for her own maternal contentment while so many people around her continue to suffer cannot taint the sense of completion she feels when she looks at him now and senses her heart slide into a state of bliss.

As she studies him, his cupid lips suckling in sleep, his fingers clenched in a tiny fist, there is a shout from the crowd and the baby starts, his face breaking instantly into a frown that threatens to turn into tears. Looking up, she spots the source of the noise – a young boy, laughing and shouting as he cheers on the boat. For the first time in a long while she thinks of Helmut, who was around the same age when his mother died. Pulling her coat close around her, she leans in and places her fingers to Tommy's cheek, his body instantly settling at her touch.

No, she will not feel guilty for clinging to the best thing that has happened in her life, not when she knows how quickly both life and love can be snatched away.

At the same time as Edith and Tommy walk away from Hyde Park, in another corner of London a meeting is about to take place between two men, on a frosty park bench.

One of them is Theodore Maly – a London-based Soviet agent, and colleague of Arnold Deutsch, responsible for the day-to-day running of assets. The other is Percy Glading, co-founder of the CPGB and a former employee at the Royal Arsenal in Woolwich.

Maly's mind is still on the report he has been providing to Moscow Centre from his British mole, embedded as a journalist in *The Times*, relaying his every move: 'Söhnchen left for . . .', 'Söhnchen should be in Lisbon today . . .', 'Söhnchen is headed for the meeting point . . .'

But as Glading approaches, these thoughts fade, the men greeting one another discreetly so that anyone passing might believe them nothing but two perfect strangers seated at the far ends of a single bench. At around six foot four inches, with small but striking grey eyes and a dark moustache, Maly strums his fingers against the wood as he instructs Glading, in slow but thorough English, about the task ahead.

There is a gust of wind and Edith adjusts the blanket around her baby's face, moving off through the city, her eyes taking in the details as they pass: a snatched glance between a man in a bowler hat and a younger woman in a fur stole, on Park Lane; the accordion player busking in front of D.H. Evans on the corner of Oxford Street and Old Cavendish Street, the sign on the front of his hat reading IN TOTAL DARKNESS.

At every turn, she stops to frame the scene with the Rolleiflex she carries over her shoulder, and, when she does, she feels once again Arnold's hands as he passed her the gift on that day that he told her was just the beginning. She doesn't allow herself to address the question that rises, unbidden, in her mind then: if that was the beginning, then where does it end?

Around the moment that Edith imagines Arnold Deutsch's hand on hers, in another part of London Percy Glading opens the door to a payphone on the corner of Albany Street and dials the number of the CPGB headquarters. When the secretary answers, Glading sighs with relief, telling her to go to a call box and phone him on the number he reads out, glancing over his shoulder to check that he is alone.

Once they are on a safer line, Percy Glading speaks in clear instructive tones. English is the secretary Olga Grey's second language, and he can't afford for a single one of his words to be misinterpreted.

She will need to rent a flat to be used as a safe house, for which he, Glading, will pay the rent, the telephone bill and any other such expenses. She will need to get three sets of keys cut, and she will need to be at the flat on a certain date to receive a fellow comrade who will teach her how to use a miniature camera in order to photograph papers and drawings of a secret nature that will be borrowed from the Royal Arsenal and delivered to the flat, around once a week, in the evening time. They will be collected and returned to their rightful place early the following morning, before anyone can notice they are gone. She will need to take and develop the photos but not print them. Does she understand?

Of course, Olga Grey replies into the receiver, with a smile he cannot see. She will go straight away.

Edith walks for hours, capturing the city in frames, Tommy dozing as they head north, stopping briefly in front of the glass window of the off-licence, apparently considering the price of a bottle of Scotch whisky, her eyes scanning the reflection of the street as she moves away again. By the billboard in front of the Hampstead Picture Playhouse, where couples queue to watch *The 39 Steps*, she pauses, distracted, searching for the bottle of milk she prepared earlier, decanting the warm liquid from the manual breast-pump that she uses to supplement the seemingly constant feeding. As she dithers, she has no reason to notice the gloved hand that dips briefly into the edges of the pram, the figure brushing past and moving away again before Edith, counting a beat in her head, returns her attention to her child, leaning forward and offering him the bottle, her other hand reaching into the bassinet and tucking the envelope further beneath the blanket.

Hanging up the call to Percy Glading, in St James's, Olga Grey pauses and then smiles to herself as she dials another number and asks the operator to connect her with Maxwell Knight. He answers after two rings: the man to whom she has been reporting ever since she started working as an MI5 penetration agent inside the CPGB headquarters on King Street.

Daylight is fading as Edith and Tommy reach the bench at the top of Kite Hill, Hampstead Heath. Once again Edith reaches into the pram, this time pulling out a book from inside the bassinet.

Enjoying the sound of the spine cracking as she opens it, she discreetly removes the envelope anyone passing might assume she has been using as a bookmark, and lays it beside her on the bench. She focuses on the words in front of her, seemingly unaware of the stranger who arrives a while later, sitting a little further along the bench, unfolding his newspaper, reading for a while before placing it beside him.

When Tommy begins to cry, the new mother stands, distracted by the movement of her son in the pram, too preoccupied to remember the envelope tucked beneath the newspaper as she walks away, whispering reassurances to her child that everything will be fine.

Fine day for it, Kim Philby smiles to himself, the morning bright and springlike as he steps out of his ramshackle apartment on to one of the narrow lanes that weave through the Spanish city that for now he calls home.

1937. What a difference a year makes. This is what he is thinking as the sunshine touches his face, a shiver brushing his spine as he recalls, briefly, his life back in London: his previous role as sub-editor on the left-leaning *Review of Reviews* offset by his joining of the Anglo-German Fellowship – and later the editing of its pro-Hitler magazine (a nice touch, even his friend Guy Burgess – not prone to excessive generosity of spirit – had to concede). Not to mention the frequent visits to Berlin for talks with the German Propaganda Ministry and von Ribbentrop's Foreign Office.

Taking a step on to the pavement, the dust scattering around his polished brogues and linen suit – the perfect attire for a bright young *Times* journalist poised to report the Civil War from Franco's side – Kim takes a moment to drink it in, considering how much has changed here, too. It is less than a year since Seville was seized in the coup, signifying not just the fall of Andalusia's capital but also the capture of the most revolutionary city of southern Spain. And all the while, around him Fascism sweeps the country like the fires that lick through the brush in summer months.

Breathing in sharply, he strides away from the apartment building his handlers had been all too pleased for him to take on: the perfect cover through which to gather information on all aspects of the war effort, before handing it over to contacts in France or, occasionally, back in England. While it is all very well in most instances, going back and forth to deliver news and receive instruction, for more urgent communication their Cambridge-educated golden boy has been given a code and a series of cover addresses outside Seville – the details of which are written on the tiny piece of substance resembling rice paper Kim aka Stanley aka Söhnchen aka Sonny had been handed before leaving England.

Out of habit, his hand moves to the pocket of his trousers, feeling for the scrap as he walks into crowds that thicken as he makes his way towards the main square. For a moment his heart lurches, but then he feels it, the soft grain rubbing reassuringly against the tips of his fingers. As he looks up, his attention is seized by a poster pinned in the front window of a shop daubed with smocked girls' dresses: an illustration of a matador, his bright red cape held proudly at his side. The bullfight, Kim notes as he strikes a match to light his cigarette, is exactly what is needed to lift the spirits after a busy few weeks. Besides, with the front line running just twenty-five miles east of Cordoba, between Montoro and Andujar, it also provides the perfect cover for visiting a front to which he has not yet ventured.

Yes, this is shaping up to be a good day, Kim thinks, taking a final drag of his cigarette and crushing it underfoot. He turns, giving the window display a cursory glance and, as he moves away, for a split second his gaze locks with an elderly woman seated at the back of the shop, her eyes, in the darkness, following him down the street.

Going to Cordoba for a few days, see what's going on up there. Kim sends his message through to his editor, that afternoon.

The Friday before the bullfight, he boards a train at Seville. Moving through the carriages, he finds a seat in an empty compartment, placing his bag by his feet and watching the few remaining passengers board the train.

It is a few moments before he hears the sound of feet in the corridor. Turning in the direction of the noise, his jaw tightens as the carriage fills with Italian infantry officers, their eyes partially concealed beneath their hats.

Nodding courteously, Kim moves his bag closer to his feet, making way for the men as they settle themselves in seats beside and opposite him so that he is wholly surrounded.

'Good afternoon,' he says, nodding approvingly at their uniforms, and then, reaching into his bag, pulling out a bottle. 'Can I offer any of you gents a drink?'

By the time the train pulls in, the carriage is heaving with conversation, Kim, at the centre, regaling the men with stories of his latest romantic conquest, in broken Italian.

'Won't you join me for dinner tonight, in Cordoba, chaps?' he asks, as they gather their things, swaying slightly as they stand. 'Least I can do, as a payback for all your efforts. Besides, the paper will pay . . .'

The eldest man raises a hand by way of apology. 'We'll be too busy in the whore-houses before moving up to the front tomorrow.'

'Shame,' Kim replies, his smile tightening as the men file out. '*Che il signore sia con te.*' May the Lord be with you.

Hotel del Gran Capitan stands back slightly from the road, up a flight of steps.

The fight itself is not until the Sunday. Famished from a day's travel, not to mention the several bottles of red wine he had consumed on the train across, Kim walks out some time after nine, enjoying the smell of the city, which bustles with life – old men seated in groups, children playing chase at their feet.

After enjoying a solitary meal of fish and bread, he stops for a final brandy in one of the main squares on his way back to the hotel, and is struck by a sudden wave of exhaustion, the journey and the drink catching up with him at last. By the time he returns to his room around midnight, he can barely keep his eyes open.

It is pitch black when he awoken, faltering for a moment before registering the sound of hammering at the door.

'*Señor! Abre la puerta.*'

Standing, through the crack in the curtain Kim can see that it is still dark. For a moment he considers the drop to the street below. Reminding himself to stay calm, that any unnecessary panic might be the death of him, he moves slowly, the taste of last night's drink stale on his tongue.

'*Un minuto.*' He keeps his voice as level as he can manage, his toes gripping the tiles as he moves hesitantly towards the door. His grip tightening against the handle, he breathes deeply before opening the door, just a crack, his eyes met by two men in Civil Guard uniforms, rifles hanging at their sides. 'Can I help you?'

'Pack your things.' The face of the larger of the two men is unreadable as he forces his way inside.

For a moment Kim hesitates. He thinks of the scrap of paper, pictures his trousers strewn over the chair by the window. 'Sorry, what is going on?'

'*Ordenes. Now.*' The smaller guard replies, stepping forward as Kim, working hard to manifest the appropriate balance of confusion and self-belief, lifts his hands in a gesture of capitulation.

'Very well. Do you mind if I . . .' He picks up his clothes from the chair on which they hang, moving towards the bathroom, but the guard places a hand on his upper arm.

'Dress here.'

While the second guard turns over the bedclothes, searching every crevice and lining, the other watches the Englishman as he steps out of his silk pyjamas and pulls on the outfit he had worn the previous evening, his skin a shade paler as he is chaperoned into the hallway.

The air outside is cold. Kim shivers as the men guide him, silently, through quiet streets. Walking a step ahead of the guards, he steals a look in a shop window as they pass, sees their reflections following just a hair's breadth behind, their eyes trained sharply on his every move.

The fingers on his left hand flex, uncertainly, the other holding tightly to his suitcase with a clammy palm. His mind whirring, he closes his eyes for a second, imagining a moment in which he can feasibly work his hand into his pocket and retrieve the paper with the codes inked on to them, and let it fall from his hand, unseen.

'This way,' the smaller guard says, interrupting Kim's thoughts, as they approach the sallow reception area of their headquarters.

With one man blocking the exit, the other walks briskly towards the desk and leans in to speak to the officer on duty, who looks over at Kim and, with a small smile, stands and guides them into the back room.

'Sit down. Keep your hands on the table in front of you.'

The guards stand on either side of the door, staring forward, a desk-lamp angled so that it is facing him, its artificial heat triggering a line of sweat along Kim's forehead.

For several minutes they stay like this, the guards ignoring his brief attempts to engage them in conversation, refusing to be distracted long enough for him to get rid of the paper. Finally, the door handle moves and an older man, small and sharp in features, steps quickly into room.

'Your name is Kim Philby?'

'Yes.' He feels a twinge, thinking back to the guards with whom he had conversed on the train across from Seville. 'I don't suppose there's any chance of a coffee . . .'

'Where are your papers?' The speed of the man's delivery catches Kim off guard.

'What papers?' The vein above his eye pulses under the harsh gaze of the lamp.

'Your papers, your permission to visit Cordoba.' He is growing impatient, moving close so that Kim can smell the alcohol on his breath.

Staying put, Kim places his hands slowly on the table. Noting how the guard follows them with his eyes, he pushes his palms together, stretching his fingers, stifling a small yawn, before moving his hands to his lap.

'Well?'

'I don't have any papers, I spoke to one of the majors at the Capitania in Seville. He told me I didn't need them.'

It is the truth, but the officer shakes his head in disbelief. 'Impossible. Everyone knows a permit is necessary for entry to Cordoba.'

'I didn't know.'

The skin around the man's eyes seemed to splinter. 'What are you doing in Cordoba?'

'I've come to watch a bullfight.'

'A bullfight?' Temporarily, his face softens. 'Oh, very well, and may I see your ticket?'

'I don't have one, I . . .'

'You don't have one?'

The larger guard shuffles from one foot to another, sniggering under his breath.

'I haven't had time; I only arrived last night. I was exhausted. I had a meal and went straight to bed. I was going to get up this morning and buy a ticket. Really, I don't see why . . .'

Kim's voice drops off as the older man turns to the guards, who respond by stepping forward, each taking a pair of light-weight gloves from their pockets.

Shuffling back slightly in his seat so that his spine is now flush with the back of the chair, Kim feels the air in the room turn thick.

'And this is your suitcase?' His interrogator watches as one of the Civil Guards lifts the bag on to the table.

'It is.' Kim clears his throat.

'You won't mind if I have a look inside?'

'Not at all.' He keeps his voice even as the officer presses the release on the lock, the lid opening to reveal a single pair of clean pants, a razor and a toothbrush.

'This is everything?'

Kim shrugs, risking a small smile. 'I'm only here for one night.'

Without another word, the officer lifts the leather case, inspecting it for hidden panels, tapping its surface with a neat fingernail.

Feeling a sense of relief drift slowly across his skin, Kim relaxes enough in his chair that he feels his arms soften. He is about to ask if he might light a cigarette when the officer drops the case and looks up.

'And now, what about you?'

Fumbling for time, Kim arranges his face in an expression of incomprehension as he darts through possible distractions in his mind.

The officer gives an exasperated sigh and shakes his head. 'Come now, Mr Philby, please do not waste my time. Your pockets – empty them.'

Keeping his fingers steady, Kim raises a hand, admonishing himself for his lack of speed. 'Oh. Of course.'

Reaching slowly into the pocket of his jacket, controlling his breath, he smiles reassuringly and pulls his wallet out slowly, the moisture on his fingertips marking the leather. 'Here it is,' he says, lifting it above the table with a single flick of his wrist, the wallet spinning across the room, landing at the men's feet.

There is a scuffle of noise as all three guards instinctively drop to the floor. Thrusting his other hand into his trouser pocket, his fingers fumbling for the scrap of paper, he scrunches it as his hand moves to his mouth, his throat constricting as he swallows, just as the first guard's head rises over the table.

'Honestly, how very clumsy of me.' Kim winces, his heartbeat thumping against his chest.

His chest already stands empty the day Edith walks into her marital bedroom to find Alexander packing his bags.

She had headed out early that morning from 68 Acre Lane, Brixton, the sound of the January wind howling as she steered the perambulator through empty streets. Hours later, she is

148

still holding the Leica camera and the films – the receipts from the Westminster Photographic Exchange Ltd on Charing Cross Road, and the General Electric Company Ltd on Kingsway, both made out in her name, tucked inside the bag hanging from her wrist – when she opens the door and finds him there, bent double over the battered suitcase he takes with him, the day he ups and leaves his wife and child.

'How long will you be gone?' Edith asks, her fingers tightening around Tommy's waist.

'As long as I'm needed – ideally until Franco is defeated. But I will be back.'

We need you – what about us? she thinks, and then, *You will be back, but will we still be waiting for you?* Instead she says, 'What about the practice?'

'You could come to Spain with me. I'm sure the British Medical Aid Unit could make use of you.' He speaks without looking at her, packing into his bag the shirts she has washed and folded for him.

'I am useful here, to our son – one of us needs to earn a wage.'

'It appears you have plenty of money, the rate you're spending it.' He glances up, briefly, at the shopping bags in her hand.

'These aren't mine,' she says, through gritted teeth. She hates how petty she sounds, how painfully bourgeois their arguments are; how she is forced to admit that although in many ways she doesn't, in some ways she does need him.

In that moment, she decides, she doesn't.

'I thought you believed in self-sacrifice, Edith. What happened to us both being drawn to protect the damned?'

She shakes her head, and laughs. 'Alexander, don't you see? We *are* the damned.'

149

Dear Edith,

I have been receiving repeated requests from a particularly revolting journalist, claiming all sorts of connections that I know to be false – not least, claiming to be a friend of one of my children, who assures me he has only seen her in passing, in their local pub. I suppose, to be fair, any employee of the *Daily Mail* just has to be untruthful. If he sees her again, I suggested to John, he might tell her that I was sorry not to meet her request; and then he could explain delicately that I give interviews when I feel like it, not when a journalist feels like it. To soothe her ego, I said, he could tell her that I have left unanswered two monumentally long letters from the great David Frost.

I have a grievance – not a new one. The conventional wisdom here (out of the mouths of *babushkas*) has it that a good hard winter is followed by a hot, dry summer. Well, we had a lovely hard winter, with lots of snow and dry cold, week after week of it. So we came into the woods in mid-May with high hopes, which were boosted by ten days of beautiful sunshine. But no! May went out with a rainstorm which has lasted ever since. All June and most of July we have watched the rain by day and listened to it by night. Of course it is rather cosy to lie under warm blankets and hear the rain thundering on the roof; but one can have too much of a good thing. We are thinking of selling our watering can, which just takes up room. In spite of it all, we have done well with lettuce, parsley, dill, garlic and onions, but the strawberry crop is a lot less than meagre, and some nice mint seeds brought out by my eldest daughter and her husband seem to have been waterlogged – not a sign of life. The birds started late, but are now here in force, eating an enormous quantity of bread daily. The squirrel is a very occasional visitor, and a day or two ago a nice hedgehog scurried along the path in front of our veranda. No wolves or bears yet. (Bless me! I have just noticed an unfamiliar look about the place – the sun has just come out!)

All this nature reminds me of my father, who gave the scientific name to a number of birds – mostly named after women he admired (and one after himself). So now, somewhere far from here, there is an Arabian woodpecker by the name of the *Dendrocopos dorae*, after my mother, Dora, as well as a subspecies of an owl named the *Otus scops pamelae*, who Pamela was is anyone's guess.

I have acquired a new typewriter, a portable from West Germany. I have not been able to break it in yet, as my recent work has involved talking rather than writing. But I expect that a few more hours pounding the keys will do the trick. Meanwhile, it is rather like a new set of false teeth, useful but uncomfortable. *Au revoir* before too much water has flowed down the Vol— I mean the Thames.

Yours,

Kim

Into the woods

Edith wakes before the baby. Through the gap in the curtains that hang limply from their poles, she sees a sliver of blue. Unable to fall back to sleep, her mind returns to thoughts of Arnold in his flat on Lawn Road, on the other side of London, looking out at the same sky.

In early summer the cherry tree in the garden will be in full bloom, visible from the bedroom window that she can still picture perfectly from her last visit: inside flat No.7, Josefine's coat hanging over a chair, the child's cot in the corner of the bedroom. The tree had been bare then, in the depths of winter, as Edith and Arnold sat in the living room overlooking the gardens, sharing a cigarette, he musing over their newest recruit.

'Another Cambridge graduate. He came to us via the drunken homosexual we met through your Söhnchen, who, by the way, is proving his worth in various ways. This new one is an art collector and a distant relation of both the Queen and Oswald Mosley – it is possible that he might be our most valuable yet. Another homosexual, though.'

'I don't see how that can be relevant,' Edith had retorted, her attention fixed on the secluded woodland known as Belsize Wood that ran along the back of the flats, offering easy access to Belsize Park tube station.

Arnold had disagreed. 'Anything that will draw suspicion from the authorities cannot be overlooked. From what my sources tell me, this Anthony Blunt wasn't too discreet at Cambridge. He was part of a secret club, the Apostles – considered themselves to be the brightest minds. Through that, he took a lover by the name of Julian Bell. My concern is what has been discussed in this secret group, and how much of it could be held against him . . .'

The Isokon's long, thin design, with the position of the building angled in such a way that it is difficult to observe from the street, and just two sets of stairs – one internal and one external – makes it hard to observe from the outside, and near-impossible to keep tabs on residents and guests, once within its confines. Yet Arnold had been even more cautious than normal as he handed her the folder and the small pocket diary before she left, his eyes set on hers in the concealed doorway of No.7, which cannot be seen from the road.

A thought crosses her mind now, a rush of adrenaline as she stretches out on the sheet, the shadow on her subconscious pulling her back into the present.

Drawing herself from bed, she is careful not to wake the child who sleeps in the space beside her. She moves on tiptoes across the room, lowering herself in front of the chest of drawers, the heavy Victorian mahogany creaking under years of pressure as she pulls open the bottom drawer and feels inside to the back, waiting for her fingers to brush against the leather.

But it is empty.

Tommy cries in her arms all the way to Victoria station and is still screaming by the time the 24 bus emerges in the distance, the fleet name 'BRITISH' painted along its side in livery green. Ignoring the disdainful looks of her fellow passengers as she enters at the rear, she moves up to the top deck, steadying herself with her free hand on the rail.

Keeping her mind focused on the missing folder, she sits, out of habit, in the back left-hand corner, from where she can watch everyone who comes and goes, briefly acknowledging the bus conductor as she selects her ticket from the coloured bundles in sets on a small rack, held in place with springs.

It had been the day before Wolf and Puck went to Amsterdam to open their ill-fated photographic studio that she had responded to Arnold's call and gone to the flat – discussing Blunt and Philby, and their fellow Cambridge recruits – staying less than an hour before leaving with the folder and notebook in her bag, Arnold impressing on her with a single look the importance of what he has entrusted to her.

Darkness had fallen by then and she had walked briskly, holding the leather satchel and its contents tightly against her side as she made the journey from Lawn Road to Wolf's flat in West Hampstead.

In the present, absent-mindedly watching the twists and turns of the city as the bus sweeps through Trafalgar Square and along Tottenham Court Road, Edith tries to picture that journey with more clarity. She had walked from Lawn Road to the studio on Haverstock Hill, where she had collected Tommy from a friend before heading to Wolf's place to say goodbye to him and Puck. She had been on a high, she is sure of that much, still buoyed up from her meeting with Arnold. She had been in generous spirit, she and Wolf discussing her ongoing book project with fellow artists Pearl Binder and James Fritton, while Puck cooked and Edith browsed her brother's prints, which he had set out neatly across the kitchen table.

'These are very accomplished,' she had told him, and he had looked surprised by her unguarded generosity.

'I realise they might be a little sentimental for your taste.'

'Our photos are different, because we are different people,' Edith had said simply, sensing, without looking up, that her brother was smiling.

It had been a long evening that had passed quickly, and while it seems impossible now to think that she would have left behind something so important – items that she can still almost visualise placing in the chest in her living room – the vision blurs slightly as she thinks of it, something about the memory unreliable as she plays it back in her mind, now. She had been distracted by the other possible new recruit she had mentioned in passing to Deutsch – nothing on the scale of Kim or the other men she had her eye on, but someone potentially useful nonetheless. And she had been tired, the kind of bone-deep tiredness that comes with being woken through the night and working through the day: work she needs to pay the neighbour to watch Tommy so that she can meet the bills, feed her son, serve the cause for which she gives her life and which offers her nothing in return but enough to cover her expenses – expenses listed, alongside those of other agents, in the diary Arnold Deutsch had entrusted to her for safekeeping, that night. The diary she has now lost.

At some point, the view from the top deck gives way to private gardens, a group of boys playing in the tennis courts at Mornington Crescent, the streets thinning out as they reach

South End Green. From here, she walks the same route through residential streets, hoping to trigger a memory as she makes her way to Wolf's house, as she did that night.

When the front door opens, Wolf looks surprised, the sun receding behind the rooftops above his unshaven face, his demeanour even more delicate than usual.

'Where is the pram?' he asks, looking between his sister and the sleeping child in her arms.

'I can't take it on the bus. The city is not designed for people like us.'

Edith moves into the living room, settling Tommy on the sofa, hemming him in with cushions before following Wolf into the kitchen – not a galley kitchen like hers but a proper kitchen with black and white diamond floor tiles, a shaft of sunlight pointing from the window to the counter, dancing with dust.

'I was sorry to hear about you and Puck. Mama told me.'

'It wasn't to be,' Wolf sighs, taking the kettle from the stove and moving it to the sink.

'You have been back how long?' Edith asks, with feigned lightness.

'Two days.'

'And it has been just you here?'

Wolf hesitates, a slight jarring at the question. 'I told you – Puck and I broke up. I have been sorting out my things, working out what to do next.'

Edith nods, her eyes moving around the kitchen, and then settling on her brother. 'I liked Puck.'

'So I understand.'

There is a short silence as Wolf runs water from the tap into the kettle.

'She told me that you tried to recruit her, the night we left.'

'Recruit?' Edith laughs, bitterly. 'You make it sound terribly grand.'

'You're not denying it, then?'

'Wolf, when have I ever denied anything to you, or to Adele, or Wilhelm?'

At the sound of their parents' names, Wolf flinches.

'In fact, the reason I'm here is that I left something behind. Something important.'

He shakes his head. 'Edith, I don't want to hear it.'

Lowering her voice, she moves around the table towards him. 'A folder and a diary.'

'Edith, stop.'

'Have you seen it? That's all I need to know.'

'I said stop,' he says, firmly, and she does.

Through the charged silence, she hears Tommy cry out from the sofa and Edith stands, brushing down her skirt. 'Wolf, I need to leave Tommy with you for a few hours.'

He opens his mouth but doesn't speak.

Standing, she says. 'I wouldn't ask if it wasn't urgent.'

It is dusk by the time she reaches Lawn Road, turning right before approaching the building and cutting up along the alleyway that leads into Belsize Woods.

In the haze of evening light the landscape is hard to discern, and her foot catches on a twist of ivy, causing her to trip. Standing, she moves more cautiously, the crackle of bracken and the occasional calling of an owl audible as she makes her way over gnarly tree roots.

By the holly bush that stands in view of the rear window

of No.7 she reaches into her pocket and pulls out a small red handkerchief, which she hooks on to the branch, her finger catching on the thorn as she draws it away, leaving a tiny droplet of blood.

The air is cool and damp under the canopy of small dense forest near Kenwood, less than a mile away. Without a watch, Edith has no idea how long she waits, picturing Arnold spotting the handkerchief through his bedroom window, considering the possible emergencies the signal could indicate as he makes his way through South End Green and across the heath to their allocated meeting place.

Perhaps he won't get it until morning, if at all. But even before she hears his footsteps, crunching against knots of thorny branches, she knows he will.

'I can't find the things you gave me to keep safe,' she says, without hesitation. 'I must have thrown them out by mistake. They're not there.'

'You're sure?'

'Yes.'

In the days and weeks after Arnold contacts Moscow Central to report the missing file, and is immediately recalled to Moscow, time bends and folds. In London, the fruit on the cherry tree that stands in view of the window at the now abandoned No.7 Lawn Road Flats falls, uneaten. Arnold is gone, and it is her fault. At home, Edith continues to search for the missing folder, refusing to give up, until one day, the day she finally concedes defeat, she sits on the sofa in her living room, pulling her legs up underneath her, and feels something sharp prodding into her thigh.

Marylebone Road is a hubbub of trams, trolleybuses and motor-cars, the smell of diesel swelling in the air as she makes her way up the steps at Baker Street tube station. She carries the copy of *Harper's Bazar* under her arm, a brisk afternoon wind biting at her ankles as she turns left on to Old Marylebone Road, the sound of her own heels following her. Wallace Court stands on the right of the street. Leaning down in the porch, to tie her shoelaces, her ankle-length skirt obscuring the postbox from the street side, she glances left and right before pushing the napkin through the letterbox, smoothing down her skirt as she stands and continues along the street, looping left and cutting over Marylebone Road towards Regent's Park.

Her stomach turns with relief and remorse as Theodore Maly approaches, the moon rising above the Nash Buildings, visible from her bench near the Rose Gardens in Regent's Park.

'I've found it,' she says, under her breath as he sits a little further along on the bench, pulling out a newspaper. 'I don't know how I missed it.'

She doesn't meet his eye, her cheeks blushing with shame.

'Perhaps it is all too much for you, with the child—'

'It was just misplaced in the move from Acre Lane to Maida Vale; it was never anywhere compromised,' she replies, firmly, her voice growing quieter. 'Do you think he will come back, once you tell Moscow that I have found it?'

'I'm going to Paris tomorrow, I'll be in touch when I'm back.' Maly flicks the page of his newspaper so that it conceals his face.

Edith and Kim

Secret Intelligence Service file on Edith Suschitzky

PORT OF DOVER. COPY

METROPOLITAN POLICE
SPECIAL BRANCH
Metropolitan Police
Scotland House

27th day of August, 1937

Edith TUDOR-HART, travelling on a British passport No.2433, arrived at this port from Ostend at 2.20 p.m. today. She was accompanied by her mother, Adela SUSCHITZKY, Austrian, aged 58, who was given permission to stay in this country for three months. SUSCHITZKY gave as her intended address - 132c, Sutherland Avenue, W.9.

Submitted.

132 Sutherland Avenue is a large corner-plot on a junction with wide-open streets on either side lined with handsome

163

red-brick buildings, and – immediately outside Edith and Tommy's flat, at window-level – a postbox and phone box. Above them, oak trees splay towards the turrets and chimneys that form a constrained west London skyline as the women climb the front steps in silence, exhausted from the night ferry and the subsequent journey from Dover to Victoria, and on, by tube-train to Maida Vale.

Edith, who is carrying her mother's bag, sets it at the top of the stairs as she fumbles for her keys, leading the way into a dark hall, a low humming from the light as she switches it on.

'Tommy and I haven't long moved in,' she says as they step inside, and she sees the room through her mother's eyes: the contents of the chest gathered in a pile where Edith had attempted to tidy ahead of Adele's arrival; photographic prints partially spread across the table, the image of Kim, the night he had hidden them in his bedroom when the officers came to Litzi's flat on Latschkagasse, staring up at her from the top.

'Your photographs are very good, Edith. May I?' Edith moves towards the table and collects together the prints, shifting the one of Kim to the bottom of the pile.

'Not now. Wolf and Ilona will be here soon with Tommy, I should make soup.'

She flinches as her mother places a hand on her arm. 'Edith, it's not easy having a baby to care for, on your own. Especially when you're working at the same time,'

'Tommy and I manage just fine.'

'Are you sure you wouldn't like me to stay with you? What if the authorities check? This is my allocated address—'

'You know I would love to have you here but there's just not space.'

'Edith. I'm worried about you.'

'There is no reason to worry.'

'I've already lost one person I love,' Adele whispers. 'I couldn't bear to lose another.'

The leaves on the branches that float in the eyeline of the terrace at Molly and Jack's flat turn red as summer yields to autumn, Hampstead Heath bathed in a tender glow on Edith's daily walks with Tommy, who takes his first steps on the path under the old oak tree overlooking the pond. At the North Stoneham refugee camp in Hampshire, the sun beats down on the Basque children who laugh and frown as Edith photographs them: boys in soft caps and trilbys at picnic tables, eating soup and bread; playing games of cricket alongside English schoolboys; girls preparing vegetables for lunch, on the day of the Duke of Atholl's visit. Back on Lawn Road, Marcel Breuer and F.R.S. Yorke convert the ground-floor staff flat of the Isokon building into the Isobar restaurant. In a matter of months, hundreds of thousands of people are shot dead by Soviet secret police, all across the Union. Stalin's paranoia is so severe that purges of officers – and suspected double agents – become commonplace, the removed bodies leaving a halo of scarlet in the snow. On a single day on 12 December 1937, Josef Stalin and his henchman Molotov approve the death sentences of 3,167 people, before heading to the cinema. In London winter arrives, plucking the leaves from the trees and tossing them on to the concrete; a blanket of gold that withers to dirt. Maly still hasn't returned.

Should auld acquaintance be forgot
And never brought to mind?

Charlotte Philby

Should auld acquaintance be forgot
And days of auld lang syne?

Secret Intelligence Service
file on Edith Suschitzky

26th February, 1938

URGENT & PERSONAL

Dear Inspector Thompson,

Reference our telephone conversation, I enclose the bills for some of the photographic apparatus, which was found in the flat at 82 Holland Road. You will see that one bill includes the purchase of a standard Leica camera, No.?58231. I enclose photograph copies of the bills which are easier to read.

These bills came into our possession in the following way:- On Monday 22nd November, GLADING visited 82 Holland Road for the purpose of examining the photographic apparatus. In doing this he discovered in a suitcase an envelope with the enclosed three invoices. He instructed Miss "X" to destroy these, but she handed them to us.

E. TUDOR-HART is obviously the communist

Edith TUDOR-HART, who is a photographer and used to have her business at 68 Acre Lane. According to your report Ref. 301/MP/2270, dated 14th January 1938, this woman is now living at 132c Sutherland Avenue, Maida Vale, W.9, telephone number Abercorn 1238. Her photographic business has been transferred to 17 Duke Street, Oxford Street, W.1, telephone Welbeck 7278.

I also enclose a personal message slip from [A.G. McPHILLIPS] to BRANDES when the latter was staying 683 Mount Royal in January 1937. It occurs to me that if Dr McPHILLIPS let BRANDES his flat furnished, he must have asked for some references. It would be interesting if Dr. McPHILLIPS could remember who these references were.

I am sorry I did not let you have the enclosed bills earlier.
  Yours sincerely,
  Inspector T. Thompson,
  Special Branch

Two days after the Nazi German Anschluss, Prime Minister Neville Chamberlain addresses the House of Commons stating that, while his government emphatically disapproves, 'nothing could have prevented this action by Germany unless we and others with us had been prepared to use force to prevent it'. It is March 1938. Following a little rainfall on the first of the month, the weather remains unseasonably mild and dry in the weeks that follow, a shaft of sunlight spilling through the gap in the curtains that quiver as the police ram heaves against the door of Percy Glading's home, causing his girlfriend, Rosa Shar, to sit bolt upright in bed.

At exactly the same moment, a couple of miles away in the flat at 132c Sutherland Avenue, Edith turns off the radiogram. Enjoying a moment of calm before the day begins, she sits a while, in silence, her knees tucked against her chest, watching her son stagger across bare floorboards with a look of determination, before falling back again.

At eighteen months Tommy's body is changing shape, his limbs thinning down, his face often puckered in an expression of grim determination as he attempts to pull himself up using the sofa.

Despite the urge to lean in and help him, she watches on without interference, understanding that her role as a mother is a supporting one, her job to observe and cajole, to provide the tools for her child to enable himself. She makes no effort to aid him, or chastise, when he accidentally kicks the single book that Adele had held on to from Wilhelm's store since she left Austria, finally, after stoically continuing the business for years after his death.

When Edith thinks of her mother, she feels a wave of remorse that she had not let her stay, but it is for Adele's safety as much as her own. With Arnold gone, Edith has to step up.

Uncurling her legs, she stands and lifts Tommy from the edge of the sofa, kissing his cheeks and breathing in the smell of him before placing him on the bed while she dresses for the day ahead.

In the weeks following the annexation of Austria by the Third Reich, Vienna becomes an untenable place for Jews. Throughout the city Jewish people are attacked: children forced to write the word '*Jud*' on the windows of their parents' shops; parents at the Prater Stern made to lie down and eat grass. Within days, the apartment and publishing house of the renowned psychoanalyst Sigmund Freud, near Innere Stadt, is raided, his daughter, Anna Freud, arrested and questioned by the Gestapo. By the time, on 4th June 1938, the Freud family escape, boarding a train that will escort them across Europe to Paris, and from there, to London and their new life at 39 Elsworthy Road in Hampstead, Jews have been removed from public office, tens of thousands have lost their jobs, and hundreds have committed suicide.

The absence of sleep over the past months has brought with it a numbness that Edith relishes. In the sleepless hours this morning, as Tommy gurgled and fretted in the bed beside her, she had traced the route in her mind, walking to the end of the street and turning right on to Maida Vale, following Edgware Road to Marble Arch, weaving through the side roads as she makes her way along Oxford Street. She plays it over in her mind again now as she wedges open the front door, leaving Tommy inside as she negotiates the perambulator down the front steps, parking it between the phone box and postbox while she returns to collect the child.

Once outside again, she tucks Tommy into the pram and crosses the street, following the route she has mentally mapped. It is almost lunchtime when she arrives, two streets west of Portland Place, stopping at a bench in front of a pub with brightly coloured hanging baskets.

When Tommy cries, she feels a flicker of guilt for bringing

him with her. He is too old for this, too big to be strapped up for hours in his pram when he should be untethered, exploring nature and the capabilities of his own body. And yet, she remonstrates with herself, she has no reason to feel guilty. Tommy is safe, and stimulated by the sights and sounds of the city. Besides, she has no choice. Alexander is still in Spain, for all the use he is when he is here, and she was not given sufficient warning of this meeting to make alternative arrangements.

It is the man she was due to meet ten minutes ago who is late. It is he who should feel guilty, which he undoubtedly won't, guilt being a female affliction, a result of patriarchal conditioning to which she will not succumb.

Tommy wails again, his body contorting in a show of rage as the figure finally approaches.

'There, there,' Edith says, glancing up and finding the man just a few feet away, facing the bench. He doesn't acknowledge her, resting his dishevelled suit jacket on the back of the seat between himself and Edith, and, with chewed fingernails, placing the envelope he is carrying down a moment, next to her shawl, while he prepares to adjust his shoelace.

The jacket has not been placed there properly and it drops down on to the shawl. She wraps the material around her shoulders, silently pulling it closer to herself, along with the envelope concealed beneath the jacket. Obscuring the envelope inside the shawl, she continues to reassure Tommy, speaking at a volume only the three of them can hear above his cries.

'I'm taking you to stay with a friend while Mummy goes on a little trip. Tomorrow. The 8.15 train from King's Cross. Yes?'

The man beside her grunts, the smell of the alcohol on his breath carrying through the air as Edith turns and walks away, only faintly catching the noise as he strides into the pub, the roar of indignation flying out from his colleagues at *The Week in Westminster* that he is the last again to arrive: 'Guy Burgess, you tight bastard, get us a drink!'

The day Paul Hardt aka Theodore Stepnavich Maly aka Peters is executed on suspicion of being a German spy, Edith and Tommy take the train from Swiss Cottage to King's Cross, walking east towards York Way and along Gray's Inn Road, pausing to allow a tram to pass before turning towards Coram Fields. The date is 20th September 1938. The woman seated on the bench has coppery blonde hair that shines a rusty gold in the sun, her spine pulled straight as Edith approaches, her hands held tightly on her knee in a subconsciously defensive position.

When she looks up, her fierce eyes soften under heavy lashes, Litzi's face opening in a smile that makes Edith's chest expand with love.

'We've missed you. Haven't we, Tommy?' Edith says, and Litzi leans into the pram, cooing affectionately to the child, who gently turns his head, allowing her to stroke his cheek with her thumb.

'I thought you'd forgotten about me – you're always so busy, I haven't seen you in months.' She kisses Edith on the cheek, exhaling a line of smoke over her shoulder.

'How could I forget?'

'Everyone else seems to have.'

Litzi offers Edith a cigarette, which she accepts, leaning into the extended match and inhaling gratefully. She holds it in her chest, feeling it expand in her lungs, soothing her, before exhaling gently, the smoke blanketing her face.

'So how is Herr Honigmann?' Edith says finally and Litzi shrugs.

'Georg is fine. Getting plenty of work as a freelance journalist, and he's been editing for the *Exchange Telegraph*, which means we have better prospects for eating, and such indulgences, than we had when I was with Kim.'

Edith looks away, across the expanse of green, her attention pausing briefly on Tommy as Litzi takes her final drag of her cigarette and then sniffs, pushing her hands deep into her pocket.

'I'm not questioning it,' Litzi says. 'I understand what needs to be done. Speaking of errant husbands, have you spoken to Alexander?'

'Briefly.' Edith raises her eyebrows, and flicks the tip of her cigarette. 'He came back to London but he is not living with us.'

'Good. I never liked him.'

'I couldn't tell.' Edith laughs.

'Such an ineffectual man. And you have enough work?'

'In his defence, he has been mending the bones of injured Republicans.' Edith leans her head, tenderly, on Litzi's shoulder, and then realigns herself. 'I've given up the studio. I still have some work, but not enough to justify the expense alongside rent on the flat. I think I will have to diversify.'

'That's ridiculous. Your photography is brilliant.'

Edith shrugs. 'I'm not sure my style chimes with the increasingly sentimental aestheticising of today. You saw the recent competition in the *Socialist Worker*? None of the winning images had any political content. It's absurd. Under the Popular Front, the British Left have completely failed to see the potential for the photographic medium.' She sighs. 'Speaking of sentimental photography, you've heard that Wolf has a new partner? Your old friend Ilona Donat.'

'Of course. Georg and I went for dinner the other evening.

It seems serious between them, I imagine they will have children soon, and then I will be the last one left. Your mother
was there, too – she was worried about you.'

Edith takes a cigarette from her pocket and lights it. 'You'll
have children when you're ready.'

Litzi shrugs. 'Maybe.'

'And when you do, you'll be a great mother.'

'I'm not sure I know what a good mother is.'

Edith looks away, righting herself before turning back to
her friend, her mind returning to Anthony Blunt, who at this
moment should be making his way down the steps at the
University of London, where he is working as general publications editor at the Warburg Institute.

'Perhaps. But in the meantime Tommy and I appreciate you.'

'Aren't you scared, Edie, of what will happen to you if you
are caught?'

Edith looks at Litzi and smiles, feeling tears form in her
eyes. 'I'm terrified.' Standing, she dusts down her skirt, lifting
her chin a little higher. 'Thank you so much for watching him
– I won't be long.'

Edith is at home with Tommy, thinking back on her meeting
with Blunt, when it lands on the doormat in the communal
hallway: a copy of *Harper's Bazar*, hand-delivered, the corner
of page six folded down slightly.

Her face dropping, she considers the meaning for a split
second before gathering her things. Minutes later, trembling,
she picks up Tommy and walks in silence to Maida Vale tube
station. At Baker Street and again at Warren Street, she changes
trains, Tommy clinging to her as she walks, briskly, through
dark residential streets to Lawn Road.

In late summer, the sky is still light and she rings the bell of the top-floor flat first, walking Tommy upstairs to where she finds Molly waiting in the doorway. 'Is everything all right, Edith?'

'Could you watch Tommy for a while? I have to meet someone.'

Molly pauses momentarily, before nodding. 'Of course – we were just preparing supper. Will you be back in time to join us?'

'I won't be long, and we won't stay.'

'Edith,' Molly says, stepping forward and taking Tommy from her arms. 'You look . . . Is there anything I can do?'

But before she can say anything else, Edith turns, calling over her shoulder. 'Just watch Tommy, please.'

Two floors down, at one minute past the hour of six, the Isobar is empty but for a solitary figure seated at the end of five stools that line the wooden bar, his hand resting on a glass.

Inside, it could be any time of day or night, a Duke Ellington riff playing quietly on the record player.

Arnold's gaze remains fixed on his glass, the area dark and still as she moves towards him. 'I didn't know you were back.'

'Only for a few days.' His manner towards her is cool and professional. He barely glances in her direction, as if even to look at her would cause him pain or revulsion, or both. 'Percy Glading has been arrested. Police raided the safe house – among the things they found was the camera.'

Dropping herself on the stool beside him, she works hard to remain calm, though beneath her skin her blood runs hot.

'Is there any way they can link it to you, Edith?'

She shakes her head, her fingers curling under the bar, for stability.

'You're sure, Edith?'

'It's impossible,' she says, turning away from him, imagining a finger, like ice, running down her back.

Edith and Tommy are on the corner pavement, taking in the morning sun in front of the flat, the day the officers make their appearance. Edith understands immediately who they are, these men in their dark double-breasted coats. The older is tall and unfit. Neither man smiles.

'Edith Tudor-Hart?' The officer states his question as her fingers squeeze more tightly around Tommy's hand. 'We are from Special Branch. We need to take you in for questioning. Is there someone who can mind the child?' Sensing a curtain flicker in the window of one of the flats in the building opposite, she lifts her chin, defiantly. 'You can talk in front of Tommy. What is this about?'

'It would be best if you contacted someone who could look after the child. Perhaps a neighbour?' the other adds.

Edith clears her throat, keeping her voice calm, for Tommy's sake. 'My brother. He and his wife live in N.W.11.'

The officer with the moustache nods. 'We'll drive you there.'

'I'll need the perambulator to get home, afterwards,' she says, turning and making for the door of the flat.

'It won't fit in the car.'

'Then I can push Tommy to my brother's and meet you at the station,' she tries, keeping the strain out of her voice.

'We'd rather escort you.'

Her jaw tightening, she nods. 'Well, then, I'll get our coats.'

She doesn't speak as the car drives west, through central London, turning into Birdcage Walk, and along St James's Park, before heading right again into Queen Anne's Gate: the headquarters of the Secret Service of His Majesty King George VI.

The paternoster lift rattles as it transports them to the top floor, reflecting the beat of her heart. Feeling the men's eyes watching her, sidelong, she stares straight ahead, her expression cool.

'You might already be aware of why we've brought you here,' the younger man says, once they are seated opposite one another in an interview room.

'No.' Edith's tone is polite but firm, her hands crossed in front of her on the table.

'Percy Glading . . .' He lets the name hang there a while, watching for a response that doesn't come.

G sharp, C sharp, E. One, three, five.

'You know him?'

'Not that I'm aware of,' she says. 'I'm a photographer so I meet a lot of people.'

'You're a photographer. Yes.' The second detective's mouth curls into a smile. 'You are, aren't you? You came here from Austria, is that right? In 1933. You married a British man by the name of Alexander Tudor-Hart.'

'That's right.'

'And where is he now, this husband of yours?'

'Working, I imagine,' she says.

'Working? And where might that be? Oh yes, in Spain, treating the injured in the war? From which side would that be?'

'Anyone who needs his help, presumably.'

'Presumably?'

'Alexander and I are separated.'

'And yet you remain in England?'

'I am a citizen,' she replies, her tone a little more sharp.

'Of course. By virtue of your marriage.'

She holds the officer's eye, saying nothing.

The younger detective speaks next. 'So you've never heard of Percy Glading? Even though you've been present at a number of Communist rallies at which Mr Glading spoke.'

'I've already told you. I'm a photog—'

'You're a photographer. Yes, you said. And what about the Arsenal, in Woolwich. Have you heard of that?'

'Vaguely.'

'Right, but you've never heard of one of its former engineers, Percy Glading?'

Before Edith can answer the older officer intervenes, looking down at his notes. 'Mr Glading has been arrested. During a raid of a property connected with Mr Glading, invoices were found in respect of a Leica camera and other photographic material which had been supplied in January 1937 by the Westminster Photographic Exchange Ltd, Camera House, Charing Cross Road, and by the General Electric Company Ltd, Magnet House, Kingsway. These invoices showed the goods were supplied to E. Hart, 68 Acre Lane. These materials are believed to have been used in a crime covered by the Official Secrets Act.'

Edith feels the air, thick and wool-like, expand in her chest. *It's not just about the lies we tell other people, but the lies we tell ourselves.*

'Yes,' she says, after a brief pause. 'And?'

'And, *Mrs* Tudor-Hart. Could you explain to us how a camera purchased by yourself ended up being used for illegal purposes?'

Edith pulls herself straighter in her chair. 'Absolutely not. And I have no idea why I should have to. I own all sorts of cameras – as I say, it's my job. Sometimes I keep them for a long time; sometimes, such as in this instance, I sell them on.'

'You sell them on?'

'Yes.'

'And you retain receipts for these sales?'

'No. They would be of no use to me.'

The younger officer uncrosses his legs and pulls himself more tightly in his chair, agitation showing in his voice. 'And you expect us to believe that you, a known Communist sympathiser, bought the camera that was used to photograph sensitive documents, but that it is just a coincidence.'

'I am not suggesting anything. All I am saying is that I have no memory whatsoever of purchasing such a camera. So as far as I can tell, either I bought it, at some point that evades my memory, and sold it on. Or perhaps someone else bought it, using my name. But the point is that it is not my business what you believe.' She moves closer, her chin resting on her hands. 'It is merely up to me to explain, and for you to conclusively demonstrate, if you can, that the facts are otherwise.'

The rain has returned by the time Edith steps out of the police station, her bravado falling away as she turns left. She hails a cab, her eyes occasionally flitting to the driver's rear-view mirror as they move through London, the bright lights finally giving way to dark suburban streets: rows of identical white new-builds shielded by box hedges.

At 28 Willifield Way, Ilona answers the door, her eyes fraught with worry. 'Edith, what happened?'

'It's nothing. They made a mistake. I'm sorry to ask, but I need money to pay for my taxi.'

'Of course,' Ilona says as Edith takes her son back, kissing his head, feeling her own body calm in response to the physicality of him, and then lifting him in front of her and smiling to demonstrate to her child that everything is fine – a smile that he doesn't return. 'What a silly thing to have happened!' she says, trying to catch his eye.

Returning inside once she has paid the driver, Ilona's expression is strained with concern. 'Stay, have some food, Wolf will be home from filming soon. He told you about the documentary he is making with Paul Rotha?'

'He mentioned it,' Edith says, distractedly. 'I'm sure he will make an excellent film-maker. Thank you but we mustn't stay, I have work to get on with at home.'

'At least come and stand in front of the fire a while, and warm up.'

'We must get back,' Edith replies, more firmly. 'Thank you so much for watching Tommy.'

'How will you get home?'

'We'll take the tube-train.'

'But Edith, the nearest station is Golders Green, and it's raining. You don't even have the pram.'

Edith smiles, kissing Ilona on the cheek. 'We'll be fine. Give our love to Wolf.'

'Wait, please.' Ilona ducks into the living room and returns holding a woollen shawl. 'At least take this blanket.'

Edith walks as fast as she can, along unfamiliar residential streets, only partially lit by street-lamps.

She holds Tommy close to her chest, her shoulders aching under his weight, her breasts hot with the strain of excess milk. She doesn't stop to reposition the child when she feels the wet patches caused by leaking in response to her toddler's cries. Instead, she keeps her vision fixed ahead as she continues along Hoop Lane, the cemetery stretching out on her left.

The white noise of the tube-train calms him, and he falls

asleep, Edith standing upright in the carriage, afraid of waking him should she sit down.

By the time she reaches the flat, her whole body is rigid with pain, and she pulls the key from her pocket and lets herself into the communal hall. Even inside, she doesn't capitulate at first, placing her hand on Tommy's cheek as she walks up the steps towards her front door. Only once it is shut does she allow herself to exhale, dropping back against the sturdy frame, her mouth falling open as she closes her eyes, her legs suddenly weak and shaking.

For a moment, she stays there, hunched on the floor. When Tommy writhes, she lays him down on the worn carpet while she rolls up her top, milk leaking on to her skirt, lifting the child, who snorts and snuffles before finally settling on her breast.

Once he is asleep, she pulls herself up, supporting his dead weight with her right arm, using her left hand to lever herself to a standing position. Placing her son on the sofa, she spreads Ilona's shawl over him and props a pillow at the edge of the sofa to stop him falling.

Waiting a moment to check that he doesn't stir, she walks to the rain-streaked window, ignoring the figure she imagines hunched under the lamp-post as she pulls the curtains to. When she turns back, her arm catches a glass of water which had stood on the edge of the table from this morning, and she hears it smash against the tiles, sending shards across the floor. Freezing, expecting the child to wake, she waits, and then – without stopping to clean up the broken glass – she returns to the front door and double-locks it, her heartbeat rising again as she walks towards the box of negatives she had brought home from the studio earlier that month.

Her fingers fumbling, she works through the pile, less

carefully than she ought, until she finds the ones she is looking for: two films. She looks at the shape of the military plans, like bodies floating in oil, as she lifts each frame to the light.

Replacing the lid on to the box, she carries the negatives to the sink, her eyes glancing briefly back at Tommy, and then she takes a match and strikes, watching the strips shrivel as they twist and burn.

Closing her eyes, she hears the crackling, and above it, the sound of Kim's voice as they sat around the table at Litzi's apartment, in another lifetime, devising codes. So we are agreed? *May I have a cigarette?* to indicate the coast is clear. Most importantly of all, the code for you are in danger: *Thank you for the match.*

Dear Edith,

We had a disturbing incident last month: two nights running, with the temperature at about minus 20°C, a young woman rang our bell to ask for a glass of water. The second time, we asked where she lived and she waved her hand vaguely in the direction of Gorky Street. It seemed most odd that she should twice come all the way up to our flat for a glass of water; evidently she was casing the joint for someone or other. We reported the matter, of course, but there was precious little to go on. Anyway, there has been no follow-up so far; so we are just keeping our fingers crossed. There are many occasions in life when one has simply to take the elementary precautions and then hope for the best.

I have promised to take Nina to Tbilisi for ten days in the second half of March. She has never been there and it is an absolute 'must' – a gorgeous city in itself with wonderful excursions into the Caucasus. My only fear is the far-famed Georgian hospitality, which is more awesome even than the Volga kind. I have strenuously asked the people here to insist that I am a total valetudinarian, capable of only one banquet a week. But once we are there, we are in the hands of the locals and Gawdelpus!

Alas, any vision one might have of us gliding through the Taiga towards blini lunches is unfortunately a mirage. It is true that, for the first time in five years, we are enjoying a real Russian winter: lots of snow in December, January and February, with temperatures ranging from minus 10 to 25°C. But in mid-December Nina got a nasty attack of angina (sore throat, a cold, etc.). It was nothing serious, but it lasted about a month. She had scarcely got better when I lost another anchor-tooth, and spent ten days or so, in and out of the polyclinic getting another plate. Finally, I ran into this spate of work. So we have not skied at all this winter, although we hope to do so soon. The forecast is for a cold and snowy March, which will give us a chance, if it comes true.

Yours,
Kim

Elementary precautions

Her fourth home in less than five years in London. This is what Edith is thinking as she looks up at Tommy, the ringing of the bells through the speakers of the wireless signalling the start of the morning news, distracting her briefly from the pile of unpaid bills mounted on the table in front of her, in the new flat on Alexandra Road.

Thursday 24th August 1939. According to the Russian TASS news agency, the Soviet Union has revealed a pact of non-aggression with Germany. The agreement, which took place, completely unexpectedly, in the early hours of Wednesday morning, would give the Soviet Union seven-year five per cent credits amounting to 200,000,000 Marks for German machinery and armaments . . .

The words reach into her gut and give a sharp twist. And yet as she sits here, her eyes still fixed on her son, life carries on, just as it was a few seconds ago, Tommy stacking blocks on the other side of the room and knocking them down again with a meticulousness that is as violent as it is hypnotic.

When she stands, the words continue to warp in her ears: *Germany will buy from the Soviet Union 180,000,000 Marks' worth of wheat, timber, iron ore and petroleum in the next two years.*

She is light-headed as she steps forward, her fingers trembling as she reaches out, and with a single turn of the knob the room plunges into silence. From where he works on the tattered rug, Tommy looks up, clutching one of the blocks in his hand. Before he can cry out, protesting against the sudden absence of noise, Edith moves towards the gramophone, her hands trembling as she places the needle on the record Arnold Deutsch had given to her the last time she saw him at his flat. Lidiya Ruslanova's 'Charming Eyes' crackles through the speakers, and Edith lets her eyelids drop.

In that moment, time thaws and she feels herself withdraw to another place, sensing once again his skin brushing hers as he had handed her the record, his blue eyes trailing her as he talked in that voice that had promised revolution.

'It hasn't yet been publicly released,' he'd whispered, and she had smiled.

'Then how do you have a copy?'

Leaning in, he had pushed a curl of hair gently behind her ear. 'Don't ask me questions that require me to lie to you.'

There is a low click, click, clicking sound in the present as the tune fades and Tommy objects, the sudden sound of his voice making her start. *Use words*, she wants to tell him. *Why won't you speak?* Instead, she reaches out with one hand as if to soothe him, with the other returning the needle to the edge of the disc.

At the resurgence of the sound the child's expression mellows and he brings his legs up in front of him, wrapping his arms around his shins, his head resting in the crook of his knees.

They listen twice more before Edith removes the needle from the vinyl and beckons Tommy towards the door, comforting his cries with the promise of the trees they will count on their way to Lawn Road. The same trees, the same number of steps. Continuity, reliable sequences: the things Tommy values.

For his age, Tommy walks well. Choosing the quieter streets

on account of the boy's nerves, they take the forty-minute journey to Lawn Road Flats on foot, hand-in-hand. Molly smiles with surprise as she opens the door, crouching down and talking to Tommy at eye-level. Though he doesn't smile, he knows her well enough not to resist when she leads him through to the roof garden at the back of the house where the children – Jonathan and Jeremy, and Tommy's cousin, Jennifer, who at ten years old is the youngest of the three – play on the terrace.

'Aren't they darlings?' Molly says and Edith nods, distractedly, her eyes moving back through to the living room. 'Edith, I'm so glad you're here. Lucia is coming over in a minute, she's in a dreadful state – Lázló and Marcel have been using her photographs of the Bauhaus without giving her any credit. She mentioned that she'd seen you recently and shared some contacts.'

'May I use your phone?' Edith says and Molly smiles.

'Of course, I'll take Tommy to see the children.'

Sliding the door closed and dialling the switchboard, Edith shuts her eyes with relief when Litzi answers.

'Have you heard?'

There is a pause on the other end of the line and Edith pictures her friend straightening herself, disapproving of her for making contact on this line, when anyone could be listening in.

'You mean about Tommy and the other boy?' Litzi replies. 'Yes, I have. I hope you're not worrying unnecessarily about it.'

Edith breathes in. 'No, I suppose—'

'Good. There's nothing you can do at this stage except trust that there is a reason for their friendship.'

'But I don't trust it: we both know what the other boy is capable of—' Edith's voice strains with the urge to scream the image of her father forming, in a bath of his own blood.

'We all know what he is, yes. But we also know that sometimes we have to trust the ones we really care about. You don't need me to remind you of that. There is nothing else to be done at this stage other than what you're already doing. You're a good mother, a *committed* mother. Don't question yourself, Edith.'

'I'm not.' Her voice wavers. Closing her eyes, she thinks of Arnold. There will be a plan behind the pact. She hears his voice soothing her: *A whole new world awaits.*

'I know you're not. You're just not thinking straight. It's to be expected – it's a strange time. How is Tommy, otherwise?'

'Tommy is fine,' Edith says, before ending the call. 'We're both fine.'

The room stings with silence once they have hung up. She runs her fingers along the walls of the apartment as she walks back through it. With its sliding doors and absence of any hinges there is nothing to hint at the mechanisms beneath the surface, polished concrete and carefully positioned glass creating the perfect illusion.

From the living room doorway Edith watches a while, the older children playing on the roof terrace, Molly crouched again beside Tommy, who is seated away from the others. There is a gentle breeze as Edith steps out on to the roof terrace.

When she spots her, Molly smiles, less convincingly this time. 'Everything all right?'

'Yes, thank you. Come, Tommy,' Edith says. 'We won't stay – we're meeting my brother and his wife, and my mother, also.'

'Oh, charming,' Molly says, though her tone doesn't match her words. 'Have you spoken to Alexander? Beatrix tells us he's coming back to England.'

'Not yet.'

Molly pauses. 'Edith, does Tommy ever attempt to verbalise, besides those noises?'

Studying Molly's face for a moment, Edith feels her jaw

tighten. 'He is only three years old. I speak to him in English and German – often bilingual children take longer to be confident in their speech.'

Molly pauses. 'You know I've studied psychology and psychopathy,' she says, laying a hand on Edith's arm. 'I've run several children's groups . . . Tommy—'

'Tommy what?'

The air between them sharpens.

'He's a wonderful child, Edith, please don't get me wrong. I just wondered, if you ever wanted to speak to someone, I know good people who might be able to help with his needs—'

'I think we will be going now,' Edith says, lifting Tommy into her arms. 'Edith, I don't want to interfere, but perhaps you know Anna Freud? She's from Vienna, the daughter of Sigmund—'

'I know who Anna Freud is, Molly.'

'She is in London now, just a few streets away from here, in Hampstead. She is coming tonight, for dinner—'

But by the time she finishes her sentence, Edith has already turned.

Ilona's expression is strained as she answers the door, beckoning her sister-in-law and Tommy inside, blinking at the street over Edith's shoulder before closing it against the outside world.

'We have gin – one of Wolf's colleagues gave it to him. I'll get you some, and some fruit syrup for Tommy.'

Edith accepts the glass and leaves Tommy's cup on the table when he refuses to acknowledge his mother or his aunt, Molly's words clawing at her mind. Taking a long, grateful sip of the alcohol, she leans back against the hob, her lower back catching on the ignition.

'Shall I take Tommy?'

'No,' Edith says, more harshly than she intends, gripping the child in her arms as Ilona moves closer, lowering her voice.

'Just to warn you: your mother—'

Before she can finish, Adele bursts into the room, an apron tied around her waist. Without acknowledging Tommy or Ilona, she addresses Edith, accusingly. 'You have heard the news?'

'Yes,' Edith replies, her tone calmer than she feels.

'And you stand by your position?'

This time when Ilona outstretches her arm Edith relinquishes Tommy to his aunt, her attention fixed on her mother as Ilona takes the child into the living room, away from what is to follow. 'So, my daughter doesn't condemn it: a pact between the Nazis and the Soviet Union. And so you must condone it, this agreement between your leader and the same man who forced us from our homes, who stole our country – the men who are responsible for Papa's death?'

'Hush,' Edith hisses, her eyes looking nervously around her.

Adele laughs in disgust. 'Why, Edith? Who are you so afraid of?'

'You don't understand.' She replies through gritted teeth, steadily returning her mother's stare.

'I don't understand? Oh, please, Edith, enlighten me.'

'It's a trick. Hitler thinks he's outsmarted the Union but there's a plan.'

'A plan?'

Edith says nothing.

Adele speaks louder in response. 'And where is your beloved Thälmann in this plan? Was his release a condition of the pact?'

Edith feels her cheeks burn but still she says nothing.

'No.' Adele picks up the kitchen knife on the counter top, and turns towards a tray of potatoes. 'Now whose silence is deafening?'

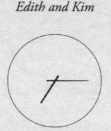

I am speaking to you from the cabinet room at 10 Downing Street. This morning the British ambassador in Berlin handed the German government a final note stating that unless we heard from them by eleven o'clock that they were prepared, at once, to withdraw their troops from Poland, a state of war would exist between us. I have to tell you now that no such undertaking has been received, and that consequently this country is at war with Germany.

```
Secret Intelligence Service file on
            Edith Suschitzky

                                    9th May 1940
P.F.40997/B.4.a(2)
Dear Mr Moriarty,


I  was  much  interested  in  your  letter
X.2326/2617 of 16th April 1940, about Doctor
A. HART of 47 Beaufort Road, Edgbaston.
  It seems most probable that he is identical
```

with Dr Alexander Elthan TUDOR-HART, born at Piesole, Italy, on 3/9/1901, who has been known to us for many years as a member of the Communist Party. We did not know however that he was now in Birmingham. In fact, the last information we have of him dates back from the spring of last year. I enclose a copy of his photograph from which you will be able to check his identification.

Alexander Tudor-HART has been a Party member at least since 1930, but he is not a person who carries a great deal of weight. I do not think he is identical with Alexander HART to whom you refer as having been a Lenin School student from 1932—34. At that time, Tudor-HART had a house appointment at St Mary Abbott's Hospital, London. His principal work of recent years has been the organisation of the British Medical Unit to Spain of which he was in charge in the field. He spent nearly two years in Spain in spite of a certain amount of friction between him and the Spanish authorities. We are not quite sure of the details of this, but it is evident that the Unit did not give entire satisfaction. However, his experience proved to be of service, as early in 1939 he was advising the China Campaign Committee on the Medical Unit for China.

My impression is that he is not a very effective person and is of much less importance in the Party than his first wife, Edith

SUSCHITSKY. Her name is associated with underground activities and she was almost certainly
involved in the GLADING organisation. We have
no record of the present Mrs HART.

You raise the question of Dr HART's
employment under the Ministry of Health.
I am not aware of the details of this
appointment, but on first sight he would
apppear to be better employed there than
in any more confidential position. If,
however, you have reason to think that his
work does include confidential matter, and
you feel it inadvisable for him to hold
the post, perhaps you would let me know.
I might then be able to take up the subject
with the Ministry of Health.
  Yours sincerely,
  Major General Sir Vernon Kell

Cecil, C.H. Moriarty, Esq. C.B.E., LL.D, TCD.,
Chief Constable
City Constabulary
Birmingham

EHC/MF

It is eight months after war is officially declared that the
Luftwaffe mounts its first significant attack – which will later
be recorded in the incident registers of the London Fire
Brigade. 13th May 1940. At 2.51 p.m. the Dutch ship

SS *Prins-Willem-Van-Oranje* is struck by an incendiary bomb at Gravesend Reach in Kent.

Some three months after that, in August, the first raids on central London begin with a night-time attack over the East End, the City of London and suburbs to the north, west and south, leaving nine dead and fifty-eight in hospital.

At five p.m. on Saturday 7th September – a full year after Neville Chamberlain's declaration of war – three hundred and twenty German bombers, and six hundred fighters, fly up the Thames, wreaking havoc on swaths of the city starting at Woolwich Arsenal, through Beckton Gas Works, leaving large parts of the docks on fire before littering their bombs over the City, Westminster and Kensington, in an attack that lasts an hour. Two hours after it ends, a further two hundred and fifty fighters resume their assault and don't let up until four-thirty the following morning. Within twenty-four hours, four hundred and thirty-three people are dead and sixteen hundred seriously injured.

During a period of fifty-seven consecutive nights, from September 1940 until May 1941, almost ceaseless bombing deforms and obliterates London.

Suddenly, the war that until then had been largely happening elsewhere is happening here.

It is the intensity of the silence that follows as carnage gives way, briefly, to normal life, that Edith will remember when she looks back, later: calm and chaos bundled side by side.

The term 'Blitz' derives from the German word *Blitzkrieg*, meaning lightning war. Lightning never strikes twice, but it hasn't struck here yet, Edith thinks as she lies awake beside her son, her subconscious tuned in to the sirens and the blasts that ravage other parts of the city until it is no longer in another part but here on her own street, silver sparks clattering against the windows, lighting up the darkness, pulling her by the throat out through the gauze of sleep and into the waking nightmare in which she hears Tommy's screams, the clawing at her stomach and the smell of the napalm.

Beside her, her child holds himself in a ball, his hands pressed over his ears as Edith clutches him tightly, the sound of the explosions growing louder around them.

'It's OK, Mama will protect you,' she tells him. 'Mama will keep you safe.' But what she really means is, if you die, then I'll die too.

Too fine an evening to take a taxi-cab, Kim walks from his mother's flat on Drayton Gardens to the address in Mayfair, enjoying the late-afternoon sun on his face as he passes South Kensington tube station.

It is warm by London standards and at Knightsbridge he removes the jacket of the Wyser & Bryant suit he had purchased as a little treat to himself the day Burgess got him the job at SIS, tucking it over his arm and letting his eyes look up at the heavenly blue sky. Warm, though nothing compared to the Iberian Peninsula – he wouldn't be needing a jacket there, at this time of year. Unfortunately, his new role – once he is transferred to the SIS Iberian sub-section, taking charge of British intelligence in Spain and Portugal, in a month or so, thanks to good old Tommy Harris – will be based a little closer to home.

Tomás Harris had joined MI5 after the break-up of the training school at Brickendonbury. When he mentioned, over lunch, that the head of Section V, Felix Cowgill, was looking for someone with a knowledge of Spain to take charge of the expanded sub-section, Kim had nearly spat out his food. They had been seated not far from where he is headed now, at Harris's house on Chesterfield Gardens, surrounded by art treasures in an atmosphere of *haute cuisine* and *grands vins*.

The job was still quite a coup, even once it emerged that the headquarters were not in Spain or Portugal, but in fact in St Albans. It was better than Beaulieu, Kim's current placement in another of the Special Operations Executive's training schools – this one in Hampshire, where it is Kim's job to devise the school's syllabus and teach the art of political propaganda. In its bid to cause chaos behind enemy lines in Nazi-occupied Europe, Beaulieu has also been playing havoc with his ability to access any bloody information. So no, the job at the SIS Iberian sub-section is hardly the one he would have chosen – not least given that Spain and Portugal are now lying far out on the flank of his real interest – but it is a means of disentangling himself from Beaulieu.

And, as it transpires, the archives of SIS are also handily located at St Albans, next door to Section V.

There is a rustle of movement as Kim crosses the road at Hyde Park Corner, and he turns to see horses cantering past, two abreast. The sudden rush of memory takes him by surprise. For a moment he is back there, that day in June 1934. The beginning of everything.

Everything looks altered, in the aftermath. The pitted windows, in the surrounding buildings, hollowed out by the blast; shards of glass littering the area beyond the barricade guarding the hole where until just a few hours earlier her photographic studio had stood.

'Ma'am, you'll have to stand back, it's not safe,' the fireman says as Edith hovers in front of 17 Duke Street: suddenly an absence of space, a void that has opened up and swallowed a part of her life so that, looking at it now, it is hard to believe that it ever existed at all.

'Luckily no one was killed. If you had any belongings in there, as you can see, they won't have survived.' The fireman's voice interrupts her thoughts. 'I'm sorry, but you can't stand this close to the bomb site.'

Duke Street extends from Grosvenor Square, northwards across Oxford Street to Manchester Square. She had kept nothing at the studio; her prints and negatives are all at home, safe within the confines of the flat.

Her camera itself hangs around her neck, beneath her coat, as she walks with her hands pushed deep into her pockets, along Bond Street, Londoners rolling their eyes at yet another detour on their route to work, the city bustling with life in the face of death.

She walks and walks, framing the city's streets. It is around lunchtime when she stands on Portman Square, looking down through the lens, adjusting the frame, the man's voice breaking her concentration.

It takes a moment for his face to register, and, when it does, she smiles at the sight of an old friend, a face that belongs in a previous, somehow less complicated life.

'Stefan, what are you doing here?'

'I've just been having a meeting at the Courtauld Institute.'

He rolls his eyes in a show of self-deprecation. 'We all turn into those we despise in the end. Well, some of us . . .' His wide-set eyes fan with fine lines as he smiles back at her, his face unaltered and yet completely unrecognisable from the young man on the lawn in front of the Prellerhaus in Dessau. 'But it's been years . . . How are you? Are you living in London?'

'It's been a decade,' Edith says, leaning in to kiss him. 'I tried to get in touch with Maks, after he returned to Hamburg, but he never returned my letters.'

Stefan's expression changes. 'You haven't heard?' He pauses, studying her face. 'Maks is in prison. Auschwitz. I've heard conflicting stories but he managed to escape to Germany a couple of years ago, and made it to Czechoslovakia; he had a lover there and they lived together. As far as I know, this man had helped others escape to Denmark, but Maks wanted to stay and help, too; he never made it himself. A year later, when Hitler invaded Czechoslovakia—' He pauses. 'I'm so sorry to tell you like this.'

'Dear Maks . . .' Her words trail uselessly in the air.

Stefan blinks, righting himself, as if remembering where he is, returning his face to a strained smile.

'But Edith, it's so good to see you. Lydia would love to see you too. We don't live far from here; you must come and have a drink with us.'

'I can't. My son is with his father and I need to collect him.' She lies easily, instinctively, picturing Tommy on the other side of the country, in Birmingham, spending the first couple of nights away from his mother.

'You have a son, how wonderful. And we have a telephone. You can call his father and tell him—' Stefan's expression changes. 'In fact, Edith, you must come with me, this evening – be my date. I have an invitation to a party. Flora Solomon has the most incredible flat and is known to throw the best soirées. Lydia is claiming to have a cold so she can't come with me. It's just the other side of Berkeley Square from where we live. No, don't say anything.' He raises a hand. 'I'm not taking no for an answer. For Maks, for old times' sake.'

As she stares back at him, she sees the dark fleck in his left eye expand so slightly that it's impossible to know whether she imagined it.

'So you and Lydia have been together ever since the Bauhaus?'

'More than a decade,' Stefan says, looking straight ahead as they continue along the Strand. 'I tried to get Maks a job here in London but he couldn't get a visa, and I wasn't able to sponsor him. Lydia's mother is British, as you know – once Lydia and I married in Germany we came here, her family helped me get a job, and I fell into this picturesque bourgeois life that you see before you now.' Stefan laughs, self-deprecatingly.

A silence falls between them, each lost in their private thoughts, the late summer air freshening their cheeks as they pass St Martin-in-the-Fields.

'Maks visited us once,' Stefan says after a while, picking up on Edith's mood. 'He said he was happy for me, that I was achieving what he never had the chance to. But, I don't deserve it, and I certainly don't deserve his generosity of spirit. At least I've seen sense, in some respects. Maks was always more generous than I was – and more generous than I would have been, if the tables had been turned.'

'It's impossible to know how we would behave, in different circumstances,' Edith replies, coolly, though as she says it she knows exactly what she would have done in his position.

'And what about you? How do you behave these days?'

There is something in his tone that makes her hesitate. 'I'm not sure I quite know what you mean.'

'You're not still buying all that stuff they fed us, are you?' He holds her gaze in a way that makes her rearrange her hands, behind her back. Indicating towards Trafalgar Square, he continues. 'This was the last place I saw you, wasn't it? You were here with some English people, members of the CPGS, so I remember.'

'You have a long memory,' Edith says.

'Some things are hard to forget. Did you ever hear the story of Rose Cohen?' Stefan's tone hardens slightly, the two of them slipping into a side street, the sudden cool air forcing Edith to tighten her coat around her waist. 'She was one of their founders, a friend of Lydia's mother, in fact, when they were young. She worked with, and was greatly admired by, Harry Pollitt, apparently. He was here that day, wasn't he? That's why I wondered if perhaps you knew the story.'

'I haven't heard of Rose Cohen,' Edith replies, her chest tightening in response to the edge in Stefan's voice. 'Should I have?'

'It was before your time,' Stefan shrugs. 'In the 1920s, Rose married a Russian and went to live in Moscow. Years later, in 1937, she was arrested. Pollitt, knowing her well, tried to intercede, but he failed and Rose was shot. Executed. Three months later, the same Harry Pollitt wrote an article in the *Daily Worker* defending the trials of – and I quote – "political and moral degenerates", which were, he went on, "a mighty demonstration to the world of the power and strength of the Soviet Union".'

They both look straight ahead, neither quite knowing what to say, and then Stefan reaches out and hails a passing cab. 'Actually, I'm in need of a drink; let's speed this up a bit, shall we?'

The house stands on the corner of two residential roads just behind Mount Street, in the aristocratic heart of Mayfair: an old coach-house transformed in a mock-Tudor style with red brickwork and dark latticed window panelling, above and either side of a decorative passageway that leads inside.

The sound of the traffic recedes as Stefan closes the door behind them, a cool air taking hold.

'It belongs to Lydia's family,' he says, watching Edith's face as they move through the hallway, lined with paintings and oversized statues, a table at the far end adorned with an enormous bouquet of dried flowers in peaches and mauves and creams. 'I'm afraid it's always chilly. Something to do with preserving the artworks.'

'Stefan, is that you?' Lydia peers over the banisters, her red hair falling over slanting shoulders, casting her face in shadow. A silk kimono is wrapped around her narrow waist. After a beat, she breaks into a smile. 'Edith Suschitzky? Well, I never.'

Edith doesn't correct her on the change in name, smiling as Lydia makes her way down the stairs.

'We bumped into each other outside the Courtauld,' says Stefan. 'I told Edith you were too ill to come with me this evening, so she will be my date.'

Lydia nods, slowing her steps. 'Oh, Edith, it's marvellous to see you! No, don't come too close, I have a nasty bug, but let me get you a drink. Follow me into the drawing room. What will you have? I'll make cocktails, Tom Collins or a Pink Lady? Never mind, I'll choose something. Gosh,' she says, 'you look exactly the same.' Her eyes linger a moment on Edith before she turns and walks away, padding down the hall in her embroidered slippers.

'I'm underdressed,' Edith says, a statement rather than an apology, and Stefan dismisses her with his hand.

'You are always utterly yourself, Edith, it's admirable.'

The drawing room is covered in exquisite silk wallpaper, in teal and gold, floor-to-ceiling bookcases along one side, the other with a marble fireplace decorated with oddities.

Edith's attention rests on a large crackled grey lavender bottle, Stefan following her gaze, amusedly.

'The Chinese call it Ju ware,' he says, moving behind her. 'This piece was brought to England in 1936, and sold as an eighteenth-century piece for about £10.'

Edith leans forward, examining the craftsmanship, the perfect curve of the base.

'It's incredibly beautiful.'

'Yes,' Stefan agrees. 'And it turns out it was actually made in the Sung dynasty, about six centuries earlier than originally dated. Lydia's father bought it a month or so ago, at Sotheby's – paid some £900 for it.' He pauses. 'It should have been obvious to anyone who knows their stuff, but I suppose the truth is always obvious, once you know.'

The truth is always obvious once you know, Kim reminds himself as he moves along Hill Street towards Berkeley Square, feeling a chill and pulling on his jacket. But he never did know with Flora Solomon – not yet, in any case – besides the fact that the woman understands how to throw a party.

He knows also that her attitude towards him has cooled since he tried to bring her on board, persuaded to do so by her openly left-wing leanings. She had rebuffed him, and Burgess, too, who had been trying to bring her into MI6 at the time, to no avail. And yet, it hadn't stopped her introducing him to Aileen. For that, at least, he is grateful to the old goat.

He smiles at the thought of his fiancée. Aileen will be at

the house already, having arrived straight from her mother's place on Cadogan Square. He should have travelled with her, really, but in her condition she would need to take a taxi and he fancied some time to himself. With fatherhood impending, and the prospect of the move to St Albans, a man needed some space to breathe.

Skirting across Berkeley Square, Kim's attention catches on two figures slightly ahead of him, leading off into Bruton Street. The man's silhouette – suit and hat – is caught in shadow. The woman turns, as if aware that she is being watched, and he sees that her hair is roughly cut into a bob; notes the long skirt, the dark roll-neck jumper at odds with the season.

Pausing while he collects his breath, he hears a motor-car slow down behind and turns to see Aileen smiling at him through the open window of the cab.

'Kim? There you are, impeccable timing.'

'Hello, darling,' he says, righting his expression and admiring the swell of her belly as she steps out on to the pavement. 'Shall we?'

'Shall we?'

Stefan places a hand on the small of Edith's back as they leave the house.

She is drowsy with champagne and gin, the night air sobering her slightly as they step on to the street, Lydia's eyes following them from the doorway.

Despite the warm evening, there is a chill in the air as they cross Berkeley Square towards Bruton Street.

Pausing, Edith turns as if expecting to find they are being followed, but the street is empty and they continue, the sky darkening around them.

At No.32, white pillars flank a large doorway, music drifting into the street from several Juliet balconies that open out into the night sky.

'I can't believe you've never met Flora Solomon,' Stefan says, holding Edith's arm as they move through the main front door, towards the sweeping staircase. 'She is a legendary hostess; her father is a multi-millionaire Russian banker, and a Jew – the kind of foreigner still courted in England's capital. That is to say, a very rich one.'

Stefan smiles as the swell of voices and piano music rises up behind Flora Solomon, her set hair and arched eyebrows lifting as she approaches.

'Stefan,' she purrs, 'and I see you've replaced Lydia.'

He laughs. 'Flora, this is Edith Suschitzky. We were at the Bauhaus together, when we were young.'

'Nonsense, you're still young, and so am I.' Flora leans forward and kisses Edith on the cheek. 'Edith, you are most welcome. Will you excuse me for a moment? Members of the Etz Chaim Yeshiva have just arrived and I'm trying to tap them up for donations to the hospital. Help yourselves to anything and everything.'

'I refuse to believe you won't know anyone here.' Stefan passes Edith a glass of champagne from the tray proffered by a young woman in a round-collared shirt and headdress.

'Thank you.' Edith nods to the waitress, taking a sip, her eyes looking over her glass at a sea of heads, craning and turning through a mist of smoke. In the corner, the pianist plays a tea dance number on a grand piano and she feels a jolt of longing for her upright, back in the apartment in Vienna.

'You play?'

When she looks, she finds a man in front of her with dark hair and intense eyes.

'I did once,' she replies. *G sharp, C sharp, E. One, three, five.*

'You should give us a tune,' Stefan interjects and Edith shakes her head, finishing her glass.

'I'm afraid my repertoire is not well suited to such an upbeat occasion.'

'Forgive me, I have not introduced you. Tomás Harris, this is Edith Suschitzky. Edith is a photographer; we met at the Bauhaus. Tomás is also in the art world; he specialises in Spanish art.'

'Is that right?'

'If Stefan says so.' The man smiles. 'My father runs a gallery on this street, specialising in Goya and Velázquez.'

'I had a meeting with Blunt today at the Courtauld.' Stefan addresses Tomás. 'He mentioned he might be coming tonight.'

Tomás takes a sip of his drink, evenly. 'Really? I haven't seen him.'

The hairs on her arms prickling, Edith clings more tightly to her glass, her left hand touching the camera case that hangs around her neck.

'Would you like me to take that for you, and put it in the cloakroom?'

Edith replies sharply. 'No . . . thank you, Stefan.'

The sound of the piano fades out and in the split second of silence Edith feels a chill run over the back of her neck.

Stefan takes two more champagne glasses from a passing waiter, and hands her one before she can object. Raising his glass in a toast, Tomás opens his mouth as if to speak and then catches sight of someone over Edith's shoulder. 'And here he comes, the official expert on Spain.'

When she turns, he is there, moving beside her without so much as a blink, the lines around his grey-green eyes pronounced as he smiles.

'Now, now,' Kim replies, self-deprecating, his attention moving seamlessly from Edith to Stefan and back to Tomás.

'Modest as ever,' Harris taunts him. 'I heard that when Britain decided to recognise Franco it was Mr Philby to whom the new British ambassador turned for advice.'

Placing a hand to her throat, which feels suddenly dry, Edith nods politely. 'Excuse me, I must find the ladies'.'

As she moves away, the floor beneath her tilts like the bowels of a ship.

The night air is sharp as she steps on to the balcony, looking down at the street, which feels suddenly far away. Lighting a cigarette, she inhales, her fingers shaking as she blows out a line of smoke inhaling again so that her head is light.

'I didn't expect to see you here,' the voice behind her says, without a trace of a stutter.

'Believe me, it was a surprise to me, too,' Edith replies, quietly, without turning around, holding the cigarette filter close to her lips. 'I bumped into an old friend—'

'Hello, darling.' Kim's voice is suddenly louder.

Edith turns and finds a woman moving towards them. She has pale eyes and dark hair, a hand held protectively over her pregnant belly.

'I'm sorry, I didn't catch your name.' Kim looks Edith straight in the eye.

'No.' She smiles. 'I'm Edith Tudor-Hart.'

'Very good. This is Aileen Furse, my fiancée.' He places an arm around the woman's shoulder. 'And I'm Kim Philby.'

'A pleasure to meet you both,' Edith says, turning to face them. 'Congratulations.'

'Thank you.' Aileen places a hand on her protruding stomach.

'It's our first,' Kim says. 'Our very own bastard child. Do you have children, Edith?'

'One,' she replies. 'A boy. Tommy.'

'Tommy. What a lovely name,' Aileen replies with a shy smile. 'How do you know Flora?'

'I don't. I came with an old friend.' Edith glances over Aileen's shoulder and spots Stefan, who is speaking to a guest she doesn't recognise, his back turned to the balcony.

'Flora was the one who introduced Kim and me,' Aileen says. 'In this very flat, the day the war broke out. She and I had been working together at Marks and Spencer. Flora gave me a job, as part of her reformation of the company.'

'A store detective . . .' Kim interrupts, conspiratorially. 'And I've known Flora since childhood; we first met in the Middle East when I was a boy. Years later, I'd recently returned from Spain and came to a party here . . . The moment I saw those blue eyes across the room, I was smitten. Flora's first words were: "Aileen's a true patriot, you'll have much to talk about."' He takes a sip of his drink, fixing Edith's gaze. 'And so we did.'

'So this is where the party is.' Tomás Harris's voice booms as he steps on to the terrace behind Aileen.

'Edith, you have already met Tomás Harris, I see,' Kim says, seamlessly.

'We met just now,' Edith replies, holding her arms crossed against her chest. 'It was good to meet you all,' she says, smiling at Aileen and turning back towards the door, the lights of London blinking behind her.

'Likewise,' Kim says, his eyes settling on hers. '*Thank you for the match.*'

Secret Intelligence Service file on
Edith Suschitzky

3rd March 1941

Dear Major Golden,

With reference to your letter of February 18th to Major Wethered about Dr. Alexander TUDOR-HART, I attach a note about this man. With regard to the three points which you specifically mentioned in your letter, the following are the answers.

(1) According to my information, TUDOR-HART divorced Edith SUSCHITSKY some time before April 1940, and he married Constance SWAN. This information was obtained from the Chief Constable Birmingham in his report of April 16th 1940. Constance SWAN was an artist's model and attended the West Bromwich School of Art twice a week. Her widowed mother, Beatrice SWAN, usually appears to live with them. I have no evidence to show that Constance SWAN is a member of the Communist Party. Dr. TUDOR-HART is known to be still in touch with his former wife, who lives in London.

(2) The GLADING organisation was the espionage organisation run by Percy GLADING, who was convicted and sentenced several years ago to a term of imprisonment. Certain cameras and photographic

equipment in GLADING's possession had been purchased through E. HART at an address at which TUDOR-HART's former wife ran a photographer's business.

[SECTION REMOVED]

Yours sincerely
[UNKNOWN]

Dear Edith,

I write to you from the dacha. Just as I thought I had no cause for complaint on the weather, I thought too soon! Mid-June was bitterly cold; and we had the coldest June 24th since records began. For the past week it has been so-so, the sun alternating with torrential rain, which did our seedlings a bit of no good. Too optimistically, we removed their coverings just before a violent midnight hailstorm. However, they are not lost beyond all recovery. We have two shops within ten minutes' walk for essential supplies, groceries, licker, tobacco, etc., and we have a bi-weekly delivery of spring chickens, eggs, dairy products and such. So we don't starve as much as we should for the good of our figures.

Yesterday, I spent two hours with the official photographers. Why? They want illustrations for the Mongolian edition of my book, which is due to appear next year. Little did I think that my deathless prose would be read in Ulan Bator! I wonder, sometimes, what I was thinking, writing the thing at all: but there have been more than plenty books about that scoundrel Philby, and it felt only right that I get down my side of the story, or at least some. The truth is, I sat on the idea for some time, giving

consideration to the desirability of publishing something
on my life. I understood it was likely to cause a rumpus
with potential international complications. However,
those articles in the British press completely altered the
situation. (It is not my usual character to have a change
of heart, as you know as well as anyone.)

I like to think you wouldn't mind me talking to you
so candidly. You were always one of the few people I felt
I could talk to, openly, in my life; and one of the fewer
still whose opinions I respect. So, yes, I regret that my
writing will no doubt be the source of some discomfort
to those featured, and I would apologise to those for
whom embarrassment is caused. It should be remembered that I, too, have suffered personal inconvenience
through my connection with the Secret Service.

I am alone here at the moment, Nina having obtained
through a producer friend a season ticket for the Moscow
Film Festival which opened yesterday. As a film addict
of many years standing, it was a must for her. She
intends to come down here from time to time (in fact,
she will be here this evening), but it will be convenient
for her to spend the odd night in our Moscow flat. It feels
odd without her, as we have seldom been apart, for more
than thirteen years. But I am competent to look after
myself (my view, not Nina's!) and anyway have my work
to keep me occupied.

And I enjoy just being here. Our forest really is rather
splendid: mostly oak, birch, poplar, fir, pine and hazel.
And we have collected a grand collection of birds by the
simple method of assiduous feeding: sparrow, chaffinch,
goldfinch, blue tit, wagtail, a family of magnificent wood-
peckers (they are probably forgetting how to peck wood

because of the free meals we provide), the odd starling, wood pigeon, magpie and crow, and one or two more which I cannot identify in English. We also have a fairly regular visitor in the shape of a glorious young red squirrel, a most delicate eater with a taste for fruit cake. It is strangely unafraid of us, though we haven't got around to hand-feeding it yet, as I used to with a particularly brazen red squirrel in the park at St John's Wood Church Gardens, where I used to play when I was a boy. We hope to achieve that before we return to Moscow in September.

So you can envisage me as a nuclear age Cincinnatus, contented with life on my estates, yet ready to respond if called upon to save the Union.

Yours,

Kim

Red squirrel

'I hear from your initial enquiries that you're looking for somewhere more suitable to raise a child.' The letting agent who meets her at the entrance to Grove End Gardens holds a clipboard in one hand, and a set of keys in the other. 'I gather your current property isn't too far away, so you must already know the St John's Wood area? The Church Gardens is full of wildlife, a lovely place to take a child.'

Edith follows him through the central front door of the building: a red-brick façade, seven storeys high and twice as wide, and then a communal hallway, where the porter nods at them from behind his desk.

'How old is your son?'

'Tommy is nearly five years old.'

'Well, this should meet your requirements. The flats were only built a few years ago. The shell of the block is solid ferro-concrete – residents have been known to sleep in the corridors to avoid the air raids. There is a warden stationed on the roof of the block. I'll show you around the more general premises and then the flat itself,' he says, leading her right, and through a hallway that leads out to the side of the building, past a small brick pond where the shadows of the carp sweep back and forth below the surface.

'As well as being safe and quite affordable, each apartment

has its own modestly sized kitchen with its own fridge and waste disposal unit, plus an electric fire and a radiogram; there are communal facilities, including a reception room on the ground floor and squash courts on two upper floors, as well as access to the club, restaurant and bar, just along the hall on the ground floor, over there. Which I'm sure your husband will appreciate.'

Reaching the communal gardens at the back of the building, the man stops. 'This will be a lovely place for a family,' he says, indicating towards the back door of No.12, with its own modest strip of green in the front.

'It's just the two of us,' Edith replies, imagining herself and Tommy planting bulbs and perhaps some lettuces like those she picked in the gardens of the school, the year it was commandeered.

'My condolences.' The agent places the key in the lock. 'There is a little sand-pit over there to play in when the weather is nice, and other children around the same age. As long as you can meet the rent each month, I can't see any reason why you and your boy shouldn't be very happy here.'

Edith walks briskly, in intentionally convoluted fashion, aware of every passer-by, every car horn, as she makes her way to the hall of the Mary Ward Settlement on Tavistock Place. There are some hundred people already in the crowd by the time she arrives, scanning for anyone she knows before slipping into a row of chairs towards the back of the room. The organisation – The Future Austria – was founded in 1939 with the chief aim of keeping the minds of Austrians living in England alive to the idea of a free and independent fatherland; the subject of today's debate is the reconstruction of Central Europe.

'Recently, political events remind one of the importance of the Austria of the future,' the first speaker begins as he steps on to the stage, his voice self-assured. Bruno Heilig is a former Berlin correspondent of the liberal Austrian daily *Der Wiener Tag*.

Edith is vaguely aware of a person moving into the seat beside her as Heilig continues.

'It is the duty of all Austrian emigrants to co-operate even more fully than ever before for the liberation of our fatherland. After the overthrow of Fascism, it is not only the right but the duty of every progressive Austrian to return home and put their service at the disposal of our reconstruction. One must not, on any account, reject the country along with Hitler. Criminal characters are to be found in in every country.'

'Do you mind?' The voice belongs to a man around her own age, in a black neckerchief, with curious eyes and thick dark hair swept fashionably to one side.

'No.' Edith says, annoyed by the distraction. Aware of his eyes lingering on her, she turns back to watch Heilig, who resumes his diatribe, lifting his hand to emphasise his point.

'The next question is what form the new Austria will take. One thing for certain is that it will not be a Hitler-Austria. It must be remembered that on the 12th of March 1939 the development of Austria was forcibly interrupted, and we must start working on the Austrian front as it stood on the eve of the Nazi invasion. We must take our destiny into our own hands.'

As parts of the crowd start to applaud, the figure next to Edith speaks again. 'Please forgive me for bothering you, but I know you from somewhere.'

'I don't think so.' Edith speaks without facing him.

'You are from Vienna.'

'Yes, I imagine most of us here are . . .' she replies, looking straight ahead, the noise level in the hall drowning out her words.

As the clapping subsides on stage, Heilig continues.

'The class of guardians for the people must disappear and then the different people of Central Europe will find the way to peaceful co-operation and construction – a way leading to true democracy, without crisis and without unemployment, not another dictatorship—'

His words are followed by a ripple of applause as the second speaker stands. Edith does not clap.

'I think we both know which dictatorship he is referring to,' the man besides her comments, under his breath, as Erich Fried, a young revolutionary writer from Vienna who belongs to the Der Jüdische Kulturbund makes his way to the stage.

Edith stands, discreetly, taking her coat.

'I hope I didn't distract you,' the man says.

'I have somewhere to be,' she replies, evenly, feeling his eyes on her back, like the barrel of a gun, as she walks through the room.

Outside, the cold air hits her face as she steps out into Bloomsbury, and walks as fast as she can into the alleyway, turning at the last moment to check he isn't following. Two men in bowler hats sit side by side in a parked car. Via the side streets, the journey home takes less than an hour. As she walks her panic fades. It was probably nothing, just a misguided attempt to pick up a new lady-friend. Perhaps the man was simply lonely. By the time she returns to the flat, she has pushed the thought of the man in the neckerchief firmly from her mind.

Ilona – heavily pregnant – and Tommy are waiting for her in the living room when she walks through the door.

'How was it?' Ilona asks, and Edith shakes her head. 'Lucia wasn't there,' she says. 'The speakers were terrible. I left early – thank you so much for having Tommy. You know I'll repay the favour when your little one arrives. Not long now.'

The letter, dated March 1941, is addressed to Mrs Tudor-Hart, 12 Grove End Gardens, return address: the director of Studio Sun Ltd, 49a Blandford Street, London.

Holding the sealed envelope between her fingers, Edith pads quietly along the hallway as she returns from the porter's lodge, her mind skipping back to the meeting the previous day at the photographic studio off Baker Street.

Despite his insistence that the business was going through a period of restricted turnover, the studio's director had been clear that they were at pains to keep it going. Upright and sincere, he had clearly been impressed by the suitably sanitised selection of work she had shown him: child portraits, family compositions demonstrating the necessary qualities to suit the studio's focus and mood.

She had mentioned her previous studio being destroyed in the Blitz, without going into detail about the nature of her work for a dwindling number of left-wing publications, as editorial tastes shifted towards the degrading, contrived representation of poverty that had become increasingly fashionable. Rather, she had stressed her photographing of women and babies: a respectable hobby for a woman of her age.

Closing the door to the flat behind her and walking across the living room to the ground-floor window, Edith pulls the curtain back just enough to see the postman move out of the driveway and turn right towards Abbey Road. Tugging it closed again, she moves towards the Isokon lounge chair Molly and Jack had given her for her last birthday, perching on the seat and using her thumbnail to tear the corner of the envelope and slice along the seam. Pulling out the letter, she scans past the courtesies to the important point.

I have been wondering just what would be the best way of giving you an opportunity of trying out our studio equipment, before undertaking the production of fashion or advertising shots of your own.

The letter continues with the offer of £5 a week for five days a week of work, nine a.m. to four-thirty p.m., acknowledging her need for two days off the following week.

Leaning back into the chair, a warmth creeping over her, she smiles, noting the request that she might contact the company secretary, if she were able, to confirm whether she will be in the following Wednesday.

If you feel that an opportunity of working in a studio such as this, and gaining experience of fashion work, is desirable, it is probable that we can work together quite well . . .

Inhaling triumphantly, she allows her mind to briefly skirt over the reason for the time off.

As soon as Tommy is awake she will boil the pan and make them a cup of tea to share, by way of celebration. Not yet, though. The sound of the boiling water risks waking him, and he had been up most of the night again, the memory of the bombing cutting through both of their dreams. Unable to stop her mind racing forward to the follow-up meeting she has booked with Anna Freud the next day, she shakes her head, physically dismissing the thought. It is hopeless really. What Tommy needs above all else is rest: rest, and love. She will not send him away, like Jack and Molly's children, who have been evacuated to the countryside for their own safety. She understands the reasoning, but she will not follow suit. She is Tommy's mother; each of them is all the other has. Tommy, her camera, and the cause.

But for now, in this brief moment, she has quiet, too; and she will enjoy it, this peaceful interlude. She sinks back further into the chair, her fingers working their way along the seam of the envelope, oblivious to the slight bubbling where the seal has already been steamed open and then resealed.

The weekend is one of quiet celebration, Edith and Tommy eating porridge and sharing a cup of tea before making their Sunday morning pilgrimage to St John's Wood Church Gardens. They leave early to avoid the bustle that might trigger Tommy's nerves.

Turning left and following their usual route, Edith scans the junction before they turn right on to Wellington Road, her eyes catching sight of a single figure who emerges from behind St John's Wood tube station, the street otherwise empty. Something about the silhouette sparks a shiver of recognition.

Edith tightens her hand around her son's as they walk, fingers entwined, the child's thin face fixed in concentration as he places one foot carefully in front of the other until they reach the public gardens.

At the entrance, iron spikes pierce a gentle blue sky. Following the track that runs through the middle of the gardens, they veer left where the path divides, a cemetery opening up on either side. Under a canopy of plane trees the light is soft, a stillness settling but for the jeering of a jay-bird as they walk between the graves, Edith pointing out signs of spring: smatterings of primroses between two head-stones, one small, one large – mother and child laid side by side.

Pulling her cardigan more closely around her, she turns and Tommy lets go of her hand, walking further into the small graveyard.

'Watch out for the nettles,' she calls softly, settling herself on a wooden pew as Tommy keeps walking, running his fingers over the moss and crusty lichen, the imprints of the letters marking out of the names of the dead.

Inhaling the morning air, the city smog less oppressive at this time of day, Edith lets her attention drift upwards to where a red squirrel runs along the lower branch of a tree. Its rustling obscures the footsteps, so that, when she turns a moment later, the man in the neckerchief is already beside her, seated a little way along the bench.

'You?' she says, smarting at the sight of him, those unmis-takable eyes that had watched her at the debate in Tavistock Place. 'It was you who was following us?'

'Edith,' he replies. 'I hope I didn't startle you. My name is Engelbert Broda.'

She rolls the syllables around in her mind, but comes

up with nothing. Away from the oppressive crowd of the meeting, she looks at him clearly, noting the dark intensity of his eyes. He speaks in Austrian-inflected German, turning so that his glance grazes the tip of Lord's Cricket Ground and then the church spire, all the way round to the mansion blocks on their left, finally resting his full attention on Edith. 'I'm sorry if I was indiscreet at the meeting last week. We have mutual friends who suggested I get in touch. You left before I could—'

Edith glances briefly at Tommy, his attention occupied by the worm he prods with the twig of a hawthorn bush. Startled by the sound of their voices, the squirrel has scarpered, leaving the air around them still and silent as the bones beneath.

'Who are you?' Edith keeps one eye on Tommy.

'I am a scientist.' He waits and when she says nothing, he continues. 'The longer version is that I've gained quite a reputation in England since my arrival from Vienna in 1938, so that I am now considered a valuable addition to the scientific community here.' His tongue moves over his lips. 'The short version is that I have my eyes on a particular prize which, should I be able to pull it off, could be one of the greatest contributions we could make.'

'We?'

'With you as my point of contact, I plan to hand over some of the finest information the Soviet Union could hope for. You have heard of the so-called Manhattan Project?'

'I have no idea what you are talking about,' Edith says, but she doesn't move, working hard not to mirror the excitement that flickers across his features. 'I am working towards gaining employment with the Cavendish Laboratories in Cambridge, in the department of scientific and industrial research. There is a specific project, known as the Development of Substitute Materials, under the direction of a Major General of the US Army Corps of Engineers, which is now known by many as the Manhattan Project. Their work has been ongoing since the beginning of the war, in collaboration with scientists across the US, Britain and Canada, the significance of which is huge.'

Broda looks over his shoulder. When he speaks again his eyes shine with excitement. 'I am talking about the creation of the first ever atomic bomb.'

It is a Monday morning. June 1941. Tommy had screamed for most of the night, again, and Edith's head is whirring with exhaustion as she takes the tube to Baker Street, walking along the main road, turning left on to Blandford Street and through the archway that leads into Studio Sun.

Noting, as she enters, the look she is given by the director's secretary, the pity in her dull blue eyes, Edith holds her chin a little higher.

The thought of this young woman, who spends her life being dictated to by a man she determines to impress through sheer compliance, believing that it is Edith who is the one whose life should be pitied, bolsters her now and she feels her spine straighten as she places the horn-rimmed spectacles on her nose.

As she does so, her mind moves to Engelbert, a few weeks earlier – how he had gently lifted the frames from her face and kissed her cheek and her forehead, his intense eyes assessing hers before their lips finally touched. How the cool touch of the ring on his wedding finger as his hand brushed her cheek, was offset by the heat that rose up through her as he regaled her with the details of his advancing plans.

'You're late,' the director says, striding past as she enters, her camera case held over her shoulder.

Inside, the models are already *in situ*. The man has a heavy moustache and hair combed back from his face. He wears a three-piece suit, a cigarette clutched between his fingers; his eyes meet those of his female companion, robed in a black calf-length dress with fishnet sleeves and a gold brooch pinned above her right breast.

Edith frames the shot so that the woman looms above him, his face cast in shadow; her expression one of quiet disdain.

When they break for lunch, Edith heads outside, savouring a single cigarette.

Behind her, the company director leans back against the wall a little way along and pulls open his copy of the *London Evening Standard*.

'Well, would you look at that? *Hitler has broken Molotov-Ribbentrop pact.*' Sneering, he lights his cigarette. 'Looks like the old Commies can't bribe their way out of this after all.'

A shiver moving down her back, she steps inside, the director's voice following her. 'Everyone pays in the end.'

Secret Intelligence Service file on
Edith Suschitzky

COPY   INTERNAL MEMORANDUM

From F.2b/MJEB   To B2. Mr Postern

I am making some enquiries about Mrs. Edith
TUDOR HART née SUSCHITZKY, a British subject
by marriage, formerly Austrian and believed
to be a member of the Central Committee and
accountant of the Austrian Communist Party
in this country. In addition to her political
activities she runs a photography business
of which the last address is 17 Duke Street,
Oxford Street, W.1.

It is believed that this woman has an account
at Martins Bank, 88 Wigmore Street, W.1. I
should be grateful if you could look into
her account.

Date: 5.4.42
                    Signature (Sgd) M.J.E. Bagot

Four months after Engelbert Broda is granted a permit to
work at the Department of Scientific and Industrial Research
at the Cavendish Laboratories, Cambridge, on Government
research work, Edith wakes suddenly, her senses instantly alert
to the world around her.

No screams. No sirens. Only the musty smell of the bedroom, the gentle whirring of the fridge in the adjoining room, the sound of one of the little girls from the flat down the corridor skipping past, a woman's heels clacking behind – the happy movements of a child and her mother on their way out.

She wonders where they might be going. Ruby is not much older than Tommy, but so different that Edith finds herself holding back or leaving by another exit when she spots her lingering by the fishpond in the courtyard, running her fingers along the surface of the water, her mother chatting readily to one of the other neighbours.

How must it be, to have a child for whom life is so easy?

At the thought of Tommy, Edith's mouth trembles.

Without him, this morning, the flat feels eerily quiet, the right side of the bed empty and cold. Laying her palm flat on the space where her son's body should rest, imagining the thin fingers   surgeon's fingers, inherited from his father, but a childish version, the skin soft and doughy over the joints – she pictures him here, his mouth slack with sleep.

Standing, steadily, she moves to the chair and pulls on the long black dress and matching stockings she had laid out the night before, her fingernail snagging on a hole in the nylon that is obscured beneath the heavy material of the skirt.

Taking a glass from the counter, she runs the water until it is cold before drinking thirstily. Briefly she casts her eyes over the rations she has put aside for breakfast the following day – milk, bacon, butter, sugar. There will be enough for both of them, her and Tommy, and double for her if his stomach complaint hasn't eased.

Lighting a cigarette, she runs a brush through her hair,

pulling on the coat Wolf and Ilona bought for her last birthday, glancing up at the clock as she passes.

9.10 a.m.

The morning at Studio Sun passes slowly, Edith's mind jolting whenever it drifts to Tommy, between shoots: directing the models with as much enthusiasm as she can muster, their silhouettes bleeding into the film.

'You off for a smoke?' the director's secretary asks as Edith passes on her way out the door, just after midday. 'Just so I can tell him if he asks.'

'He won't,' Edith replies, without looking back, reaching into her pocket for her cigarettes and lighting up as she walks through the archway and on to Blandford Street, her fingers running along the wrought-iron railings. Looking up, she catches sight of a figure reflected in the glass, her eyes lingering on his for a moment. When she turns forward again, she feels her toes brush the edge of the kerb and hears the beeping of a horn as she pulls herself back on to the pavement.

When she looks again, the man has gone.

Cutting down Marylebone Lane, making a detour through Cavendish Square Gardens where she loops the park, Edith pulls herself upright, reassured. She is imagining it, the eyes she feels on her back as she walks through the city streets, glancing up at empty windows that line the pavements of Soho; the smell of gas lingering from a recent bomb that struck the gas main.

Twisting back towards Princes Street, the bell tinkles above the door of Wyser & Bryant tailors as she steps inside, cushioned from the outside world by rows of dark suits. 'Edith!' The man behind the counter grins, looking up from his measuring tape, his long eyebrows seeming to shift sideways above pronounced cheekbones.

'Luca.' She smiles.

'You are here to let me make you a new skirt, at last? I'll do you a great price.'

Edith shakes her head, amusedly. 'I'm here to collect the contact sheet, if you've had time already to mark it up?'

'Of course.' He walks into the back room and returns holding a large envelope, which he lays out on the counter, pulling the sheet carefully from inside, pointing to a shot in the left-hand corner with impeccably manicured fingernails. She had known already, when she had brought in the contact sheet a few days earlier, which ones he would go for. Men like Luca are nothing if not predictable.

'So we are going for the one where the woman is looking straight at the camera,' Edith says, barely concealing her distaste.

'What about that boy of yours – how is he? You should bring him in one day, let him meet Uncle Luca; I could do him a special suit, too.'

Edith feels her smile fade. 'My son is well, thank you for asking. I don't suppose I could use your telephone, while I'm here? Something I left at the office. I won't be long.'

'Just don't tell the boss,' he replies, conspiratorially, as Edith follows him through to the back of the shop.

'I'll be there in a minute,' she says, turning her back and waiting for his footsteps to fade away before she dials.

The sky strains with the prospect of rain when she steps back outside, keeping her eyes to the ground as she makes her way back towards Blandford Street, stopping at her favourite café, a few doors along from Studio Sun, just as the clouds finally burst.

Taking her usual seat in the window, she orders bubble and squeak and watches the world contort through droplets that smear down the glass as she waits for her lunch to arrive, distracting herself from images of her child in the company of strangers, just a few streets away.

He'll be fine, she tells herself; he is in the best place, for the best reasons. Besides, it is only a few hours more.

Her thoughts are interrupted by the waitress, arriving with her food and a piece of greaseproof paper, which she slips under her plate with a wink. 'Made the portions extra big, today.'

'Thank you, Maggie.' Edith smiles, laying the paper out flat on the table, placing half the food inside and wrapping it before returning it to her bag, casting her eyes back at the clock on the wall, which reads 1.15 p.m.

She eats, gratefully, her jaw working every mouthful, holding back so that she has reason to linger a little longer. When the door opens again, bringing with it a gust of damp air from the street, she hears a man's voice.

'Of course, follow me,' Maggie says, and Edith sees them, in the reflection of the glass, moving through to the back room at the far end of the restaurant, the waitress bustling ahead.

Scraping the last of the potato on to the fork and shovelling it into her mouth before gathering her things, Edith leaves the exact money on the table and makes her way towards the back of the room.

'I'll just use the bathroom before I go,' she says to Maggie as she passes. 'It was delicious.'

'You know where it is. Just give it a knock, make sure no one's already inside.'

The corridor that links the two dining rooms is dark, illuminated by a miniature chandelier that hangs precariously on a low ceiling, a row of gas masks on hooks along the wall.

From the crack under the door, she can see that the light in the lavatory is on. Edith waits a moment before stepping forward and knocking, twice. 'Hello? Is anyone inside?'

When there is no response, she turns the handle and pushes it open, closing the door behind her and turning the lock before smiling at Engelbert Broda, and the envelope in his hands.

She can barely conceal her excitement. 'Berti. You made it.'

Secret Intelligence Service file on Edith Suschitzky

P.F.63349

24th April 1942

Re Mrs. Edith TUDOR-HART, Grove End Gardens, Grove End Rd.

Observation was taken up 16th April in Duke Street, W.1 when it was found that No.17, the last recorded business address of Mrs Tudor-Hart, had disappeared owing to enemy action. The watch was therefore transferred to No.228 Grove End Gardens but up to the morning of 22nd instant no person answering to the description of subject had been seen.

[SECTION REMOVED]

It was also ascertained that subject was in some way connected with the Studio Sun Ltd., Commercial Photographers, 49a Blandford Street, W.1, Tele WELbeck 2861, of which particulars from the Companies Register are also attached. Observation was then taken up in the vicinity of the last address and at 5.55 p.m. 22nd. a woman answering to the description of subject was seen to leave 49a, travel by bus to Grove End Road and enter the flats at 6.10 p.m.

Description:- b. 28.8.08, 5'8", medium build, brown hair, light-coloured eyed, slightly fresh complexion, wearing light-coloured horn-rimmed glasses. Dressed in black dress, pinkish-red coat, light stockings, black suede rubber-sole shoes, no hat. Foreign Jewish appearance.

At 9.10 a.m. 23rd, subject left the flats by the Grove End Road exit for Blandford Street and at 12.10 p.m. on foot to 11 Princes St, W.1., occupied by Messrs. Wyser & Bryant, tailors. At 12.45 p.m. she reappeared carrying a large photographic proof and an envelope, thence to the 'Posibile' restaurant, Blandford Street [SECTION REMOVED] eventually returning to 49a at 1.40 p.m. At 4.40 p.m. TUDOR-HART left with the photographic proof; called at the London Clinic of Psychoanalysis, 9 Gloucester Place, W.1, and left for home at

5.15 p.m. with a small boy, about 6 years
of age, who bore a striking resemblance to
subject.

The observation is being continued.

The afternoon sky above the chimneytops of Soho has been
cleared by the rain as Edith leaves work, just after four-thirty
p.m. She makes the five-minute journey from Blandford Street
on foot.

Despite the calmness of the day around her, she feels
uneasy as she makes her way from the studio and cuts right
down Rodmarton Street, and over Dorset Street, through
Clay Street. It is narrower here, the sun obliterated by
shadow, Montagu Mansions on the right with curved
secluded balconies recessed into the building. Ducking
behind the wall, in front of the stairwell, Edith waits a
moment, feeling her heartbeat expand in her chest, the smell
of the nearby dustbins causing her to hold her breath as
she counts the seconds.

Mouthing 'sixty', she steps out again, quite suddenly,
facing the way she came. But in both directions the street
is empty. Letting herself rest her back against the wall, she
exhales, her breath coming fast and hard, laughing a little
in relief.

When she continues along the alley, stepping out again on
Crawford Street and turning immediately right on to Gloucester
Place, she pauses in front of No.96.

Bracing herself a moment before taking her first step on
to Victorian tiles that lead towards a large white and brick
terraced building with a wrought-iron Juliet balcony, she

looks up at the first-floor window above a high arched doorway, and she rings the bell.

Anna Freud's expression is open and knowing when she answers, placing a hand warmly on Edith's arm as she guides her inside to where Tommy stands, looking small and lost in the great open hallway, superimposed on to a scene in which he does not belong. His trousers, which Alexander had bought him on a recent visit, graze skinny ankles.

'My love,' Edith says, placing her bag on the floor at the foot of the stairwell where they are waiting for her, crouching in front of her son and pulling him close.

He doesn't resist, doesn't react at all, allowing himself to be tugged, rag-like, into her embrace.

'I missed you last night,' she whispers, trying to catch his eye. 'We'll go home now, shall we? It's all right . . .' She keeps her focus trained on her son, holding his hand kindly and firmly as he thrashes with resistance. 'It's the main road, he can't stand it,' she adds, without looking up. 'Too much noise.'

'Can I get you a taxi?' Anna Freud asks, and Edith shakes her head.

'We'll walk. We can manage; we've done it plenty of times before.'

At five and a half, Tommy is small for his age, and Edith lifts him with ease, despite his resistance, soothing his cries as they step out into the street outside, suddenly loud and chaotic. When Edith looks at her son, she feels the world as he experiences it: the overwhelming smell of damp plaster in the air, emanating from the innards of a collapsed building, accentuated by the recent rain.

The shrieking of brake noises, reminiscent of sirens and falling shrapnel, causes him to cry out and pound his fists against her as she holds him close, wrapping his legs against her waist and pressing his left ear against her shoulder. With her right hand she covers the exposed ear, shielding him from a world that threatens them both.

As she walks, she sings, the rhythmic reverberations of her voice soothing him as they move along York Street, turning right on to Lisson Grove and continuing towards the flat.

She stops only occasionally, Tommy's whimpering returning to cries as she adjusts the handle of her bag against her shoulder. A man on the opposite side of the street looks over as she hums, more loudly, the opening notes of Chopin's Étude Op.25 conjuring an image of Rudolf Serkin hunched over the piano in the Vienna apartment, the figure of Wilhelm hovering in the doorway; the sudden backfiring of a car exhaust.

It is nearly eleven by the time Tommy falls asleep, the remnants of the bubble and squeak he had refused to eat still smeared across his plate, pieces on the floor where they had fallen.

Pulling the blanket up over his chest, she watches a while, the sudden facial movements indicating nightmares that have followed her only child from wakefulness to sleep. She wishes she could reach into his chest and pull them out with her fingers, and place them inside herself instead: but the demons have woven their claws around the bones of his ribcage, too tightly. She alone cannot banish them.

Scraping the last of the potato into the bin, she is too tired to tackle the items strewn across the room, including the greaseproof paper from the café, from earlier in the day. Pushing the door of the bedroom to, she clears a space at the kitchen table and lights a cigarette, pulling out the document Berti had handed her, the words Directorate of Tube Alloys

in the left-hand-corner, the stamp in the right reading
CAVENDISH LABORATORIES, CAMBRIDGE, and above
it: TOP SECRET.

It is still light as she and Tommy make their way along Maresfield
Gardens, Edith turning to look over her shoulder before guiding
her son through the gate towards a large double-fronted
red-brick house at No.20, set back from the road.

Inside, Edith's stomach tightens in response to the smell of
freshly baked bread.

'Can I get you something to eat? It is suppertime,' Anna
asks as they follow her up curved stairs to the study.

'No, we're fine,' Edith says, her fingers curling more tightly
around Tommy's slender hand as she follows Anna into the
consulting room, overlooking the garden.

'You mentioned that people have said they are scared of
Tommy.' Anna takes a moment to go through her notes, talking
quietly to Edith while the child sits on the carpet in front of
a selection of wooden toys in which he shows little interest.

'I didn't say "scared". That's ridiculous, he is a child. They
just don't understand him. Tommy is a particular person.
Some people don't know how to react; they have their own
expectations.'

'Because he doesn't make eye contact, and he doesn't speak.'
Edith nods, slightly.

'He also shows signs of compulsive behaviour: listening to
the same music over and over. He sometimes struggles to
understand the difference between people and objects—'

'I never said that.'

I'm working on my own observations of Tommy at the
clinic, and those I've received from colleagues there,' Anna
says, looking at Edith with dark, attentive eyes.

'As I told you, he has had a very difficult childhood. His father and I argued a lot when he was younger, and then the impact of the Blitz, and the ongoing threat of bombs—'

'You and I both understand the impact of early trauma, at first-hand. We have both been, and worked with, children in difficult situations. You are younger than I am and you must have felt, in Vienna, the fallout of the First World War. That was when I trained. Currently I'm setting up a nursery for children here in Hampstead, and in Essex, for those whose lives have been disrupted by war. I am no stranger to the impact on a child's mental health. But I have to tell you, what I am seeing with Tommy is different. Tommy's condition is not something that can be wholly attributed to external sources . . .'

'Condition? Tommy doesn't have a condition . . . You know I respect you very much. From what I have heard you are a warm and compassionate teacher and that's why I agreed to bring Tommy to see you, but you're wrong. You do not know my son.'

'Edith, I understand that it is difficult to hear—'

She stands. 'I don't even know why I came here.'

'You came because you need help.'

'I came because my son is traumatised by the war and I was told you might be able to help him overcome his trauma and its manifestations.'

'Edith, please. Sit down. I understand that this is difficult, but—'

'I don't have time for this. If you can't help us, then I will find someone who can.'

The night porter tips his hat at the sight of them. 'Mrs Tudor-Hart, your sister-in-law came past and left a note.'

'Thank you, Michael.' She takes the envelope and opens it carefully, removing the single leaf of paper inside.

Dear Edith, your mother asked me to tell you: your father's brother, Philipp Suschitzky, and his wife, your Aunt Olga, were deported from France and have been killed in Auschwitz. I am so sorry. Love, Ilona


```
Secret Intelligence Service file on
            Edith Suschitzky


                              11th May 1942


Re:- Edith TUDOR-HART of No.288 Grove End
Gardens, N.W.8


Further observation has been maintained on
the above named and on:-

Wednesday 6th May she was seen to leave Studio
Sun at 12-50pm for Messrs Selfridges Ltd.,
provision dept, where she shopped before
lunching at her usual cafe in Blandford Street.
At 1-55pm she returned to the Studio and at
4-40pm she left and despatched a small parcel
from the Baker Street Post Office to Dr. E.
Broda, c/o Cavendish Laboratories, Cambridge.
She then took tea in the Dutch Oven restau-
rant before collecting the boy from the clinic
and proceeding home; she was not seen to
leave again up to 9-15pm.

(NB Dr Broda was the subject of observation
by B.6. about two years ago.)
```

Thursday 7th May she left the studio at 12-20pm for lunch at the cafe, and later shopped before returning at 1-15pm. At 4-50pm she left, collected the boy from the clinic and returned home. At 6-45pm she left home with the boy and wasted time before entering No.20 MaresfieLd Gardens, N.W.3 at 7-15pm. This is the address of Mdme Martha FREUD, Austrian, r.c. No.668147, born Hamburg 26-7-61, of no occupation, and the widow of the well known professor. She lives there with her daughter Anna, r.c. No.668142, an Austrian, born Vienna 3-12-95, a psychoanalyst. Tudor-Hart left with the boy at 7-45pm and when en route for home she met casually at Swiss Cottage the contact 'A'. [SECTION REMOVED] This boy is undoubtedly the son of Tudor-Hart and she shows a good deal of affection for him, but he must cause her a could deal of worry as his nerves are in a bad condition.

Tudor-Hart takes a prominent role in the running of Studio Sun but from her dress and habits she does not seem to be in affluent circumstances. She shares a flat with her cousin, who might easily pass for a brother, and this flat is poorly furnished and in an untidy state, probably owing to the nerves of the boy.

The observation has been withdrawn for the time being and will be resumed when the opportunity permits.

Dear Edith,

My long silence must have suggested to you that we
had walked off into outer space and fallen through one
of those Great Black Holes that the astrophysicists are
still scratching their heads about. Nothing quite so
romantic, in fact: just creeping laziness which an austere
diagnostician might even describe as galloping laziness.
One does what one has to do; anything less pressing is
shelved. Too many *mañanas* these days!

I can think of no very apt comment on the world this
summer. We are doing what we have always said we
would do: match any Western escalation of the arms
race as long as that escalation goes on. Meanwhile, we
are doubtless doing our best in the probably impossible
task of making sense of Reagan. When someone has
consistently and stridently bad-mouthed you for at least
twenty years, and then starts exuding sweetness and
light, what are you to make of it? Is it only election-
eering? If not, what else is it? My own instinct, a purely
personal one, is to let him stew in his ignorance, idleness
and irresponsibility. No skin off our nose!

So there is the prospect of a nice little war with
Argentina. It is difficult really to believe it. I am afraid

that the Grantham broad got carried away at the first shock: all that stuff about regaining sovereignty, people of British stock, etc. Her boyfriend, Ronnie, will be seriously cross if she starts blasting the Argentine navy out of the water, while there are a lot of conservatives, of the Julian Amery type, who will be seriously cross if she doesn't. According to the BBC, which doesn't even yet seem to know what's going on, the most likely outcome appears to be a triple condominium: Britain, Argentina and the United States – who else? A pretty raggedy compromise likely to please nobody except the USA, which thereby gets another base in the South Atlantic. Of course, it would be unfair if the honest broker didn't get a major slice of the cake. And who is going to pay for the Thatcher Armada? That, of course, would be the good people of Britain.

As I type, I am partly distracted by the sound of the record player. Chopin's Étude Op.25, No.11 (Winter Wind), which feels highly appropriate. I suppose my last message must have beamed through loud and clear because the snow I asked you to send has arrived, though not in time for Xmas itself. It was my nineteenth in Moscow and the first non-white one. It (the snow) began on Dec. 30th and fell pretty steadily for 48 hours with the temperature plummeting. As a result, my birthday was one of those miraculous winter days, minus 20 and the sunshine fairly dancing on the snow. Alas, all too short. I started this letter at midday with my desk light on, a dark grey sky outside the window and our outside thermometer back to zero, with the weatherman forecasting still warmer periods to come. In January! Shades of Napoleon and Hitler! Of course the meteorologists all assure us that there is nothing really amiss, just a hiccup over the centuries; maybe, but what good are centuries to you and me here and now? As Maynard Keynes curtly reminded conservative economists who argued the infallible virtues of a free market economy in the long term: 'in the long term we are all dead'. Quite so.

I received two very nice letters from an old friend, thanking me for some caviar I sent back to him in London via one of my children, and transmitting many amusing comments on certain contemporaries of mine whom he has run into lately. He seems to be altogether *compos mentis*, so perhaps he has laid off the snakebite for a bit. He tells me that his English teacher at Cambridge was H.S.D., whom I knew slightly, chiefly because his wife ran off with C.M., a poet who was also a member of the local Communist party. I think C.M. must have left the party, because the next time I heard of him was that he had just started Mass Observation with Tommy Harris, who, of course, was killed in 1964 in a road accident in Thailand. As I seem to have strayed on to the subject of old friends, I wonder if you saw that Princess Anne and her inarticulate husband attended the wedding of Christopher Collins to a horsey-looking type (but perhaps the photograph in *The Times* was unflattering). As there was no reference to his mother among the guests, I suppose that she is dead. Douglas, of course, died two or three years ago; I seem to remember that they were divorced a little earlier, but I cannot remember where I got that from – the newspaper?

It is strange to think of London, now. I imagine I should find it much changed; in fact, I didn't much like it on my last visit, 1961? 62? Now you have the Hilton, the

Holiday Inn, the Post Office Tower, the flyovers, the new Barbican, etc. Not to mention Carnaby Street and the culture it has spawned. Not the sort of thing for a conservative old gentleman like yours truly.

Enough! I must get back to the kitchen where a tongue is gently simmering with celery, onion, bay leaf, etc. Nina is out, on her usual busy round, having her swim, visiting the polyclinic, also possibly the Post Office, etc.

Yours,

Kim

Nothing really amiss

As summer hands over to autumn, the sky beams bright above the rooftops of Paddington Green Children's Hospital, red brick with red terracotta dressings over three storeys. In the entrance, a sculpted mother and children are set in a Dutch gable.

Donald Winnicott leans forward slightly as he speaks, his fingers locked in front of him on the table in his office, the corners of his mouth upturned in an expression of kindness, the lines around his eyes permanently crinkled as if from a lifetime of intense listening.

'Before I commit to seeing Tommy, I thought it important that we meet, and determine that we are both comfortable. I know that Tommy has previously seen Anna Freud, an associate of mine at the London Clinic of Psychoanalysis. He is six years old?'

'That's right. We were seeing Anna for over a year.' She swallows her anger that Anna could not, or would not, help her son.

Winnicott nods. 'You may or may not be aware that we are currently in the process of redefining various approaches within the practice of psychoanalysis. Roughly speaking, we are now three separate factions. There are the Freudians, the group to which Anna belongs, the Kleinians who follow the work of Melanie Klein, and those such as myself who belong to the Independent Group.'

'I wasn't aware, specifically,' Edith says. 'But you come highly recommended.' She thinks of Anna's words: *There is nothing I can do for Tommy, his outbursts, his anger. All I can do now is try to refer you to Donald Winnicott. If anyone can help Tommy, it's him. I'll prepare a full file for him, ensure that none of the work we have done over the past year is wasted.*

'Generally, I don't do private practice work. I'm currently employed in my consultant paediatric work; the children's evacuation programme is keeping me very busy,' Donald Winnicott tells her, from the other side of his desk. 'But from what I read in your letter, and Anna's file, Tommy's situation – and yours – relates very distinctly to my work. I have great respect for Anna Freud – how could I not, when her family has done so much for our profession? But I fear that under Miss Freud you were perhaps not getting the right approach. I believe that she doesn't understand the need to defend the instincts of the ordinary, devoted mother against the threat of intrusion from professional expertise.'

Edith looks up to meet his gaze, as Winnicott continues, and feels herself blush.

'In my opinion, there is no better place for a child than the nurturing environment provided by his or her parents. When I work with patients, I am not just working with the patient but with the mother. It is my opinion that the foundations of health – mental and physical – start with the ordinary mother in her ordinary loving care of her own child. A child is the culmination of his or her experience.'

'Yes,' Edith nods. 'You see, the war . . . poor Tommy, it has affected him so very gravely.'

'It is to be expected. The impact of such trauma at a young

age cannot be underestimated. If we look at the experience provided and demonstrated by the mother in a child's early years, and extend the impact of that experience to new external forces as they grow – be it people or events – we see how, if a child is not held and supported properly, he or she can be damaged.'

Edith closes her eyes, letting her head drop. 'It's not just the war.' She pauses. 'When he was a baby, his father, Alexander, and I argued, a lot. We have just divorced and we haven't lived together for many years – though we are civil with one another – but those early days affected Tommy, I am sure.'

'Just as it affects you,' Winnicott says. 'You are a devoted mother – I can see that; if you weren't then you wouldn't be here. You love your son and you have tried to do right by him, but you believe that, unwittingly, you have inflicted damage on him.'

A lump forms in Edith's throat as she tries to swallow.

Winnicott shifts further forward in his chair. 'And you have. You are imperfect and flawed, because to be human is to be imperfect and flawed. Your son is searching for security that is lacking in both his family life and the world at large. In order to provide for him what he needs, there is work to be done.'

He reaches across the table and takes her hand, lines forming at the edges of his eyes as he smiles.

'It will involve empathy and imagination, but together, I believe, we can do it. Give me two years, and I will get to the bottom of Tommy's situation.'

Her voice breaks when she tries to speak. 'Thank you.'

Light trips along the rooftops over Paddington, following Edith as she walks from her meeting with Donald Winnicott.

On the corner of Church Street and Paddington Green, she instinctively turns towards St John's Wood and home before changing her mind. She has the rest of the day off, a rare moment to herself, and so she wanders in the direction of the museums, enjoying the light breeze as she meanders through the residential streets of Tyburnia, before cutting into Hyde Park.

Even from a distance, she recognises Lydia by her streaks of copper-red hair that blaze in the sun. She wears an emerald-green belted overcoat with large buttons and a rounded collar. Looking up and catching Edith's eye, she smiles.

'What are you doing here? This isn't your neck of the woods.'

'I was taking in the sunshine. I thought I might head to the Victoria and Albert Museum—'

'You'll struggle to get through. A bomb hit Our Lady of the Victories on Kensington High Street last night; all the roads around it are closed off. This weather, isn't it glorious?'

'It is—' Edith manages before Lydia interrupts.

'I just stopped to have a sandwich in the sunshine on my way from Portobello Market. They're introducing antiques and my father sent me to do a recce. He's training me up to take over the family business, you see. He's rather progressive like that – personally I think Stefan's furious that he isn't priming him.' She pauses. 'But he has his own work.'

Smiling, as if a splendid thought has just occurred to her, Lydia links her arm through Edith's. 'You have a good eye, you should come with me. I have a couple more shops to attend.'

'Oh, but I was going to take some pictures—'

'Perfect. We'll head to Mount Street first, and then on to

M. Harris & Sons on New Oxford Street if we can be both-
ered. It will be fun. You're at a loose end – perhaps we could
go for a drink, afterwards, if we can find somewhere that will
let us in.'

Edith thinks of the cost of Tommy's treatment and shakes
her head. But Lydia continues. 'On me, of course . . . Stefan
is having cocktails at the Connaught with a friend. It's been
spruced up by a Swiss hotelier, it's nowhere near as tired-
looking as it was. Oh, come on, Edie, you'll simply love it.'

John Sparks Ltd stands at 128 Mount Street. Inside, stark
white walls are offset by tall intricate vases displayed on pedes-
tals, an austere wooden chair set in front of a pleated curtain.
It is cold inside the gallery, and Edith folds her arms in front
of herself, feeling the eyes of the proprietor watching her as
she leans in to inspect a statue of a camel, its head tilted back,
mouth agape, as if howling at the sun.

'Don't worry, they know me here,' Lydia says, sensing Edith's
unease. 'I come all the time. Here, and M. Harris, and Harold
Davis on King Street, are the best dealers of their kind. The
man who owns this shop also has a premises in Shanghai,
which allows them to source objects directly from China,' she
adds, leading Edith through the archway and into a second
room, further stocked with antiquities.

'And your father only buys Chinese works?'

'Pretty much. His theory is that it doesn't necessarily matter
what one collects, but the important thing is to collect one
thing, and to stick with it, rather than buying lots of different
things.'

Edith smiles. 'I like that.'

'Yes,' Lydia replies, considering her, a thought stirring in
her eyes. 'I can see why. There's a single-mindedness about it

that suits you. You always seem to know exactly who you are.' She laughs. 'Though I'm damned if I do.'

'Do you ever miss home?' Lydia asks, as they walk along Mount Street, turning right into the public gardens and sitting on a bench, taking in the afternoon sun.

'Vienna isn't my home any more; the city I grew up in no longer exists,' Edith replies, smoothly, tucking her legs under the seat, not meeting Lydia's eye. 'How about you? Or do you consider yourself an Englishwoman? You speak both languages perfectly. It must be confusing to be two people at once.'

'I'm not confused,' Lydia says, and then she frowns. 'Well actually, you might be right. I grew up between England and Germany, so wherever I am I always feel like I'm in the wrong place; trapped between two worlds, neither of which really exists in the way I think of them when I'm not there. It's not so much that I have two heads, but almost as if I have two sides to my head.'

They sit in a silence a while, before Lydia speaks again.

'Do you ever think of what happened to Maks?'

'Yes,' Edith says. 'Often.'

'It's funny how we keep bumping into one another, after so long. It happens, though, doesn't it, people's lives intertwining, almost as if drawn together on some subconscious level. Sometimes even without one knowing it.'

Edith takes a cigarette from its tin and offers one to Lydia. Accepting, Lydia reaches into her pocket and draws out a box of matches, and strikes.

Leaning into the flame, Edith inhales and then looks away as she exhales, towards a couple seated side by side on the bench sharing a sandwich from a piece of greaseproof paper. 'I was at the hospital, today, seeing a doctor about my son,

Tommy. That was where I had come from when I bumped into you.'

Her already pale skin seems to whiten further as Lydia exhales a lungful of smoke, coughing slightly. 'I'm so sorry, I had no idea he was ill.'

'Don't be. It was a good thing: I met with a doctor who can help us, finally. Tommy has suffered with his nerves as a result of the bombing. But Dr Winnicott is very sure he can help us.'

'That's wonderful, Edith.'

'Yes,' she says. 'It is.' Her eyes brim with tears, suddenly, and she turns away, lifting the front of her wrist to dab at their corners.

'I'm so sorry,' Lydia says, leaning forward to comfort her. 'I didn't mean to upset you.'

'You haven't.'

'Where is Tommy now?'

'He's being looked after by my mother.'

'And what of his father – you two don't live together?'

'No.' Edith pauses. 'I'm not sure that we ever did, not properly. He went to Spain eighteen months after we came to England. He's back now, living with another woman, in Birmingham.'

'That's horrible.'

Edith shakes her head.

'You've obviously never been to Birmingham,' Lydia says and Edith laughs.

'We are not suited to one another in that way, anyway. It is a cordial arrangement: he comes and visits Tommy – and I take Tommy there, occasionally.'

Lydia's amber eyes narrow. 'There's someone else, isn't there? You wouldn't be so forgiving if there weren't.'

Her mind drifts, catching on an image of Arnold Deutsch, beside her on the bench under the maple tree, and then it moves on, to Broda, and Edith half-smiles. 'Nothing formal.'

Secret Intelligence Service file on Engelbert Broda

P.F.46663.

Engelbert Egon Ernst August BRODA.
Born: 29th October, 1910 at Vienna.
1st wife: Hildegard nee GERWING (Austrian).

[SECTION REMOVED]

In 1932, BRODA was National Leader of the German Communist Students in Berlin and at Berlin University in 1933.

On 10th April 1938 BRODA arrived in this country from France to attend meetings of the Faraday Society at Bristol University and to talk to chemists at London University. He was followed shortly afterwards by his wife Hildegarde on 23.5.1938 whom he had married on 12.9.1935 in Vienna.

BRODA's stay in this country was extended for three months until the end of July on the application of the Society for the Protection of Science and Learning. It was further extended from time to time at the instance of the same society. In July 1938 Special Branch reported that BRODA was the leader of a group of the Austrain Communist Party and that Edith TUDOR-HART was the liaison between this group and the Central Committee. BRODA also lectured for the Left Book Club.

During 1939 BRODA was much concerned with the affairs of Austrian refugees and the Austrian Centre. He edited 'The Austrian News', and was in touch with such people as Eva KOLMER (secretary of the Austrian Centre and a fanatical Communist), John LEHMANN, Andrew d'ANTAL, Edith TUDOR-HART, Donald Orr SPROULE, etc. BRODA's potentialities and value to the R.I.S. at this time can perhaps best be judged by these friends and short summaries of their careers are now given.

[SECTION REMOVED]

In February 1939, BRODA took up a research appointment with the Department of Physiology at University College. This job was found for him by the Society for the Protection of Science and Learning. Special Branch who had given us the previous report that BRODA was the leader of a group of Austrian communists in this country, were unable to add to this information and it was accordingly decided to put BRODA under observation for a short time but this provided no important information. In September he wrote to a friend saying he hoped to move to Cambridge and work in Professor Norrish's laboratory. This was arranged for BRODA by Commander Goodeve of London University who administered the Rockefeller Foundation for a research in vision for which BRODA had been working. On 6th October, 1939 BRODA was interned in view of his connections with the Austrian Communist group. Among his belongings examined at the time of his arrest was a notebook, unfortunately since destroyed. This book contained some 41 names and addresses.

[SECTION REMOVED]

On 18th December, 1939 BRODA was released from internment and went to stay with Sir William BRAGG in Surrey. In January, 1940 he returned to London, and in March, 1940 Special Branch reported that he was working in close collaboration with Eve KOLMER at the Austrian Centre.

In May of that year Andrew d'ANTAL was interviewed by this office. He told us that when he was at a German University he fell in love with a girl, with whom he spent the summer of 1932 in Dalmatia and found that she had become a Communist. d'ANTAL was at that time politically innocent and as a result of his association with this girl he began to study political trends. This girl-friend in Germany had married BRODA and when BRODA came up to London on May, 1937 she wrote to d'ANTAL and he put BRODA up at his flat in Dolphin Square. He said that BRODA held Communist meetings at his flat from which he was excluded. He felt that he was being used and relations became strained. In 1938 he spent his summer holiday in Austria with BRODA and his wife but there had been a complete break since the beginning of the war.

In June, 1940 BRODA was again interned under the General Order until September. In January, 1941 he was working as a Research Chemist. In March a report was received that BRODA was a member of the Central Committee of the Austrian Communist Party and that in Vienna he had been a Cell Leader of the Austrian Communist Party and that in Vienna he had been Cell Leader in the First District. In September, 1941 BRODA was working as a research chemist at Barking and living in London at 45, Hamilton Gardens, N.W.8.

In November D.S.T.R. suggested that BRODA should work at the Cavendish Laboratories, Cambridge, and in December he was granted an A.W.S. permit to work for D.S.I.R. at the Cavendish Laboratories on Government Research work. The A.W.S. section informed the D.S.I.R.

of BRODA's adverse record, who replied that Sir Edward APPLETON, secretary to the Department 'directs me to say that, having given full weight to the various views expressed in your letter, he feels that the exigencies of this Department do override objections of security grounds to Mr. BRODA's employment on the work for which his services are desired; and that it is essential to ask that a permit may be issued accordingly for his employment by the University of Cambridge, in the Cavendish Laboratory, Cambridge, on the work which is there being undertaken for, and at the cost of, this Department. I am to add that the work in question is in two parts and that Mr BRODA would not be employed on the more secret part.'

From April to November, 1942 Alan NUNN MAY was at the Cavendish Laboratory. In May, 1942 BRODA was known still to be in touch with Edith TUDOR-HART and was closely concerned with the Austrian Centre in Cambridge. In June a report was received that he left Austria in 1938 for political reasons as he had not been sufficiently Jewish to be caught in the Nuremberg Racial Laws. He was said to be anxious for a united Austria and to make no secret of the fact that he had been politically very active in Austria, although he was not keen to say on behalf of which party.

45 Hamilton Gardens is a short walk from the Lawn Road Flats. In November, the street is dark by five o'clock.

Edith takes the scenic route, turning right at Abbey Road and then left on to Hill Street, slowing down where it curves towards Alma Square, and bending to tie her shoelace.

From here, when she looks up, the street-light illuminates the road, which is quiet, not so much as the sound of a motor-car to disturb the peace. Night-time raids are fewer now that the Blitz is formally over, but it is still unwise to step out after nightfall: the official advice remains to stay home unless there is an emergency, which there is – and this makes her all the more exposed now as she looks up at the windows as she turns into the dark narrow street and pushes open the gate at No.45, which he has left ajar so as not to disturb the landlord.

Broda waits for her in the hallway, a letter in his hand, a broad smile moving across his face.

'What's that?'

'What does it look like?'

'Not what I think?' She smiles, curiously, and he places a hand on the arch of her back, pushing her so that her spine bends and he leans forward, her chest softening as they embrace.

The light in the bedroom is soft and peachy-hued, illuminating the line of sweat that runs down Broda's forehead as he falls back on the bed next to Edith, who lies beside him, her face resting on the crook of her hand, her naked body positioned towards him.

'You're going to wear me out,' he says, and she laughs, her fingers skimming the envelope on the side table as she reaches for her cigarettes. *Cavendish Laboratories.*

Lighting her cigarette, she stands, feeling him watch her as she moves, slowly, towards the pile of clothes on the floor.

'You're going?' he asks.

She smiles. 'I already have what I came for.'

'How is Wolf adjusting to life as a father?' Litzi asks, her voice low as Ilona takes baby Peter from her arms and places him in the Moses basket in the corner of Edith's living room.

A little way away, in the kitchen, Edith turns on the tap, focusing on the task of washing Tommy's clothes using the electric heated tub that came with the flat.

'You know Wolfi, he isn't a man of many words. But he seems happy,' Ilona whispers in reply, hovering over the infant, making sure he is sound asleep before sitting back on the brown sofa, her skin soft and dewy with the hormones of early motherhood. 'But Peter's a good baby, he's no trouble—'

She stops herself. Sharing a look with Litzi, Ilona sits forwards and Litzi calls to Tommy, who sits cross-legged in the corner of the living room, facing towards the corner. 'Tommy, come and sit with your aunty Ilona and me.' She crouches beside him, her hair, dyed a dark plum colour, grazing his shoulder as she leans into him.

When he doesn't move, Ilona stands, speaking gently. 'That's all right, you don't have to,' she says. 'I'm going to powder my nose.'

Staying crouched beside Tommy a moment before standing and walking to the kitchen, Litzi moves the carpet brush and leans against the hob, a shaft of light drifting through windows that look out over the communal garden.

'Is everything all right, Edith? You seem . . . I don't know. Tommy, is he—'

'I don't want to talk about it.' Edith flashes Litzi a look that she doesn't contest.

'Fine. How are things with Broda?' she continues, keeping her voice vague.

Looking up at the doorway and the sound of the door closing in the bathroom on the other side of the hall, she flinches. 'You know we're not supposed to talk about these things, Litzi.'

'Oh, come on, since when have you and I kept anything from each other?' Litzi takes the other side of the sheet Edith is attempting to wring out, and twists.

'He is proving useful; Moscow is happy,' Edith says quickly.

'And you – are you happy?'

A single drop of water falls on Edith's hand. 'Does it matter?'

'It matters to me.' Litzi lowers her voice further. 'Have you heard from Arnold?'

When Edith doesn't reply, she continues. 'You know, there are rumours, about what is happening in Russia—'

'I thought you said that *sometimes we have to trust the ones we really care about*. Weren't those your words?'

'But what is—'

Neither of them notices Ilona walk back into the room, until they hear the screaming.

As Edith turns in the direction of the sound, Ilona is already at the Moses basket, Tommy stepping back and running from the room.

'What happened?' Litzi moves towards Ilona, who cradles her screaming baby, his face turning red with rage.

'It was Tommy, he was hurting Peter.'

'No,' says Edith firmly. 'Tommy wouldn't do that.'

Holding Ilona's eye, she storms into the hallway and through into the bedroom where she finds Tommy on the floor, his back against the wall, his hands pressed over his ears.

'Tommy,' she says. 'What happened?' As she speaks, her voice grows louder. 'Tommy, I asked you a question. Did you hurt Peter?'

He makes squeaking noises in place of words, refusing to look at her. Before she can stop herself, she grabs his arms. 'Tommy – I asked you a question: did you hurt Peter?'

The force of her speech is such that for a split second it silences them both.

In that moment, she hears movement in the hall, behind. When she turns, Litzi is standing in the doorway with Lydia by her side.

'I'm so sorry, this is a bad time.'

Edith feels her cheeks blush. 'What are you doing here?'

'You said to drop by if I was ever passing, and I was . . .'

'I didn't mean that.' Edith holds Tommy a moment and then walks away, closing the door behind, her whole body trembling. 'I'm sorry, he just doesn't like being around lots of people.'

'Edith, I'm so sorry, I shouldn't have just—'

'Ilona and I were just leaving,' Litzi says quickly, her voice unnaturally bright. 'We've heard so much about you, Lydia, but we've never met properly. Why don't we walk out together?'

Lydia smiles, her expression strained. 'That would be nice, but Edith, I'm sorry. I didn't mean to intrude.'

'Come on,' Litzi says, squeezing her friend's arm in comfort as she turns, guiding Lydia towards the door where Ilona stands with her coat on, Peter still crying in her arms.

'Thank you for seeing us so quickly,' Edith says, her voice drained of emotion. Tommy is seated in a ball on the far side of the room, his knees curled against his chest.

'It's not your fault,' Donald Winnicott says. 'You mustn't blame yourself.'

His eyes are kindly and wise, a shade of blue that makes her want to lean forward and dive into the lake, letting the water rise over her head.

'But I do,' Edith says, the tears working their way to the surface.

'There, there,' he says, lifting a finger to wipe her cheek. 'We will make this better.'

'But what if we can't?'

'We will.'

On 4th November 1942, the tanker *Donbass* sets sail from Vladivostok to San Francisco, en route to South America, with forty-nine crew members on board. It leaves by the Arctic route from Novaya Zemlya. The following day, on 5th November, the ship is attacked by the Luftwaffe; two days after that, there is a further assault and the radio goes off air.

An older woman of fifty or so, in a dark suit jacket and skirt, stands in the doorway of Jack and Molly Pritchard's penthouse apartment. The look of her, somehow out of kilter with the usual circle of guests, makes Edith pause on the landing.

Molly's face widens with surprise when she lifts her eyes from the woman's face and spots her old friend on the second-floor corridor of Lawn Road Flats. 'Good grief, we haven't seen you for so long, we wondered if you'd gone up in a puff of smoke. Come in, come in – Jack will back soon, he will be delighted . . .'

'I can't stay long,' Edith says, nodding courteously to the stranger, who smiles politely in return, before retreating from the doorway.

'Molly, I didn't mean to disturb you,' Edith says, as the figure walks away.

'Not at all,' Molly replies, lowering her voice, amusedly. 'That was Agatha from No.8. I went in to check on her earlier about a leak that had been reported in Arnold Deutsch's old flat, next door, but she was writing so she didn't want to be disturbed. Piles of notebooks everywhere, there were. She writes crime novels, apparently – I got the feeling she turned me away just so she could come up here and have a jolly good nose around.'

Molly smiles as they walk into the living room, the calendar on the wall reading 12th November 1942. 'Anyway, enough of me – how is Edith? We miss seeing your face around here. Nothing seems to be the same any more.'

They drink tea on the terrace, overlooking the woods, Molly filling her in on the children's lives in the countryside, and her plans to restore the Isobar once the war is over.

'I wanted to say thank you,' Edith says, as she finishes her cup.

'Whatever for?'

'For helping me with Tommy. When you mentioned seeing a psychoanalyst I was resistant – I didn't believe we needed help, Tommy and me. But we did – and now we're getting it.'

'Oh, Edith, that's wonderful news. So you are seeing Anna Freud?'

'No,' she says.

'May I ask who?'

'Donald Winnicott.'

Edith's expression changes, and Molly pauses. 'I see. I've heard very good things. And by the look of it he's made quite an impression on you.'

Edith feels the heat in her cheek as she answers. 'Yes, he has.'

Her mind moves from Donald to Arnold when she leaves, an hour later, passing along the corridor where the two of them had walked side by side, willing herself not to picture the red handkerchief she had hung in the woodland visible through the window at No.7, the handkerchief that had signalled the beginning of the end.

She is nearly at the exit when she hears her name and turns to find Jack, her face falling in response to his expression.

'Apologies, Edith, I was in my own world.'

'Jack—'

Reaching for her hand, his eyes search her face and then seemingly finding the answer, he swallows. 'I'm afraid I've just heard some terrible news from one of the other residents. It's about Deutsch and the boat he was working on. I take it you haven't heard?'

'What boat? Jack, what are you talking about?'

'Edith, I'm so sorry. He was aboard a tanker that was struck by the Germans, just over a week ago. They haven't found him. It's presumed that Arnold Deutsch is dead.'

The world around her warps as she puts one foot in front of the other, her vision blurred, eyes focused on the pavements below her feet; a tangible force keeping her upright, while everything around her tilts.

'It's not your fault,' Donald Winnicott tells her as she sits in front of him in his office, unaware of how she even got there, unable to picture the journey from Lawn Road to Paddington. Unable to imagine anything but her first love, lost in an ocean that swells as she pictures it, no discernible beginning or end, just a single expanse of darkness.

Looking up at him, her chest burns. How did he know? Was it possible that she had let slip during one of their sessions, without her realising? And then he speaks again and she realises the guilt to which he is actually referring.

'You must understand, Edith, that my calling you to come here without Tommy isn't an indication that I blame you for his problems – on the contrary. In recent months I've been developing my theory that there's no such thing as an infant, which builds on Sigmund Freud's recognition of the transference as a manifestation of psychic transmission related to the infant's early psychic history. The theory revolves around the fact that it is not possible to understand an individual without taking into account his – or her – psychic history.'

He stops, leaning forward across the desk, watching Edith as if inspecting a delicate shell.

'It is not only Tommy who is in pain.'

Unable to move, Edith remains seated, her eyes unblinking as the tears fall, feeling rather than seeing him as he approaches her from around the desk, crouching so that his head is in line with hers.

'I want to help you both,' he says, and she feels herself nod, slightly, in response to him.

'I'm so tired,' she says, so quietly she doesn't know if she says it aloud.

In the months after Arnold's death, the weeks pass in waves that undulate and still, frothing quietly at Edith's heels before roaring up again and tipping her face-first into the swell.

At night she wakes to the sound of Tommy whimpering in the bed beside her, his silence following her as she leaves him with Ilona before heading to work.

'I never know what you're thinking,' Broda says, one night as they lie in his bed, her bare leg wrapped around the sheet.

'No one knows what anyone else is thinking. Not really,' she replies, without turning back to him.

He lights a cigarette, before speaking again, his voice coarse through smoke. 'Do you ever doubt it?'

'Doubt what?'

'What we're doing.'

'It's just sex, Berti, I hardly give it a second thought unless I'm without it.'

'I mean this.' His arm extends over her shoulder, indicating towards the papers tucked into her handbag which stands on the chair, the words CAVENDISH LABORATORIES, TOP SECRET stamped on the front.

She turns, suddenly, to face him. 'Never. And I hope you don't either.'

He holds her eye so that she can't be sure which of them

is testing the other. 'Not even after what happened to Arnold Deutsch, and the others?'

Standing, she moves to the wireless and turns the knob to full volume before walking back to the bed and crouching down in front of Engelbert, speaking directly into his face. 'What do you know of Deutsch?' she says, her voice a growl, and he draws away from her slightly, keeping his tone firm.

'Nothing.'

'No,' she says, standing and moving towards her clothes. 'Don't ever say his name to me again.'

It is bitterly cold as Edith makes her way back to the flat, too distracted by Broda's words to take the scenic route. Litzi and now Berti, spreading rumours of Stalin's temper, rumours of a paranoia that has seen him take out some of his finest agents.

Rumours – that is all they are. Designed to stir up doubt, to create divisions, just as they had done tonight. He will be lucky if she doesn't report him, she thinks, as she walks along Garden Road, shivering as she turns, out of habit, half-glancing back towards Alma Square, a shadow moving beneath the lamp-post so quickly that she cannot be sure if it is a silhouette or her mind playing tricks.

She hears her mother's voice from inside the foyer as she moves through the car park, picking up her pace as she approaches the main entrance where Adele stands with her back to the door, shouting to the porter.

As she pushes it open, her mother turns and confronts Edith, her face white with worry.

'What is it, where's Tommy?' Edith's feet break into a run, pushing past the man and her mother, who follows her.

'Where were you?' Adele's voice is accusatory. 'I've been trying to get hold of you!'

'Where's Tommy?' Edith shouts, unconcerned by the doors opening in the hallway in response to the commotion.

'He's locked himself in the bathroom. I was just telling the porter, we need to call the police—'

'No.' Edith sinks in front of the door and puts her lips to the keyhole. 'Tommy, darling.' Her voice is unnaturally high-pitched. 'It's Mama. Please, open the door.'

'Where were you?' Adele rages, keeping her voice low. 'I was worried sick. I had no idea how to get hold of you.'

'I told you, I was working. *You* were supposed to be looking after him.'

The sound of his whimpering makes Edith sit up taller. 'Tommy, if you don't open the door now, we will have to break it and it will be really loud. I don't want to break the door. Tommy? Please, my darling.'

'Oh, yes, working – without your camera. What sort of mother—'

But, before she can finish her sentence, the door opens and Tommy is there, his expression blank, his tiny body framed in the doorway.

In the doorway, Kim waits for Colonel Valentine Vivian to look up and nod before stepping inside the office at SIS headquarters, 54 Broadway.

It is months since – with word having reached Moscow that the British service was turning its attentions towards its defence of its isles against Bolshevism – Kim had been told by his informers that he was, at all costs, to take over as the head of a new anti-Soviet section, XI.

'Simple as that?' he had joked to Vadim, the handler who had taken over since Maly had returned to Moscow. Vadim hadn't laughed.

Following months of elaborate effort to discredit the natural successor to the job – his own boss, Felix Cowgill – he feels a line of sweat form on his forehead as he closes the door behind him.

'Good afternoon, sir, I was told you wanted to see me.'

'Philby, I'd like you to read this, it's a memo I've written to the chief,' Valentine Vivian says, handing him a sheet of paper.

Stepping forward, running his tongue over his lip, Kim nods, taking the sheet and letting his eyes scan the words. *Cowgill's been caught up in a series of quarrels . . . I recommend that a more favourable candidate for the position of successor is Kim Philby.*

Looking his boss straight in the eye, Kim stutters slightly, a result of the shock – only partially feigned.

'I don't know if I quite understand – you want me to take over as head of the newly formed operation against Communism and the Soviet Union? But surely there are better candidates—'

'Nonsense. Your responsibility at Section V has already been extended from Spain and Portugal to include to North African and Italian espionage. I couldn't think of a reason not to recommend your appointment.'

The call from Major General Sir Stewart Graham Menzies comes within days. It is not Kim's first visit to the *arcana* – but for the first time the secretaries smile as they point him to a chair to await his invitation into the chief's office.

It is several minutes before the green light flashes. Kim stands, brushing down his trousers.

'Philby, come in. I have a minute here from Colonel Vivian; I'd like you to read it.'

Taking the letter, Kim scans the page, as if for the first time, his facial expression changing in response to the wording of the recommendation.

'You are offering me immediate succession to Currie?'

'Well, have you anything to say?'

Kim is prepared for the question and offers a suitably self-effacing response, highlighting his reluctance to take the job away from Cowgill – his own boss, no less – proving himself not just a team player but a man with the sort of loyalty one cannot buy.

'Perhaps,' he says, after a beat, 'if I may suggest such a thing: in order to regularise the position of the new Section IX, it might be prudent to draw myself a charter for your signature?'

The document, when it is finalised weeks later, gives him responsibility, under the chief, for the collection and interpretation of information concerning Soviet and Communist espionage and subversion in all parts of the world outside British territory, and names Kim Philby as the person charged with maintaining closest liaison for the reciprocal exchange of intelligence on these subjects with MI5.

'Just one more thing,' the chief says, stating a final provision. 'On no account are you to have any dealings with the United States services. The war is not yet over and the Soviet Union is our ally. There is no question of risking a leakage, if you understand my point.'

'Absolutely, chief.' Kim smiles, approvingly. 'We cannot afford to risk a leakage from the United States services to the Russians. One can never be too careful.'

Careful to stay alert for familiar automobiles and men in doorways, Edith moves quickly as they make their way home from their appointment with Winnicott. A summer storm is brewing on the streets of northwest London and a wind presses against their backs as she ushers her child inside, with a final backward glance.

The date is 18th August 1944. At this exact moment, six hundred miles away at Buchenwald Concentration Camp, the former leader of the German Communist Party, Ernst Thälmann, is shot dead on Hitler's orders, after eleven years in solitary confinement.

The news has yet to reach Edith as she falls asleep, fully dressed, on the sofa, finding herself back in the hall of mirrors in the Musée Grévin in Paris, several pairs of eyes staring back at her, impressions of Tommy and Arnold growing and receding in waves.

In this dream, she walks once more through the woods at the back of Lawn Road and finds herself in the forests that skirt Vienna, Tommy running a little ahead, Edith out of breath, struggling to keep up. Looking down at her hand, she sees blood weeping from the wound where she had pricked it on the holly.

When she wakes, she gasps for breath as though being dragged up from the bottom of the ocean. Keeping her eyes closed, she longs to be held there, her fingers running along the sand, searching for his.

Secret Intelligence Service file on Edith Suschitzky

F.2.b through F.2.a. Miss Ogilvie P.F.63349

9th September 1945

Edith TUDOR-HART

Further to my report of 3.8.45 it must be added that this woman joined the British Communist Party about a year ago but also continued working with the Austrian Communists until a few months ago. Since then she has been active within the British Communist Party, attending meetings and conferences and taking part in a general drive to raise money for the re-establishment of the Communist Parties on the Continent. The Austrian Communist Party is also participating in this collection which is restricted to party members.

Edith TUDOR-HART, who has no job at present but intends to establish a photographic studio of the kind she ran before, has gathered around her rather an interesting circle of intellectuals, some of whom are members of the Communist Party and some only sympathisers. These people are in the habit of meeting more or less regularly at each other's flats and discussing politics from the Communist point of view but avoiding narrow-minded official party line and propaganda slogans which usually prevail at Communist gatherings. They admit frankly, and sometimes cynically, their totalitarian aims and methods with all the hardship and 'unavoidable' atrocities involved, yet which are justified by the cause. Neither do they refrain from criticising Russian policy if they find it to be inconsistent with Communist theory.

Amongst others the following are conspicuous in this circle:-

[SECTION REMOVED]

Lizzy FEAVRE or FEABRE née KALMANN of 96 Wellesley Court, N.W.8. She was born in Vienna and left about 1934 for the U.K. Later she went to France where she lived for about three years and married an Englishman there, thus acquiring British nationality. She is separated from her husband and was living with Dr. Georg HONIGMANN whom she left recently owing to a disagreement. She is at present ill and is living somewhere in Fitzjohn's Avenue, N.W.3. She is a member of the British Communist Party and a shop steward.

Dr. HONIGMANN (see report of 26.9.42), who is
a member of the German Trade Unions Group, is
mainly concerned with trade union activities.

[SECTION REMOVED]

The Labour Party victory at the General
Elections was hailed in this circle as
removing the danger of the anti-Russian block.

E.5.(L)

Edith and Litzi are the last to arrive at 44 Cumberland
Mansions. Inside, the ten or so friends are gathered on chairs
and sofas, already deep in conversation.

Distracted by the meeting she has just left, at Donald
Winnicott's office – one of an increasing number without
Tommy present – Edith is uneasy as she thinks of his expression,
the blue eyes that remind her of Arnold, creased with worry.
Tommy's case was proving more complicated than he had antic-
ipated, he had told her, Tommy's behaviour becoming
increasingly unpredictable. 'I fear, as he continues to grow, he
will pose a threat to you and—'

'Tommy isn't a threat, he is a child and he is disturbed,
that's all,' she had replied, horrified by the accusation.

'He tried to attack one of my colleagues, Edith. He is

nine years old; soon he will grow stronger than you, and I worry what might happen then. We can't leave it—'

The violence of Donald's words is at odds with the kindness in his eyes and she had longed to lean forward and kiss him then, though she is revulsed by her own feelings in the context of what he is saying. Yet she knows, just as Anna Freud told her four years earlier, that he is her son's best chance. Besides, he has told her, in quieter moments, how unhappy he is with his wife. It's just a matter of time until he leaves. And then . . .

'If everyone's here then I'll start,' the speaker says, breaking into Edith's daydream and bringing her back into the room. She knows the man with the narrow moustache and spectacles, who stands to address the group, from Berti's occasional mentions. Alan Nunn May – code name Alec – is the British scientist who for the past few years has been working in Canada on the Tube Alloys directorate, helping to build a reactor at Chalk River near Ontario. She also knows that he is currently in London for a Conference of Scientific Workers. She doesn't know the specifics: that in February 1945 he handed over documents for photography, provided samples of uranium 235 and uranium 233, and confirmed the operating principles of the atomic bomb.

When he speaks, now, his voice is grave. The crowd falls silent. 'You will have heard about Percy Glading, who was recently released from prison having been brought down by none other than the secretary of the CPGB.'

His eyes look from one to the other of them as he talks.

'We must exercise caution. There are traitors in our midst.'

It is Lydia who answers the door at 28 Willifield Way, the sound of toddlers chattering in the garden audible as Edith steps inside her brother's home.

'I didn't expect to see you . . .' Edith starts before moving into the landing, from where her sister-in-law is just visible through the open door into the living room, feeding the newest baby on the nursing chair.

'I hope you don't mind.' Lydia smiles, her hair flashing auburn as she takes a seat on the sofa. 'Ilona invited me.'

'Why would she mind?' Litzi takes the proffered glass and kisses Lydia on the cheek.

'She bought gin and rum.' Ilona giggles, lifting her drink. 'We've been putting the world to rights.'

The smile on Edith's mouth becomes strained, her eyes moving between Litzi and Lydia. 'I didn't realise you were so close.'

'Where have you two been, anyway?' Lydia asks, and Litzi moves to the table, pouring herself and Edith a rum.

'We were at Tomlin's; a scientist was over from Ontario and—'

'Litzi?' Edith interrupts, her expression berating her for disclosing such closely guarded secrets.

Litzi looks at Ilona reassuringly. 'Edith's just a bit jumpy at the moment. I'm sure she'll loosen up once she's had a drink.'

'Well, in that case drink up,' Lydia says. 'Don't worry, there's plenty.'

Secret Intelligence Service file on
Edith Suschitzky

CONFIDENTIAL.
F.2.C. (Mr. Marriott)
(Copy to F.2.a/b).

25.2.46

On the 17th February a social gathering took place in the flat of Thomas MILES, 44 Cumberland Mansions, George Street, W.1, attended by a Canadian scientist who came to this country to take part in a Conference of Scientific Workers. Edith TUDOR-HART, who was also present, is a friend of MILES, whom she calls "Tomlin". From what she said of this Canadian scientist, he must be at least a Communist sympathiser and occupied with atomic research, but she did not want to reveal his name.

MILES is a member of the C.P.G.B. and married to a German Communist. Since the exposure of the Canadian spy plot Edith TUDOR-HART and her friends are even more cautious than before, and avoid discussion on this topic. In connection with the Canadian affair, however, a Communist confidential representative was alluded to. It seems that he was released from prison some time ago after serving a long sentence. His imprisonment was the result of reports by a woman who had been secretly placed in the C.P.G.B. by the British Intelligence. It is said that this man was caught in the very act of photographing documents in a Government office. This case was cited as an example that more care should be taken in order to avoid treachery.

```
Edith TUDOR-HART is friendly with a monitor
of the TASS - name as yet unknown - who
telephones her on occasions for advice.
```

```
E.5.L.
```

Four days after Alan Nunn May is arrested on charges relating to the Official Secrets Act, in March 1946, Edith stands by the window watching passers-by bustling to and from St John's Wood tube station, through the gap in the curtains.

Repeating Donald Winnicott's words in her mind, she replays the scene, as if watching from above. She sees herself and Donald seated opposite one another in his office, her skirt holed, her hair unbrushed, her eyes wide with the sort of exhaustion that takes over so that the body no longer needs rest. He is older, and firmly in charge, his voice firm and fair, like that of a teacher reprimanding his favourite student, moving around the desk so that they are side by side.

When he kisses her, she asks, 'Why won't you leave your wife?', the words tumbling out before she can stop them, heat gathering in her stomach at the thought of the two of them together.

He regards her for a moment and then smiles, almost amusedly. 'You can't control everything. You have to learn to trust others. You are still young, you have so much ahead of you.'

'You said yourself that you no longer love her.'

'I've told you: it has to be when the time is right.'

'I don't see why it isn't right now.'

He laughs, in her memory, tucking a lock of her hair behind

her ear. 'Oh, Edith. You are impatient – it's part of what attracts me to you.'

'Is that all I am to you, an attraction?'

'You know it's not. Besides, are you telling me you don't see other men?'

'As long as you're married, I don't see that it's any of your business who I spend my time with.'

'And I never ask.'

'I tell you things.' She pauses. 'I am sleeping with another man, actually – an Austrian, like me. He's my age, unlike you, and he's a scientist and he's brilliant and we fuck.'

Edith watches Donald's face, the almost imperceptible tightening of his jaw.

'And he is married too?'

'Edie, you need to eat something.' Litzi's voice cuts through from the present where she is making cocktails in the kitchen, using the bottle of rum Lydia has brought for the evening's gathering.

When Edith doesn't move, Litzi walks up behind her, placing a hand on her arm, and indicating the paper in Edith's hand. 'What's this?'

Starting, Edith answers calmly. 'It's a letter, another job rejection.' Turning over the envelope, she hands it to Litzi. 'Look, you see – it's all wrinkled around the seal. They aren't trying to hide it any more: they want me to know that they're watching. They stand out here at night, with their flashlights. When I look out, they turn them off.' Her tone is matter-of-fact. 'It's like they're here, all the time.'

'Edie, come on. It's Friday night. There's no one out there, you need to try—'

'You know that Broda's leaving? With Alan's arrest, it's no longer safe. He knows too much.'

Edith doesn't bother to keep her voice low, despite Ilona and Lydia playing with the children on the rug, a plate of sugar sandwiches, half-eaten, between them.

Turning her focus back to the window, she keeps her lips shielded by the material of the curtain so that her words cannot be read from outside. 'There is someone else. A Hungarian doctor – Janossy, do you know him?'

When Litzi doesn't answer, Edith looks up and sees Lydia beside her, the two women sharing a concerned look. Taking the drink Lydia hands to her, Litzi raises the glass as if in toast when the sound of the doorbell interrupts.

'Are you expecting someone?'

'No.' Edith straightens her back. Checking the wall-clock, she sees that the time is four minutes past seven. Her mind scans through the possibilities as she steps away from the window: Donald, Berti . . .

Whoever it is rings a second time before Edith has moved.

'Shall I get it?' Lydia asks, and Edith shakes her head.

'You wait here.'

The porter is away from his station and the hallway is silent, the silhouette of a man just visible through the frosted glass in the door as Edith approaches, the figure unclear as she peers through the peephole, his face obscured by the brim of a trilby hat.

'May I help you?' She pulls the door open a crack. Against the dark night, the man's features are clearer: a stranger with a long crooked nose and thin lips, eyes that settle on hers without hesitation.

'Good evening, apologies for disturbing you after dark. I was looking for Alexander Tudor-Hart,' he says.

'Alexander doesn't live here.'

The man looks bemused. 'Oh, I am sorry. So there is no one by that name at this address?'

'I am Edith Tudor-Hart. Who are you?' She says, irked and unsettled at once.

'My name is Mr Francis. Are you his sister?'

'I'm Alexander's ex-wife. Can I help?'

'Well, I'm sorry to have troubled you. I must have the wrong information.'

'May I ask what you want from Alex?'

'Not to worry.' Thin lips twist into a crooked smile. 'As I say, I'm very sorry to have disturbed you.'

Secret Intelligence Service file on Edith Suschitzky

F.2.C. (Mr Marriott)   18.3.46

Edith TUDOR-HART and E. BRODA

On Friday the 8th instant, at about 7 p.m., [SECTION REMOVED] Edith TUDOR-HART answered the doorbell, and had a conversation with the caller which lasted for about ten minutes. She then returned rather irritated and told [SECTION REMOVED] that a man had just called, introducing himself as Mr. FRANCIS, and enquired about Alexander TUDOR-HART who he thought was living at her place. When she had told him that TUDOR-HART was not staying with her, and that she did not know his present whereabouts either, as it was none of her business, the man pretended to be surprised, and tried in a very clumsy way

to start a conversation, asking her if she
was Alexander's sister. She stopped him,
saying that she was not his sister but his
"ex-wife", and she had realised that the
caller was nothing more than a snooper, not
an ordinary one, but a special one, judging
by his Oxford accent.

Edith seemed rather worried, and said the
incident must be in some way connected with
BRODA, or with one of his friends who might
have got into trouble with the police. She
then wondered whether she would be forced
to give evidence against BRODA, and accused
him of being too careless. "When a man is
involved in such a business as he is," she
added, "he ought to be careful and not
endanger his friend by writing to or visiting
them."

The following Wednesday, the 13th, early in
the morning, BRODA came up from Cambridge
by the first train, and told her that a man
had been caught by his landlord in the act
of trying to get into his (BRODA's) room.

[FILE SMUDGED]

They meet at the Victoria and Albert Museum in Kensington,
where admission is free and unrecorded.

Disappearing into the crowd as she makes her way through

the Central Court, circling the displays, Edith moves her eyes over and between the headless mannequins, scanning the corridors visible through glass display-boxes containing ancient Chinese sculptures.

Turning right through the South Court, and past Oriental metalwork, she makes her way towards the staircase, checking the clock as she passes. 10.10 a.m.

Berti waits for her in a room dedicated to elaborate costumes and embroidery, a brochure held in his hand as he inspects the seams of a theatrical brown coat and britches.

'Thank you for coming,' he says, quietly, his attention fixed on the objects behind the glass. Edith walks the perimeter of the display and back around to the other side of him; the only other person in the room is the guard at his post by the door, out of earshot.

'The same man tried to get into my room too. My landlord spotted him, and he ran off.'

'Should we be worried?' Edith asks.

'Given what happened to Nunn May? I'd say.' He looks away again, softening his voice. 'This man who came to your flat – did you recognise him at all?'

'No, I told you—'

'And you have spoken to no one?'

'No,' she replies, after only the faintest pause.

Reaching out her hand to touch him, she watches him step back, clearing his throat.

'I'm going back to Vienna. After today we shan't see each other again.'

The junction through the window of Lyons' Corner House on Oxford Street is heaving with life as Edith stares out from her corner table, unable to pick out a scene. Her vision blurring at the edges, occasionally she spots through the crowd a face she has known and lost – Wilhelm, Arnold, Berti – but then it shifts to another angle, the shapes rearranging themselves, revealing the outline of a perfect stranger.

When the sound of Litzi clearing her throat brings her back to the restaurant, the noise of the fellow diners crescendos around them: herself, Ilona, Lydia and Litzi seated at a table laden with meat and vegetables on platters, the white tablecloth grazing Edith's thighs.

'We'll have another bottle,' Litzi says to the waitress, her tone an attempt at bright and breezy. 'This is a celebration, right, Edith? You don't turn thirty-eight every day . . .'

When Edith doesn't respond, Ilona reaches for her hand beneath the table, speaking gently. 'Happy birthday, Edith. Wolf wanted to be here, if he hadn't been working . . . I always find it amazing that your birthdays are just one day apart.'

'And four years,' Edith says. She tries to smile but the expression won't stick, her attention drifting back to her conversation with Donald as they lay next to one another in her bed in the room next door, Tommy finally having fallen asleep, exhausted, after another one of his episodes.

Again she feels his lips on hers, her eyes closing in a rare state of rest; the pain floats away and she disappears deep inside herself as her head drops back, her whole body yielding, allowing itself to be swallowed up, floating back into the darkness.

'How did you get such a good table, for a group of women?' Litzi asks, breaking the silence.

'I booked in my father's name.' Lydia shrugs. 'He can pay for it, too. He won't even notice, so drink up.'

May, 1947. The month Engelbert Broda marries his second wife, Ina née Ehrlich, Donald Winnicott calls Edith to his office. From the moment she steps into the room, his eyes are unrecognisable from those that had stared up at her as he kissed her naked torso, just nights earlier; the eyes that had held hers as he told her how miserable he was with the woman he had been with for almost two decades; the eyes that had promised her he would leave his wife for her.

'May I request that you take a seat?' His manner is brisk, businesslike. 'Very well, you may of course remain standing,' he continues. 'Mrs Tudor-Hart, as you are aware, Tommy's situation is deteriorating rapidly. As his doctor it is my duty to find the best result for him, and, in turn, for you.'

'Why are you talking to me like this?' She watches his gaze move to the bruises on her wrists and she tugs at her sleeve, obscuring them from view. 'As if we are strangers.'

He ignores her, moving his attention to the page of notes on his desk. 'There is a residential home that has space for Tommy. It's not forever.'

When he speaks, his words warp, as though either one of them is moving underwater. Edith pictures Tommy, who at nearly eleven is a handsome, strong-looking boy with blond hair and golden skin. Her sudden laughter is an involuntary response to such a preposterous suggestion. 'Don't be ridiculous, Tommy is staying with me—'

He cuts her off, as if she hasn't spoken. 'It is this or an

asylum. In the circumstances I believe the residential setting is the best choice.'

'Tommy is best off with me. I am his mother.'

Even as she says it, she feels her conviction waver, recalling the increasingly frequent outbursts, the smashing of plates, the hammering of his fists against her chest, the endless shrieking and sleepless nights.

'You will be able to visit regularly. You will have a few weeks to work out how to cover the costs. Do you have any questions?'

She looks away, silent. Her final thought comes both as a burden and a relief. *It's just me, I am all alone.*

Alone, he hovers outside the door, gathering himself. Washington, USA. Springtime. A meeting room.

The three men already inside sit around a long polished wooden table. At its head is the director of the Central Intelligence Agency, Allen Dulles; to his left, Frank Wisner, head of the CIA's newly formed Office of Policy Coordination (OPC) – the espionage and counter-intelligence branch – and, to his right, Wisner's deputy, Frank Lindsey, who is to oversee a special operation that is the reason for today's meeting.

Clearing his throat, to mark his arrival, the final man to enter the room is the head of a special liaison mission of the British Intelligence Service, whose job it is to liaise with CIA and FBI. Punctual and charming, Kim Philby – a top SS officer who lives with his family at nearby 4100 Nebraska

Avenue – is already known to Dulles, and the men pack their pipes and light up, asking after each other's wives and children before business is commenced.

The reason for his being called here today, Dulles explains, running a finger absent-mindedly over his moustache, is that the CIA has been tasked with planning a counter-revolutionary revolt in a small but significant country in the throes of socialist rule. As the former head of Section IX, the section of SIS designed to operate against Communism and the Soviet Union, their British visitor will find his input particularly valued. Taking over the reins, Wisner – a genteel former lawyer with a slow Mississippi drawl and a reputation for throwing the best parties – adds that, as operations go, this one is to be particularly significant: several hundred Albanian natives will infiltrate the territory where, once on the ground, they can organise centres of subversion that will work together to bring down the axis of power in the existing regime, triggering a series of counter-revolutionary outbursts across the socialist world.

'Do we have your approval?' the Americans ask.

'Yes,' the Brit replies, his eyes shining with the hint of a smile. 'But I have a have a few suggestions of my own, if I may?'

May turns to June. Through the window, Edith and Tommy look out at the same horizon as the train sets off from Victoria station.

Gripping his hand for the duration of the journey, she holds tighter still as they pull up outside the house. In the doorway, Edith spots her son's new charge waiting, arms crossed against her chest, her expression set in grim determination.

Edith pays for the taxi with money offered by Alexander's father, Percyval, for his grandson's residential care, her palms sweating as she leads her only child into the home, replaying Winnicott's words on loop in her head. *A residential home is so much better than an institution.*

The ground uneven beneath her, she hears her own words once his colleagues had left and it was just the two of them. *You said you could help him.*

There had been no way of knowing, then, that this would be the last time he ever agreed to see her alone.

His voice was curt. 'I tried. We both did. I wish there were more that could be done for Tommy—'

'Please don't . . .' she had pleaded, placing her hands over her ears. 'You can't send him away. I'm his mother, I'm all he has.'

'There is no other option left.'

'But you promised.'

'We did everything we could.'

'Did we?'

The day the first group of Albanian recruits gathered by Balli Kombëtar leaders and trained by the CIA set sail from Malta in a Greek-style fishing boat to overthrow the Soviet Union from within, Edith returns to Grove End Gardens and collapses in a chair.

It is the summer of 1949 and, while these men were being trained up in order to be sent to their deaths in the doomed

CIA paramilitary exercise Operation Valuable, designed with the help of the SIS officer Kim Philby, Edith had spent her weekends visiting Tommy in Sussex, returning the same day or staying at a nearby inn – a round trip that eats heavily into what she earns for her latest freelance photography work for the Ministry of Information.

Nearly a year has passed since she first left him there. In the beginning, Tommy had cried when she prepared to depart at the end of these visits, protesting in every way he knew how. But as time passes she finds him a little more depleted, a little less the boy she knows, a little more surrendered to being abandoned by the one person in the world whose duty it is to protect him.

'It's not forever,' Donald had reminded her on the occasions when he returned her calls, listening to her heartache with weary resignation. His terseness towards them – her and the child he had nurtured as if he was his own, spending nights at their flat, accompanying them on weekend trips to the seaside, writing letters in which he confided that she appeared in his dreams – had felt like a slap.

Lying on the sofa, too tired to cook, she hears Rudolf Serkin's words as he played the old upright in the apartment now discarded in the city that is no longer home.

G sharp, C sharp, E. One, three, five.

You are strong.

But she is growing weaker, she thinks, and when the doorbell rings she is so tired she can hardly stand, moving slowly through the mess that she hasn't the time or energy to clear up.

It isn't late, but she cannot imagine who will be calling. She hasn't heard from Litzi since she moved to Berlin, aside from the occasional anonymous note that tells her little beyond that her best friend is alive. It was through Ilona that she had learnt of the birth of Litzi's daughter, Barbara, in February of that year.

Peering through the peephole, she pulls back at the sight of him, her mind instantly alert. When she looks again, more tentatively this time, he lifts his head, staring straight into the lens, as if gazing right at her through the door.

Pulling herself upright, she inhales and pulls the door open a crack.

The policeman's skin is a mottled red, as if he is permanently blushing, but his voice is firm. 'Ms Tudor-Hart, it's your son, Thomas Martin.'

What she feels in that moment is relief.

He is still shackled to the bed when she arrives at the hospital, though he can hardly keep his eyes open.

'What have you done to him?'

The doctor, on the other side of the bed, is matter-of-fact. 'Just sedatives, they'll wear off soon enough.'

'My darling,' she says, dropping to her knees at the side of the bed, cupping his face with her hands. 'My darling Tommy.' Turning, she snarls at the nurse by the door. 'Release him, immediately.'

When the nurse doesn't reply, the doctor looks up from his clipboard. 'It's for his own good. Your son was found with severe injuries – self-inflicted, you understand.'

'He isn't a risk to anyone' Edith turns briefly away from Tommy, to address the doctor, and then returns her attention to him. When she does, she finds herself once more shocked to find him here, tracing his features with the tips of her fingers. 'My God, he is only a child.'

A child whose mother would exhale, gladly, to learn that the police officer at her door is there to deliver a message that her only son is injured. A mother whose heart will only ever be half his.

The sounds in the apartment building get louder and more frequent, footsteps and whispers all through the day and night. Edith sleeps with the radio on, waking early to work on the series of child portraits that she produces for the Ministry of Education.

The project for the influential publication *Moving and Growing: Physical Education in the Primary School* provides just enough money to keep a roof over her head and enable her to afford the long train journeys north to Scotland to visit her son. Besides, it gives her a *raison d'être*, confirming her core beliefs about the importance of children inhabiting their own bodies, of the necessity of play and love without inhibition. All the facets of a carefree, independent existence that Tommy will never know.

Except that now he does have a chance at a life of sorts, thanks to Camphill School, where he is accepted following the introduction to the paediatrician and Camphill founder Karl König by a friend of a friend. Founded in 1940 to care for mentally and physically disabled children according to the principles of Rudolf Steiner, the school is a vision of everything she believes in, in education.

For her visits – every six weeks or so, depending on what she can afford – she brings her camera and feels a rush of hope as she captures the nurturing community where children with the most severe mental and physical disabilities are housed in the families of their carers. A home where, unlike other institutions overseeing children who have become a burden, there is no place for violence or the liberal administration of psychotropic drugs. A home where treatment takes place in the form of movement, music and massage; touch and nurturing. These photographs are the foundations of her project, one of the last she will ever have published in *Picture Post*, entitled 'A School Where Love is the Cure'.

A home so complete that, despite the distance between herself and Tommy, Edith is able to believe that perhaps things will be fine after all.

Dear Edith,

You must have been wondering at my long silence. My own feelings are less of wonder than of shame. Perhaps my Spanish experiences are catching up on me in the shape of a malignant *mañana* syndrome, an absolute revulsion against doing today what can possibly be put off until tomorrow. Well, as you see, tomorrow seems to have arrived at last in the sense that I have conjoined my decrepit fingers to my even more decrepit typewriter. What becomes of this less than inspiring conjuncture you will have to read below.

As for Little England, there seems to be little joy in sight there. It seems they will have another four or five years of That Woman, while Foot and Jenkins join poor old General Galtieri in the dustbin of history. One weeps few tears for them. What depresses me is the jarring prospect of hearing that brassy voice forever intoning the Neanderthal economics of the Grantham Age and reading the unctuous glosses provided by *The Times*. Ah well! Into every life some rain must fall.

And what of you, Edith? I know things weren't

always easy. I tried to keep an eye on you, as best I could. I realise now that I could have done more. There are many things I could have done differently, which is the true tragedy of life, is it not? Everything is so clear, after the fact. Everything is easy, once you know how.

I saw you, not long after Karl Fuchs was remanded in custody on charges relating to his atomic research, which of course triggered everything that followed. February 1950. I was back on a brief visit from Washington, not long before Guy turned up wanting to stay with me on Nebraska Avenue, which was logistically ridiculous if nothing else, given that Aileen had not long given birth to our youngest child. Five children in one house! Can you imagine it? Anyway, I was back in London and enjoying the peace and quiet, not knowing then that the explosions that would soon erupt – thanks in no small part to Guy. You were walking, with your camera. I was in a restaurant and spotted you through the window. I wondered whether I had imagined it, but Stefan recognised you, too. He was one of us, all along. I wonder if you'd gathered that. Given that he, too, is now dead, it seems churlish not to acknowledge it. I am beginning to feel somewhat in the minority in that respect. By then, of course, your Broda was already back working at the University of Vienna; the war was over. For some, at least. For soldiers like us, Edith, it never ended, did it? It takes its toll.

I suppose you heard about the execution of Ethel and Julius Rosenberg, at the time? Just because one knows one is doing the right thing, that doesn't make that thing without its challenges. I have said many times that I am two people: a private person and a political person. If there is a conflict, the political person comes first. That doesn't mean it is always the easy to do so, or one without consequence. A soldier who kills another on the battlefield does not fall to sleep at night without a stain of his conscience, without the memory seeping into his dreams.

I'm sure the agents we sent into Albania would have felt the same, had the tables been turned. They knew the risks, just as we did. Am I a monster, or am I simply on the wrong side? Are the traitors who double-crossed us – the Ms Xs of this world – not treated by Britain as heroes?

But that is all water under the bridge. As I said, what others think of me is none of my business. Except for you, Edith. I've always cared what you think. You are one of the most clear-minded people I've ever known. I heard that you were incarcerated for a while. I am sorry that this happened to you, and yet I am not surprised. People are scared of what they don't understand; and people like us will always remain a mystery, to some.

Anyhow, time marches on. November always feels like the longest month, December taking forever to come around, and then, once it's there, you blink, and just like that it's over. Rather like this letter.

I sometimes can't believe we shan't see each other again.

Yours,

Kim

Everything that followed

Secret Intelligence Service file on
Edith Suschitzky

```
METROPOLITAN POLICE
463/9A/DE
Subject: Betty GREY or GRAY
SPECIAL BRANCH
REF P.F.144034
30th day of July 1951
```

With further reference to Betty GREY or GRAY,
the subject of M.I.5 letter Gen. 22/B1a/DE
dated 20.4.50, Special Branch reported dated
9.6.50 and M.I.5 form 252A, P.F.144034/R4
dated 26.6.51, of which the latter shows her
to live at 12 Grove End Gardens, N.W.8, to
be a freelance photographer, to have joined
the Communist Party in 1926 and to be a
member of the North Marylebone Branch of the
Communist Party in 1951:

Discreet but exhaustive enquiries have been
made at Grove End Gardens, a large block of

privately owned flats in Abbey Road, N.W.8, but no one of this name is known to be residing there. 12 Grove End Gardens is the residence of Edith TUDOR-HART née SUSCHITZKY, the well-known Communist who is the subject of Special Branch record file 301/MP/2186. Also registered as residing at that address is a Christina Ritchie DISHINGTON P.F.76778 born 17.12.17 (no trace in Special Branch records). Nobody else is known to be staying in the flat at present, although Mrs. Edith TUDOR-HART does have guests who stay with her, and it is certain that, had anyone had been staying with her any length of time, I should have been made cognisant of that fact.

It is noteworthy, however, that Mrs. TUDOR-HART is, herself, a photographer, and, according to M.I.5 form S.283, P.F.63349/R.4 of 7.12.49, joined the Communist Party in 1927 and was a member of the St John's Wood St Marylebone Branch in 1949. In view of the fact that all enquiries to establish the identity of Mrs. GRAY have been fruitless, one cannot overlook the possibility that "Betty GRAY" may be a name assumed by Mrs. TUDOR-HART for certain purposes, although she has not changed her name officially, and is commonly known at Grove End Gardens as "TUDOR-HART".

                              Constable.
Submitted
                Chief Inspector.

                    Chief Superintendent.

REGISTRY.   P.F.144034

I think we can assume that Betty GRAY is an
alias of Edith TUDOR-HART. [SECTION REMOVED]
Handwriting of address of Registration Form
at 1a is identical with that of writer of
letter at 56b (P.F.63949).

Please amalgamate PF.144034 with PF.65549.
Make cross-reference under Betty GRAY.

D. Edwards.

B1a
8 August 1951

                              2 October 1951

Dear Allan,
I am applying for a H.O.W. on correspondence
for Mrs Edith TUDOR-HART, of 12 Grove End
Gardens, London N.W.8. This woman, who is a
professional photographer, is reported to
have been involved in Russian espionage activities in this country, and we are investigating

her in connection with a current case of
suspected espionage.

In view of her record, the check will have
to be operated with caution, and anything
which appears to relate to her business can
be allowed to pass. We are particularly
interested in any letters which she may
receive from the continent, and it may be
possible shortly to confine the operation of
the warrant to such communications.

Yours sincerely,
C.A.G. Simkins

Colonel N.F Allan M.B.E.,
G.P.O

TOP SECRET
PS.63349/B2a/CAGS
2 October 1951

Dear Saffery,

I am applying for a telephone check on
CUNNINGHAM 1699, the subscriber to which is
Mrs. Edith TUDOR-HART, 12 Grove End Gardens,
London N.W.8. I should be grateful if this
check could operate throughout twenty-four
hours.
Yours sincerely,
C.A.G Simkins

SECRET

To THE POSTMASTER-GENERAL, and all others whom it may concern:

I hereby authorise and require you to record all telephone conversation on the telephone line number: CUNNINGHAM 1699 and to produce for the record for my inspection.

For doing so this shall be your sufficient Warrant.

One of His Majesty's
Principal Secretaries of State

The subscriber to this number is Edith TUDOR-HART of 12 Grove End Gardens, London N.W.8. This woman is reported to have been involved in Russian espionage in this country. It is desired to subject her current activities to close investigation.

P.F.63349/B2a/CAGS

The figure pauses at the entrance to the room, straightening their coat before following inside.

The bustle of the junction at Horse Guards Avenue and Whitehall is hardly audible from up here, slatted blinds revealing slices of burnt orange and blue where the autumn trees meet the sky.

'As you know, everything you say is absolutely confidential. Now, shall we begin?'

TOP SECRET Copy for P.F.63349 TUDOR-HART

Interview with Source on 31.10.51

Accompanied by Captain [REDACTED] and using the alias 'Morley'

I today interviewed source [REDACTED] at Room 055, War Office. He impressed me as being careful in his statements and able to discrim-inate between what was known to him as fact and what was no more than speculation.

Captain [REDACTED] began by saying that we had asked [REDACTED] to come to the War Office because our enquiry was more than usually confidential and one which we wished him to treat with the utmost secrecy. [REDACTED] took this calmly and agreed to the condition.

I then told [REDACTED] that our enquiry concerned Lizzy PHILBY and that I would like him to recount all that he knew about her. The following is a collated account of his recollections.

Sources.
[REDACTED] met Lizzy PHILBY sporadically

between 1944 and 1946 in London. His impressions of Lizzy were therefore first-hand, but his knowledge of her background was derived almost entirely from Edith TUDOR-HART. Source thinks that TUDOR-HART first met Lizzy in Vienna in the early 1930's.

Character of Lizzy PHILBY

[REDACTED] described Lizzy as a woman who, though an out-and-out Communist, enjoys good living and is certainly not the self-sacrificing type. She is attractive to men. [REDACTED] said that he had always been curious about Lizzy because she was so obviously above the level of card-holding Communist and never seemed to want for money. He compared her standing in the Party with that of Arpad HAAS, a Communist he had known in Vienna in the early 1930's. HAAS said [REDACTED] had definitely worked for Soviet intelligence.

Lizzy PHILBY's Pre-War Activities.

[REDACTED] had heard that Lizzy was first married (he presumed in Vienna) to a wealthy Austrian whose name he could not remember. He did however make a guess which was sufficiently close to convince me that he meant FRIEDMANN. [REDACTED] did not know when or whence Lizzy came to the U.K., nor did he (until a few weeks ago) know anything more about her second husband than that his name was PHILBY. He still has no idea when or where they were married or when they were divorced. His one firm conviction was that Lizzy had lived in a flat in Paris before the war on a fairly lavish scale. When asked how he knew she lived well while in Paris [REDACTED] said that he remembered Lizzy had had a bill for £150 for storage of her furniture in Paris, throughout the war, from which he had deduced that her possessions there must have been substantial.

Lizzy PHILBY's Association with H.A.R. PHILBY.
[REDACTED] said that (until a few weeks ago) he knew nothing of PHILBY except that he and Lizzy were divorced by 1944 (note this in fact is not the case). [INFORMATION MUCH REDACTED AND DELETED]

Lizzy PHILBY's War-Time Activities.
When [REDACTED] first met Lizzy in 1944 she was living with Dr. Georg HONIGMANN, a journalist, at Wellesley Court. She was doing some sort of war-work in a factory which [REDACTED] thought connected with aircraft. She gave this up in 1945 and thereafter, until her departure to Germany, she did no more than keep house for HONIGMANN. They lived very comfortably, but [REDACTED] would not say that it was at a higher salary than HONIGMANN's salary would command.

Lizzy PHILBY's Association with HONIGMANN.
Georg HONIGMANN had been interned in Canada

and had there met a man named HORNIC.
[REDACTED] thought that it was probably
through HORNIC that HONIGMANN had subsequently
entered the TUDOR-HART circle and so met
Lizzy. [REDACTED]'s impression of HONIGMANN
was that he had no firm political views until
he met Lizzy. [REDACTED] considered him not
to be a strong personality and felt sure
that he carried no real influence in the
Communist Party. [REDACTED] thought there was
real affection between Lizzy and HONIGMANN.
When, after the war, Lizzy announced that
they would go to the Soviet sector of Berlin,
HONIGMANN was obviously unwilling and held
back. Lizzy however insisted and HONIGMANN
was duly despatched to the British zone,
whence he made his way to the Soviet sector
of Berlin. Lizzy followed later (via
Czechoslovakia, [REDACTED] thought).

[REDACTED] said his views about Lizzy's influence in the Communist Party were, to him,
confirmed when he learnt how well the
HONIGMANNs were allowed to live in Berlin.
Almost at once they obtained a house, a car,
a chauffeur and so on. [REDACTED] is convinced
that HONIGMANN had neither the influence nor
the ability to obtain such preferential treatment and that therefore Lizzy's standing in
the Party must have been the cause.

[REDACTED] knows that the HONIGMANNs married

in Germany, though he does not know the date.
HONIGMANN edits an important Communist newspaper.

<u>The Episode of TUDOR-HART's Photographic
Negatives</u>.
Edith TUDOR-HART was now a sick woman, highly
neurotic and suffering from a persecution
mania. Her conversation would continually turn
to the steps which the authorities were taking
against her. [REDACTED] said that he would
listen to these outpourings, although he did
not take them seriously. Five weeks ago, when
he had visited her, TUDOR-HART had said that
she was worried lest her house and studio
would soon be raided by the police and that
therefore she had been going through some old
photographic negatives which she intended to
destroy because if the police found them they
would harm her. She mentioned three particular
photographs - those of D.N. PRITT, Paul
ROBESON, and Mr. PHILBY. [REDACTED], on hearing
the name PHILBY, had stopped and asked if
this was Lizzy's husband. TUDOR-HART agreed
and then told of PHILBY's background. She
said he was "an ace-man" in M.I.5; he was
the son of a former British representative
at the court of the King of Saudi Arabia;
and that he had been Times correspondent in
Spain at the time of the Civil War. TUDOR-
HART said nothing about PHILBY's relationship
with Lizzy. Two things struck [REDACTED] about

this story: first, he could not understand why TUDOR-HART should be worried about having PHILBY's photograph since it could not do her any harm; and secondly, he remembered a conversation which had taken place in about 1945, when the TUDOR-HART circle had been discussing telephone interception and the sort of things that were being done to [UNCLEAR]

[REDACTED] said that he was quite sure that TUDOR-HART had not been in touch with Mr. PHILBY while he had known her and that, therefore, he expected the photograph dated back to the 1930s.

Lizzy PHILBY'S Present Movements.
I reminded [REDACTED] that he had reported in 1948 that Lizzy PHILBY was thinking of returning on a visit to the U.K. [REDACTED] said that Lizzy had not been back. He mentioned however that Lizzy had written to TUDOR-HART some time ago asking her not to send any more food parcels. [REDACTED] had interpreted this as fear on Lizzy's part of having too much correspondence with the West, in case the Russians should think that she had become contaminated and so refuse her an exit permit if she ever wished to travel again.

B2b
3.10.51
A.S. Martin

The man across the table nods his head. 'Thank you for your time.'

Nodding, the figure stands, a single strand of red hair falling across the paper as they adjust their hat and turn to leave.

It is still dark when Edith awakes, alone, in the apartment at 12 Grove End Gardens, the rest of the city sleeping off the excesses of the night before.

Her mind stultified with sleep and the lingering effects of the sleeping pills, she opens the back door and stands in the doorway looking out at the communal gardens, enjoying the cold against her skin as she smokes a cigarette.

A new year. 1st January 1952. In the corner of the garden stands the sand-pit, untouched. Time marches on.

The envelope waits for her in the communal hallway, the seal slightly frayed where it has already been opened. She almost laughs at their lack of discretion as she walks back into the flat, pulling the door to and applying the latch, her laughter turning hollow as she scans down through the words, neatly typed on blue paper, a single line added at the bottom, by hand.

Dear Mrs. Tudor-Hart,

I am grateful to you for your letter about Tommy. It is a great relief that he may be able to stay where he is for a long time as it will certainly be very difficult for him to

adjust to a new place and it is difficult to think of anything
better for him.

   I regret I have not yet been able to visit Aberdeen.
With good wishes for the New Year.
Yours sincerely,
D.W. Winnicott

(I think you would like to know from me that I have
remarried.)

The call from Alexander comes in the middle of the night.
He hasn't seen his son in four years and the urgency in his
voice, together with the unlikeliness of Tommy's father being
the one to contact her, jerks her awake.

   Perhaps Tommy has been hurting himself again. It was
the final chance, Camphill staff had warned, last time she
visited, regaling her with details of how he had started to
drive holes into his own skin. She hadn't known which was
worse: the fact of her son intentionally harming himself, or
the callousness of the response of the school to whom she
had entrusted him. And yet, still, she had left him there,
hadn't she?

She takes the first train from Victoria station to Redhill, the
details of what she has learnt taunting her as she watches the
world skid past: that for days the school had been attempting

to contact her at an old address, after Tommy contracted the infection; that, once they had tracked down her ex-husband, he had permitted their son's transfer from Aberdeen to the asylum in Surrey without consulting her; that the decision was justified on the basis that Camphill wouldn't allow the use of penicillin to treat the boy.

Above all, a single fact repeats itself: all this had been taking place – her son had been sick and needing her – and she had been somewhere else.

The Institution for Mental Defectives is a red-brick building divided into a five-storey central tower, with three-storey wings on either side. With Bath stone dressings, it stands on a former common, a breeze rolling across the grass towards Edith as she steps out on the driveway from the taxi-cab.

Trying not to allow herself to compare the austere setting with the intentional softness of Camphill, she pulls her coat tightly around herself, a nurse meeting her at reception and leading the way along a pale green hallway, the sound of their shoes echoing on the tiled floor.

'Since the Mental Deficiency Act of 1913, the Board of Management decided that the Asylum rather than the local authority would cater for the needs of those, like yourselves, the lower middle classes, who cannot afford the charges for private care,' the nurse says, the smell of bleach rising up around them. 'Once he is recovered, he will join the other boys.'

'But Tommy doesn't like being with other—'

'We know what we're doing, Mrs Tudor-Hart.'

Across the room, she spots Tommy, drowsy and shackled once more, scars dotted along his arms.

It's not forever, she reminds herself, pulling her back straight and painting on her brightest smile. She simply has to persuade Karl König to take Tommy back. This is not forever.

Back at the flat she doesn't sleep, despite the pills that promise rest.

Once she has written the letter to Camphill pleading Tommy's case, she sits on the floor. Brushing her fingers over the prints, she works through her archive – sections of her life that seem now to belong to someone else compartmentalised in piles that threaten to topple and spill: the 1930s and families free-bathing in the Lobau, children receiving ultraviolet light treatment at the South London Hospital for Women and Children, a mother preparing sandbags against the attacks on the streets of London, at the turn of the decade. Through the forties, and images of fashion models at Studio Sun, a boy running amidst the ruins in London's Moorgate.

Her attention landing on a box of negatives labelled 'Vienna, 1933', she stands and moves to the kitchen, and pours a glass of water. Taking two more Seconals from the packet, she places them on her tongue and swallows.

Just a little rest, that's all she needs.

When sleep finally takes hold, the memories seep into her dreams again: the look of contempt that had swept over Arnold's features the day she had told him about the lost file, just before he returned to Moscow. In this iteration, the blue of Arnold's eyes is the water and the sky as the two of them swim side by side in the river at the Lobau. With the clouds turning dark, the river swelling into the sea, she sees her love drifting out of reach, a red handkerchief clutched between his fingers, the water rising above his head until all that is left a single square of scarlet.

Days bend and shrink and multiply. Edith goes to work and then she comes home and waits for the letter from Camphill that will tell her Tommy can return. The letter doesn't come, and then it does, confirming that Tommy is no longer welcome at the school.

At the table, she sits alone, her mind like one of the flip-books her father would show her when she was little, whole worlds jumping to life in front of her eyes. Worlds in which she and Arnold had gone to Moscow together; where Berti had never returned to Vienna; where Donald had left his first wife for her instead. A world where the city she grew up in was her home and a place to feel safe; where her only child had been born happy.

She does not remember falling asleep at the kitchen table, her head pressed against her arm. But it cannot be late because by the time the news comes over the radiogram at six o'clock – *Kim Philby suspected of being a Soviet agent* – she is already somewhere else, drawn into a deep and comfortless sleep, the sea threatening to swallow her once more.

Just a little rest! she pleads, aloud, when the crashing of the waves that sweep through her nightmares become so violent that she sits bolt upright at the table, the roar of the ocean mutating into the sound of fists hammering at the window.

Still groggy, she doesn't think to pick up the empty bottle that she keeps on the table, for protection. Instead she calls out, her voice thick with sleep. 'Who is it?'

Moving slowly through the hallway, her feet bare, she slips on the chain, opens the door a crack.

The man who stares back at her wears a trilby and checked scarf.

'Is it Tommy?' she says, and he cocks his head.

'Chief Investigator William Skardon, Special Branch. Please open the door.'

He has a thin face and eyes that roam the flat, taking in the mess that litters every surface.

'I have to lie down,' Edith says, walking carefully into the bedroom, keeping her head focused upwards, as if to do so will help draw the man's attention away from the photos that blanket the floor. 'You woke me, I was resting.'

'I am afraid it's a matter of great urgency, Mrs Tudor-Hart.'

He doesn't falter when she pulls back the cover and gets into bed, pulling the sheet around herself so that he won't see her shaking.

'Mrs Tudor-Hart, we are looking into a friend of yours, Georg Honigmann, the partner of Litzi Friedmann.'

'Why?' Her expression is one of genuine bemusement.

Watching her, the man pulls a photograph from his pocket and passes it to her. 'Do you recognise this man?'

She doesn't take the print, fearful that he will see her fingers trembling, regarding it from a distance instead.

His face is older now, set in an amused smile that she recognises from his baiting of Alexander; a look that says he is making mischief and he is enjoying himself.

'Who is he? He looks like a sinister sort of person.'

The man keeps his eyes on her as he continues. 'Kim Philby. He is the former husband of your friend, Litzi Friedmann. You don't recognise him?'

Edith shakes her head. 'Litzi and I have lived very separate lives, since coming to England. I'd heard she was married, but . . .' Her voice trails off and she holds his eye, for several seconds, moving her sheet down so that the top of her leg is exposed. 'I didn't even know she was still in the country.'

Clearing his throat, the officer straightens.

'I'll see you out,' she says, standing, moving quickly back through the living room.

When she opens the door, Ilona and Peter are there in the hallway – her nephew not much older now than Tommy was when the two of them first moved in. Pausing, the officer regards them, before addressing Edith.

'Well, if you have any thoughts, you can contact us any time. We are always here.'

'Yes,' she says. 'I'll bear that in mind.'

'Who was that?' Ilona follows Edith back into the living room, where she lowers herself to the floor.

'Lock the door, Ilona,' Edith replies, without looking up, working her way through the boxes until she finds one marked 1933. Picking it up, she moves to the sink and places it on the counter, scooping out the dirty cups and plates.

'Edith, what are you doing? Please—' Ilona marches up to her and holds her wrist. 'You're scaring Peter. What are you doing, who was that man?'

'I told you they were watching me. All along.' She glances briefly back at Ilona, her expression almost jubilant. 'He was Special Branch, he wanted to know—'

She stops herself, returning her attention to the box of negatives, before reaching for the matches. As she turns, a single strip, which has been teetering on the edge of the tin sink falls from the ledge and pirouettes to the floor.

Oblivious, Edith lights the match and holds it against the bundle of negatives. Watching the flames, intently, she does not notice the child reach down and pick up the strip of images from the floor, holding it to the light as he moves back towards the table, noting the outline of a young man, a pipe clenched between his lips, his eyes focused slightly downwards.

Hearing his mother walk into the room behind him, the child drops the negative back in amongst the others spread across the floor, before stepping forward and accepting his mother's hand.

It might be minutes or hours later when Ilona returns, Adele by her side.

She must have left the door on the latch, or not closed it at all, for they enter without knocking, Adele kneeling down beside her daughter, who lies on the floor, her legs pulled in towards herself.

'Come on, my darling.'

Edith tries to protest but she is too weary to speak. As her mother and sister-in-law support her to standing, her mind wanders to Tommy in the visitors' room of the hospital at Redhill, in the seat that is too large for such a small child, his eyes fixed away from her, towards the common.

She sees herself hovering in the doorway, taking a moment to collect her thoughts before opening the door, her face set in a smile. In her memory, a group of children look up hopefully – a girl named Amelia, a little younger than Tommy. Edith smiles, running her fingers over the girl's hair as she passes. Slowing as she reaches his chair where he looks out over the grounds, she waits for Tommy to turn to her in recognition. It is a game she plays with herself every time, always bound to lose. When he doesn't turn, she crouches in front of him, leaning forward and kissing him on the forehead, breathing him in, her face locked in a smile.

'We want to help you, Edith,' Adele says, lifting her daughter's head from the apartment floor, and holding her there in a desperate embrace. 'We love you.'

When Edith protests, quietly, too devoid of energy to argue properly, her mother hushes her, as she would a child.

'My camera, my things. You can't leave them. They'll find—'

'We're just going for a little drive, to get some air. Don't worry, we will lock up everything behind us. Everything will be fine.'

Her eyes growing heavy, Edith lies with her head resting on her mother's lap, falling asleep as the taxi-cab circles Lord's Cricket Ground, towards Marylebone Road. When she opens her eyes, the motor-car is still, her mother and Ilona on either side, along the back seat.

'Where are we?' Edith asks, and her mother opens the door.

'It's for the best, just for a while, until you're feeling better.'

She knows the smell as they walk towards the hospital doors, the same bleach they use in the sanatorium where she had left Tommy. But Tommy is not here. Different tiles, the same white bonnets on different nurses. The same grim expressions, the same sense of defeat enveloping Edith as they lead her towards her room.

'No,' Edith says. The soles of her shoes struggle to grip against the floor.

'Just until you're feeling better. You need some help, some time to rest. It won't be long.'

'Ilona, tell them . . . Please. You know I'm not crazy. You know.'

Ilona turns away so that Edith will not see the tears in her eyes.

'Please.' Edith whispers. 'If you leave me here, I will never forgive you.'

19th June 1953. The day Julius and Ethel Rosenberg are executed at Sing Sing prison for conspiring to pass atomic secrets to Russia in World War II, Edith receives a letter from the British security services demanding that she cease her photographic activities.

'They can't do that,' Wolf says, when she arrives at the house on Willifield Road, her eyes casting around at the new wallpaper, the tricycle in the hallway, signs of a family in bloom.

'They've been through my things. It's not the first time. After our mother and your wife took me to that place, I came home and they had ransacked the place. All my photos. I don't know what they found to convince them but I called all of my usual clients and every single one told me they'd been prohibited from employing me,' Edith says, automatically peering through the net curtains, surveying for possible shadows on other side of the box hedge. I can't even afford to pay for the flat. What will I do?'

'You know you can stay here as long as you like,' Wolf says.

Edith shakes her head. 'I have nothing.'

'You have us.'

'What will Ilona say?'

'Ilona loves you.'

Edith shakes her head, turning away.

'Have you spoken to Litzi?' Wolf asks.

'A while ago.'

'She plans to stay in Germany?'

'She has Barbara to think of; she will be starting school soon.'

'And the other friend of yours – Lydia? Whatever happened to her?'

'I'll find somewhere,' Edith says, and turns away.

```
     Secret Intelligence Service file on
                Engelbert Broda

                 MINUTE SHEET

                         (ORIGINAL IN P.F.66949
                                   NUNN MAY)
(Copies in P.F.46663 - E. BRODA
            P.F.78372 - H. BRODA) 898


B2a through B2

Reference Minute 856


Your enquiry about the possibility that the
BRODAs played some part in the espionage of
NUNN MAY came at a happy time, for we were
already studying Engelbert BRODA's case in
another connection. As a result of that study
we feel sure that BRODA was engaged in espi-
onage during the war, although we have no
proof of it.

Engelbert BRODA was working at the Cavendish
Laboratory, Cambridge, while NUNN MAY was
there from April to November 1942 before he
```

went to Canada. Hildegarde BRODA was living and working in London during the whole of 1942. NUNN MAY returned to this country from Canada on the 17th September 1945 and on the 1st October 1945 BRODA wrote asking to see him in Cambridge or London. According to NUNN MAY's diary he went to Cambridge on the 16th-17th October 1945 and amongst others saw BRODA. BRODA and NUNN MAY both had lunch with KOWARSKI (P.F.67192) on the 14th January 1946.

I think therefore that the answer to your question is that Engelbert BRODA might well have been the person who recruited NUNN MAY for the R.I.S. You will remember that one of NUNN MAY's few admissions, in an inter-rogation which took place at Wakefield Prison on 21st March 1949, was that he was recruited to the R.I.S. only a very short while before he left this country for Canada and that the individual who recruited him was no longer within reach. Mr. Skardon to whom this information was given was inclined to believe that NUNN MAY's statement was true. In March 1949 when NUNN MAY said this BRODA was no longer in the country.

B2b
14.10.53   R.T. Reed

My dear Edith,

It seems years since I last wrote. Perhaps I am wary of the consequences, should I be caught having for so many years written to a woman who is long since dead. Heaven forbid they think us mad, Edith. Is there any more perilous charge? The lady either protests too much, or not at all. Either way, the outcome is the same.

We are really living in a most interesting period, with the Presidential intestines well to the fore again. It hardly seems like a moment's past since Eisenhower's intestines were front-page news for months on end. I doubt it makes much difference where the Great Phoney is: in the White House, in his California ranch-house or in Bethesda Naval hospital. His mouth seems to be out of control, wherever he is. His new confederation of international terrorist states is on a par with his other undisciplined maunderings, and it is odd to see his administration bashing the TV networks for excessive exposure of the hostage crisis. Without the antics of TV, the Great Phoney would never have become president. Meanwhile, one has to gag at the obsequiousness of *The Times*, under the aegis of the deplorable Charles Douglas-Home and his master, the money-mad Murdoch. Is

Murdoch really going to take out American citizenship for the sake of a few more lousy TV outlets? What with an Australian-American running *The Times*, a Ugandan running Wembley Stadium, the Japanese running the football league and Leyland, Egyptians running Harrods, what will be left for Britons? My son's small (flailing) joinery business, I suppose. Odd to think I have fathered one of Mrs T's ever-darling small businessmen! The trouble is that small businessmen usually go big or go bankrupt. *Quo vadis, Johannes?*

It is depressing that power so often goes to the foolish and the awful. One might call it the Reagan-Thatcher syndrome. It seems that the word '*glasnost*' is entering the English vocabulary, though it is difficult to find an exact English equivalent. The dictionary definition, 'publicity', is quite inadequate; it conjures up images of Saatchi & Saatchi, who would not hesitate to lie if that promoted sales. I suppose 'openness' is best, though it is rather vague. I suppose that *glasnost* is rather vague too.

Well, perhaps we can get into it all together one day. Who knows where we will end up?

So, next weekend Nina's relatives will go down to do the heavy work of preparation: scrubbing floors, beating carpets, putting up curtains and mosquito screens and all the rest of it. When they have finished, we make our stately entry, probably on Sunday afternoon. I can hardly wait to get down to country life. The air is wonderful down there, and the rustle of leaves and bird-song emphasise the deep tranquillity of the forest. It is ideal for reading, reflection and, indeed, for work. Nina's nephew has got us a new colour TV which should work well enough in the countryside – a smallish but adequate screen, about 35cm by 20. Our old black and white set is on its last legs and is apt to go haywire at critical moments. So what with the new TV and my new transistor, I shall be keeping in touch with the ways of the world.

Not that the way of the world gives one much excuse for cheering these days. Reagan's extraordinary contortions during his European tour seem to have befuddled almost everyone, including the American public. I can't see much mileage from a summit with such an ignorant and foolish old man. Maybe Reagan would like the TV coverage, but I think that our side would hope for something more than pretty photographs. And what, by the way, has bitten *The Times* editorial writers? As often as not, they are taking both Reagan and Mrs T to task for not standing up to the Russians, dashing cold water on any sign that Reagan's advisers may be having second thoughts about confrontation. Of course, there is sort of deadly consistency in the stance of The Times over the past fifty years. Then they were the standard-bearers of appeasement. In the Hitler years, appeasement was a code for a special sort of peace: the peace that the West would enjoy if only Hitler attacked the Soviet Union. In fact, anti-Sovietism is still the driving force behind those PHS editorial pens, with Reagan replacing Hitler as the White Knight. The new element, which The Times disregards, is that the Soviet Union is, and will remain, a nuclear superpower. Some fire hazard!

Speaking of fire hazards, we should have been at the dacha by now, but they decided to give us a new central heating system which has only just been installed. The old one seemed to be quite satisfactory, if a bit stiff at the joints, but the new one should be the *dernier cri*. Anyway, the old one might have been something of a fire hazard; and, having just seen the frightening TV shots of Bradford City football ground, I am happy to see all fire hazards removed from our vicinity. Oddly enough, those pictures seemed to stir ME up more than actual fire raids during the war. Of course, I was younger then, and my nerves presumably steadier; also I am speaking of remote memories. Time does seem to be shuffling past at an alarming rate.

In other news, we seem to have scrambled back to approximately normal health, but it's no thanks to the weather. We had three or four glorious spring days in early April; then the snow and sub-zero temperatures came back, and forced us to postpone stowing away our winter clothes. Since then, it has improved a bit, but only so-so, and you need a microscope to see any green on the trees. As I write, a damp mist is hanging around, and I get some bleak cheer from the knowledge that you in England have also had a sharp kick in the stomach from Old Father Winter. All the weathermen seem to insist that there is nothing particularly unusual in the ups and downs of recent years, but I can't help feeling that fings ain't wot they used to be. Not at all what Browning had in mind, anyway.

We are beginning to address ourselves seriously to the problem of our summer travels. Fortunately Nina is firmly persuaded that I cannot pack decently, so my share of the hard work is the occasional desultory discussion of my requirement in the way of shirts, shoes, etc. and the selection of books for leisure reading. (Also, even more fortunately, she cannot trust me to wash dishes either.) It will be nice to get away from the press; the regularity of my appearance in the columns is becoming truly monotonous. As for the musical with which Manchester is being afflicted, I just can't visualise it. I hope the villain of the piece sings out of tune; otherwise the impersonation would lack verisimilitude.

There is not much going on in Moscow during the summer; all the good companies, opera, ballet, etc. are abroad, and July days (and nights) tend to be a bit stuffy. If my children visit this year, we will spend a week or so here, 3–4 days in Leningrad, either at the beginning or end of the trip, and up to three weeks cutting a broad swathe through Mother Russia.

I have just completed the astonishingly exhausting process of putting away my winter clothes and taking out the summer ones, giving both sets a good brush and sprinkling naphthalene into the pockets of the former – and polishing both sets of boots and shoes. To make it worse, the central heating, which was unusually erratic during the bitter weather in January, is now going full blast; my indoor temperature is nearly 27°C. (About 80°F!) So I must either open the windows and sit in a draught or keep them shut and swelter.

Moscow in May is usually pretty foul, with the thaw uncovering the litter of a whole winter, theretofore decently mantled in snow. But they put the Komsomols, the schoolchildren and others to cleaning up the place pretty smartly. Anyhow, mustn't grumble; soon enough December will be upon us once more and with it another year slips past. Where do they go?

Yours,

Kim

A special sort of peace

There is no seat number on the ticket she had bought from the man behind the glass counter at Victoria train station, pausing a moment before stating her final destination.

Fifty-one miles.

She stands by the door between the carriages looking out through the window for most of the journey, watching the light fade, the sky over the rooftops of the buildings growing lifeless as they rattle through the city – industrial buildings giving way to a sludge of grey and brown box-houses hemmed into one another between limp brown gates as they pass through the suburbs. Then, at last, green.

Her thoughts are broken by the slowing of the locomotive as it approaches Brighton station, past soft white houses illuminated by occasional street-lamps, the final shriek of brakes as they spin through those great metal arches.

Holding a suitcase in each hand, Edith walks slowly, letting the other passengers bustle ahead. Crossing over by the queue of taxis, her hand feels for the ten-pound note in her shoe. Like a firefly, she follows the dim beam of the street-lamp towards the sea, the salt in the air settling on her lips. It is dark by now, a cool wind whipping at her cheeks. At the traffic lights a young man with a college boy haircut and a girl in a Bowknot Bowler and a dusty blue coat dash through the traffic.

'I was expecting you earlier,' the landlady says curtly as she opens the door to the flat above the empty shop front on Bond Street. 'That's all you have?'

Edith holds the bags, which contain everything that she has not burnt or sold, closer by her side, and pulls herself upright. 'It was advertised as furnished.'

In the hallway, the landlady nods. 'That's right. And you intend to take the shop, too?'

'Yes.'

'And what, do you mind me asking, do you intend to sell?'

'Antiques.'

Edith surveys the street, out of habit. Closing the door to her antique shop, she is aware of the calling of the gulls and the distant sound of the fairground drifting up through the North Laine as she moves closer to the pier.

At this time of year the streets are largely devoid of the pleasure-seekers who descend in their droves in summer months. Still, she is largely invisible, this tall older lady in rag-like clothes and a dark beret, an old-fashioned camera-case – empty now – worn around her neck.

A young couple stands on the promenade, their faces locked in intent conversation, oblivious to the sea clawing up and down the beach in front of them.

Her hand reaching for the Rolleiflex case, she pictures Arnold Deutsch's fingers on hers and turns away from the water.

The post office is quiet when she arrives, and from her pocket she pulls the card addressed to Tommy. The image on the front is a townscape, couples and families sprawled across the seafront near the old aquarium: *a place one could get lost in.* The date etched in the corner: 15th February 1956. Reaching in again, she counts out a handful of coins to pay for a newspaper, which she will use as fuel for the fire, resting it in the crook of her arm as she makes her way home.

Inside the flat, she places the paper, face-down, on the small table overlooking the street through net curtains, so that she cannot read the headline: *Soviet leader Nikita Khrushchev denounces Joseph Stalin as a brutal despot in sensational speech.*

Running her finger briefly over a collection of matchboxes spread across several surfaces, she thinks of Lydia and she stands, the bells in the church on New Road striking six.

Six years and some three thousand miles away under a cool Lebanese sky, Kim Philby takes a final lungful of sea air, the sound of the fog-horn rising above a distant call to prayer, signalling that it is time to leave. Next stop, Odessa. And then. . .

Glancing up at the sky, he stops a moment, his attention caught by a pair of birds ducking and weaving overhead, in an elaborate demonstration of their freedom. Smiling, he nods, silently, to himself, stepping through the open door onto the freight-liner, accompanied only by his final thoughts: a wood pigeon rustling through the trees of St John's Wood Church Gardens; a seagull hovering above the shore at Brighton Beach. A great grey shrike slicing through a bitter winter sky above the Ashdown Forest, on its way home.

2 July 1963

Dear Tommy,

I hope you are enjoying watching the summer arrive, I imagine the grounds of Redhill look beautiful at this time of year. Do you ever see birds or foxes, like those we spotted in St John's Wood Church Gardens, on warm summer days?

It is hard for me to believe that my boy is turning twenty-seven years old this year. I look forward to seeing you again, my darling, once I have a little more money to spare. After I sold my cameras and the rest of my possessions, in London, all I had left was enough to start again, with the hope that one day we will be reunited. On that day, I will take the train to Surrey and bring a stick of Brighton rock for my darling boy.

I hope one day to bring you here to visit. I think you would like it by the sea. My antiques shop is coming on well, I have learnt a lot, and hold steadfast to one rule: it doesn't matter what you collect, it is important to collect one thing and stick to it. A friend told me that, many years ago. At least, looking back, I thought she was a friend. I

*hope you have friends, Tommy, but you have to be careful
about who you trust.*
   All my love,
   Mama

She walks with her head held high to the post office, past the
Poulter and Pork butcher, and the barrow hire yard, and the
pub where a crowd spills out on to the street.

Clutching the postcard in her left hand, she smiles to herself
at her private joke. Should they wish to intercept her correspondence now, they will find no need to prise open an
envelope. They can't get to her any longer, they have taken
all there is to take; she has nothing but she is a free woman.
All that she has to say can be written on an open card postcard, for all to see.

'Put it on the tab, please, Simon,' she says to the young
man who pulls out a single stamp from a leather folder, her
eyes moving to the newspapers lined up on the counter, pausing
over the front page of the *Guardian*.

'Mrs Tudor-Hart?' the man says, and she looks up at him,
distracted by what she has seen, her heartbeat suddenly rising.
'I was saying that Mr Brown requested you settle your account
in full before you place any other items on the bill.'

'Fine,' she says, fiddling in her pocket for coins and bringing
them out, letting the cashier count out the correct amount as
she folds the paper and stuffs it inside her coat.

'Mrs Tudor-Hart, you haven't placed the stamp on the card.'

'You do it.' Edith calls behind her as she hurries out into
the street, making her way back the same route she came, the
sound of the revellers outside the pub growing louder as she
passes.

Aware of pairs of eyes watching her as she works the lock

at the entrance on Bond Street, once inside, she bolts the door and applies the latch.

Upstairs, she double-locks the interior door before letting herself fall back against it.

Feeling the breath rise and fall in her chest, she pulls out the paper and re-reads the headline: *Kim Philby identified as third man in the Burgess and Maclean case.* Standing, after a while, she reads on slowly.

> *Mr H. A. R. Philby was identified yesterday as the third man in the Burgess and Maclean case – the one who warned Maclean on May 25th 1951 that he was about to be questioned by the security services. That tip led to the escape of Burgess and Maclean. Philby himself was asked to resign from the Foreign Service in July 1951, but he was cleared of the suspicion that he had been the third man. For the past seven years he has been abroad, mainly in the Middle East. Before he disappeared early this year he was living in Beirut.*

Walking to the shelf, she takes a box of matches from her collection and moves across to the fire, scrunching the words inside her fist and dropping the paper into the grate.

Her fingers trembling, she lights the match and drops it, watching the flames lick at his face.

My dear Edith,

I recently had framed a copy of the photograph you
took of me in Litzi's parents' house, that evening after
the Lobau. Do you remember that day, how even amidst
what was happening around us, the world seemed to
shine with possibility? An old friend of mine – one of
few of those that I have left – brought me a copy when
he visited. They must have had it in their files for years,
but not have been able to make any official connection
between us, beyond our time in Vienna. Lucky, really,
or they could have made your life hell. I can, at least,
take some pleasure in imagining the grief it must have
caused them, not to be able to do anything with the
knowledge. I have to admit I am surprised that you kept
the photograph. After everything, I would have thought
you would have got rid of it, along with any other trace
of our shared past. Selfishly, I'm glad that you didn't.
It is not only a reminder of that period of our lives, but
a reminder of why we did it. Amidst everything that
has happened since, it is easy to forget, sometimes. I
have to admit, these days I am forgetting more and
more. But then, none of us are getting any younger.

I've just heard the news that Klaus Fuchs is dead.

February 1988 – exactly 38 years after he was arrested, aged 38. It is tempting to read something into such mirroring but I will resist. Sometimes it is tempting to try to read into what is not there. Unromantic as it might sound, more often than not life is merely a sequence of events, which on reflection might appear more thoroughly planned than they were. Where we end up cannot ever be predicted, or contrived.

In any case, I hear Fuchs was buried with great honours in Dresden, medals and decorations from the GDR decorating his satin pillow. Not a single one from the USSR – a bone of contention in some circles – but of course he was denied by Mother Russia at the time of his sentencing, the suggestion that he had been passing atomic secrets to agents of the Soviet government referred to in the official statement issued by TASS as 'a crude invention'. There has been fussing about this, too, as if one deserves the right to be acknowledged by the cause to which one has committed oneself, in death, if not in life. But why should we? That was never the deal. We never asked for anything. Not money, not glory. We made sacrifices because we believed they were worthwhile. We believed that, fervently, didn't we, Edith?

I never asked if you heard about Guy? It was a while ago now but time doesn't seem to move in quite the same way for me any more. A heart attack took him, they said, in a hospital not far from where I sit now: so he did have a heart after all. A song comes to mind, which he insisted on singing the first time we met, here in Moscow, not long after I arrived. A ballad, written in the memory of old Harry Pollitt:

Harry Pollitt was a worker, one of Lenin's lads
He was foully murdered by those counter-
Revolutionary cads
Counter-revolutionary cads, counter-revolutionary
cads
He was foully murdered by those counter-revolutionary
cads!

You remember how Guy loved to sing, even – or particularly – when others wished he wouldn't. And now I have a sudden flashback to him bursting into a version of sorts of the Eton Boating Song, at one of our last lunches here in Mother Russia, at the Aragvi, no less. Poor old Guy. His ashes were interred in the churchyard at West Meon in Hampshire, so I'm told. A churchyard, in Hampshire? Hard to know who will be having more of a fit: the saints or Burgess. This was one of many subjects of conversation when my dear friend Graham Greene came for dinner, and we re-enacted those long Sunday lunches in St Albans when the whole sub-section, under my leadership, could relax for a few hours of heavy drinking. In this spirit, once dinner was over, we raised another glass or six to our later meetings on fire-watching nights at the pub behind St James's Street.

Speaking of old friends, it has come to my attention that old Flora Solomon was as sly a fox as one suspected her to be, confiding in money-mad Rothschild that she suspected Tommy Harris and myself were Soviet spies, since the 1930s. Confiding this information, in 1962! Well, she took her time about it, didn't she? Talk about not wanting to jump the gun. No doubt an elaborate act of revenge for what she considered my pro-Arab articles in the *Observer*. Her love for Israel trumped all else, in the end.

I thought of you as I had a routine check-up; science is wonderful and all that, but I am not particularly attracted to scanners; however, it seems they are rather attracted to me, as I was submitted to a radio-isotopic one (whatever that may be – the machine looked to me like the control room of a hydro-electric power station). Anyway, clever thing, apparently – the result, I must say, looked like the Great Red Spot on Jupiter. The doctors seemed quite happy, which was perhaps strange considering this and that.

Nothing to worry about too much, mind. It's really just a matter of my old Bronx which played up a bit last winter. I have had the weakness since the cradle and have hitherto ignored it as a merely annoying fact of life. But the doctors tell me, perhaps with some reason, that what you can laugh at when you're 30, 40 or 50, has to be taken seriously at 70, and more seriously still at 76 (just!).

I have also found myself wondering what became of your Tommy. We have a Tommy of our own, you know – or perhaps you don't. I am sorry that you never made it here, Edith. But I hope you felt proud, at the end. Is it wrong to say that I envied you your freedom? You got to live your life exactly as you ought; you never had to play a part. You were always wholly you.

For what it's worth, I don't know much – believe it or not – but I do know that history will remember us favourably. I am sure of that – none of this will have been in vain. For now, my only hope is that I shan't end up alone or dependent on servants (in this day and age, I find it extremely difficult to imagine that people so recently dead as my own parents put up with living-in servants; if my mother wanted a cup of tea, she had to ring a bell, or the cook would be offended and give notice. But, goddammit, I like making my own tea). It is difficult to realise that I have reached old age, but it is an inescapable arithmetical fact that 76 = '76. So from now on, easy does it, as I have no wish to foreshorten my sojourn in this vale of tears – not at least until I have seen the Reagans and Thatchers off. On which sombre note I will stop (you will doubtless have noticed that my typing mistakes are multiplying).

Well, as Bertie Wooster used to say, all flesh is as grass. So we go onwards and downwards. Although I now remember I left the vodka in the ice-box waiting to be broached when I return with the food – so it is at least upwards for now.

Until we meet again.

Yours,

Kim

Epilogue / notes on the cast

Edith Tudor-Hart died of cancer on 12 May 1973, at 2.30 a.m. at Cooper Cliff Nursing Home – a hospice for patients who cannot pay for private care. A nursing employee scattered her ashes in a pasture high above Brighton. Since her death, Edith has been recognised as an important and immensely talented photographer. Her existence has never been formally acknowledged by the Soviet Union.

Tommy Tudor-Hart died in 1987 while still incarcerated at Redhill, which by then had been renamed the Royal Earlswood Hospital. It was closed ten years later.

A year after Tommy's death, in 1988 Kim Philby died of heart failure in Moscow. He was given a state burial, with two of his five children present among the crowds who gathered to celebrate the life of a man considered a national hero.

Acknowledgements

I am grateful to so many people – dead and alive – who have supported, inspired and informed this book, not least the late journalists (and much-missed friends) Phillip Knightley and Chapman Pincher.

Huge thanks to members of Edith's family, including Peter Stephan Jungk who is Edith's great-nephew and the author of the German biography *Die Dunkelkammern der Edith Tudor-Hart: Geschichten eines Lebens,* and who was remarkably helpful in assisting my research for this book. His documentary-film *Tracking Edith* is a must-watch.

I am so grateful also to Edith's nephew, Peter Suschitzky, who offered time, energy and memories to this project.

In the Shadow of Tyranny by Duncan Forbes was a vital source of information.

Above all, this book would not have been possible without the use of the National Archives, files released to which are variously cited from, and extracted, throughout.

Special thanks to my Austrian family, the Steinwendtners – especially my dear cousin, Anna – who so ably and willingly assisted in answering my often very basic questions. And to my agent, Julia Silk, and editor/co-pilot Ann Bissell, who understood from the outset what I was trying to achieve with this book, and knew just how to make it happen. I must not, and will never, forget the support and thoughtful musings of my long-suffering husband, Barney, and our children.

Many others have offered guidance and insights over the years as the idea for this book formed. Thanks to Hayden B. Peake, Monica Bohm-Duchen, Dorothy Bohm, David Coppin, and Johnny Mains.

The following books aided my research, and would also provide interesting further reading for those interested in learning more about the characters in this novel:

Die Dunkelkammern der Edith Tudor-Hart: Geschichten eines Lebens, by Peter Stephan Jungk
Edith Tudor-Hart: In the Shadow of Tyranny, by Duncan Forbes
View From a Long Chair: The Memoirs of Jack Pritchard, by Jack Pritchard
Bauhaus Travel Book, by Ingolf Kern
Our Bauhaus: Memories of Bauhaus People, by Magdalena Droste and Boris Friedewald
Baku to Baker Street, by Flora Solomon and Barnet Litvinoff
Kim Philby: A Story of Friendship and Betrayal, by Tim Milne
The Lawn Road Flats: Spies, Writers and Artists, by David Burke
The Philby Files: The Secret Life of the Master Spy, by Genrikh Borovic
Philby: The Spy Who Betrayed a Generation, by Bruce Page, David Leitch and Phillip Knightley
Young Philby, by Robert Littell
Philby: KGB Master Spy, by Phillip Knightley

Treachery: Betrayals, Blunders and Cover-Ups: Six Decades of Espionage, by Chapman Pincher

The Secret World: A History of Intelligence, by Christopher Andrew

My Silent War, by Kim Philby

Circles and Squares: The Lives and Art of the Hampstead Modernists, by Caroline Maclean

A Time for Spies: Theodore Stephanovich Mally and the Era of the Great Illegals, by William E. Duff

Secret Intelligence Service file on
Edith Suschitzky

<u>EDITH TUDOR-HART</u>

<u>1. Personal particulars and general back-</u>
<u>ground</u>

Edith TUDOR-HART née SUSCHITZKY, an Austrian
Jewess, was born in Vienna on 24th August
1908. Her family were politically Social
Democrats and her father was a publisher/
bookseller by profession. She is known to
have a brother, Wolfgang SUSCHITZKY, and a
cousin, Carla, both of whom are now married.
   TUDOR-HART first came to the United Kingdom
as a student-governess in 1925. During the
course of the next few years she made the
acquaintance of Alexander TUDOR-HART, then
a medical student at St. Thomas's Hospital,
and was living with him at the end of 1930.
Although under notice of deportation in early
December 1930, Edith apparently visited Vienna

for Christmas that year with Alexander,
returning to the United Kingdom, whence she
was deported in January 1931. Following her
deportation, the reason for which was her
undesirable political (Communist) activities,
she returned to Vienna.

Alexander TUDOR-HART paid another visit to
Vienna to see Edith in early April 1931,
Edith maintaining contact with him by letter
between then and August 1933, when he returned
to Vienna to marry her. Prior to this date,
Alexander TUDOR-HART's life appears to have
been complicated by one Allison MacBETH, a
woman doctor who had been divorced by her
husband on account of the birth to her in
1927 of a son, of whom Alexander was the
father. TUDOR-HART was living with MacBETH
in 1929 and also appears to have had some
kind of relations with her during Edith's
absence from 1931 to 1933. Edith's letters
from this period show that there were certain
legal complications and obstructions to her
(Edith's) marriage to TUDOR-HART at this time.

During her two-year exile in Vienna, Edith
took up photography professionally, and, on
her return to the United Kingdom shortly
after her marriage to TUDOR-HART in August
1933, she set herself up in the same line
of business in London.

Her marriage to TUDOR-HART appears to have been somewhat uneven. They were reported to be living apart as early as April 1935. Between late December 1936 and November 1938, Alexander served in the International Brigade in Spain. Two letters from Edith to Spain in January and June 1937 suggest that they may have been reconciled at the time. In early 1940, however, TUDOR-HART had left for another woman, with whom he co-habited until October 1944, when Edith's divorce from him was made absolute. Alexander and Edith are reported to have met each other at irregular, but some-times frequent intervals, until at least 1946.

Edith TUDOR-HART's photography business seems to have been a paying proposition; it certainly prospered between 1935 and 1939, enabling her to run a studio in Duke Street, W.1. She now appears to make a fairly comfortable living from it, specialising in child photography, and running a studio in her flat in N.W.8. She is also prepared to visit houses in the greater London area to take photographs to order, and occasionally has her work published in such magazines as Picture Post.

She has the following relations in the United Kingdom:-

   a) Alexander TUDOR-HART, her former
      husband; a doctor now in practice at

        32 Park Road, Colliers Wood, S.W.19;
        an active Communist.

b) Tommy TUDOR-HART, her son by Alexander, born in 1936. He appears to be backward (if not mentally deficient) and is presently boarded at the Rudolf Steiner School in Aberdeen.

c) Wolfgang SUSCHITZKY (now known as Wolfgang DONAT, a naturalised British subject) her brother, a professional photographer and film camera man of 28 Willifield Way, N.W.11; an active Communist.

d) [SECTION REMOVED]

e) [SECTION REMOVED]

f) Adela SUSCHITZKY, mother, aged 72, now living in the Cricklewood area.

Edith TUDOR-HART is at present sharing her ground-floor flat at 12 Grove End Gardens with Christina DISHINGTON, a 35-year-old British subject who worked at the Warsaw Polish Embassy in 1947 and 1948. She is currently associated with the British/Polish Friendship Society.

2. Character of Edith TUDOR-HART

From such evidence as is on record (letters, observations, etc.) she would appear to be a rather a typical emotional, introspective and somewhat intellectual Viennese Jewess. She has for a long time had what possibly amounts to a morbid interest in psychology and psychiatry, and in 1942 was constantly taking her small son to clinics and specialists for psychiatric treatment. She is currently in touch with the Council for Mental Health. This interest probably stems in part from the condition of her son, now aged about fifteen, who appears to be mentally backward. She is apparently devoted to him.

A recent source report (October 1951 [REDACTED]) has described Edith as a "sick woman, highly neurotic and suffering from a persecution mania". She is said to be obsessed with the idea that the authorities are taking steps against her. However, she appears to be quite self-possessed from her telephone conversations, which do not reveal this alleged condition though it is perhaps worth recalling that [REDACTED] reported as long ago as 1946 that she was sensitive to the possibility of police investigation.

3. Security record

According to her 1951 Communist Party registration card, Edith TUDOR-HART joined the party in 1927, probably during her first visit to this country. It is in any case clear that between 1925 and 1930 she became attracted to Communism in the United Kingdom, since the reason for her deportation in January 1931 was that in the October of 1930 she had taken a prominent part in a Communist demonstration in London and had been seen to be on friendly terms with a number of leading (but unspecified) Communists. For some time prior to her deportation she had been living at Alexander TUDOR-HART's house in Westbourne Gardens, W.2, an address shared at this time by several other Austrian Communists and Rosa SHAR, who later married Percy GLADING. At the time of Edith's expulsion, Maurice DOBB wrote to Alexander (whom he clearly knew well) expressing his fury at the decision to deport her.

It is perhaps significant that in February 1931, after her deportation to Austria, Edith wrote asking Alexander to obtain from Communist Party- headquarters in London a certificate to the effect that she, Edith SUSCHITZKY, worked in the Party as "E. WHITE and was deported for that reason". She asked for the certificate to be sent by registered post and sealed, so that the English police should not come across it. The certificate was apparently to enable her to regularise her position with the Party in Vienna.

In mid-1931, she wrote to Alexander in London that she had been appointed the official photographer for Austria to the Moscow "Press Cliché". There is no implication that this involved a visit to Moscow, though she may have gone there. She obtained this appointment through the good offices of one Herr EBEL, the manager of TASS in Vienna at that time. EBEL seems to have loaned her a first-class camera for her work, which carried a salary. In her letter she asked Alexander to "press Rosa" (presumably SHAR) to obtain from INGULOV (then the TASS correspondent in London) as a matter of urgency a letter of recommendation to EBEL in Vienna. The significance of these connections with TASS are worth considering in the light of a report [REDACTED] in February 1947, which stated that TUDOR-HART had recently admitted having worked for the Russian intelligence service in Austria and Italy during 1932 and 1933. The exact nature of this work is not known, but it is alleged that she was responsible to a Russian colonel and used her photographic studio in Vienna for cover purposes. She was also arrested for these activities by the Austrian authorities, but released after spending several weeks in prison, for lack of evidence. These activities might also explain a panicky letter she wrote to Alexander on the 14th April 1931, which began "the camera is found", though its temporary loss made her feel "sick inside in spite of its recovery later". Edith's associate in these R.I.S. operations of 1932/33 is said to have been Arpad HAAS, a Hungarian Communist of long standing with an espionage record.

There is little of security significance on record about TUDOR-HART from her return to the United Kingdom as a British subject in August/September 1933 and August 1935.

[SECTION REMOVED]

From the investigation of Percy GLADING in February 1938 a number of receipts came to light which it is known that GLADING had wished destroyed. The receipts were for a Leica camera and other photographic equipment purchased by Edith in January 1937. GLADING used a Leica camera for his espionage work. The conclusion that he deliberately used Edith, an established professional photographer, to procure his equipment for him is almost irresistible. In this connection it is worth recalling Edith's association with Rosa SHAR, later Mrs. GLADING, in 1930 and 1931.

From 1938 onwards reports were received which indicated that Edith TUDOR-HART was becoming active in Austrian Communist refugee circles in London. The head of this group, with whom she is said to have become increasingly intimate over the next eight years, was Engelbert BRODA, a well-known Austrian scientist and atomic physicist of Communist leanings, now in the Soviet Zone of Austria.

In March 1941, TUDOR-HART was reported to be a member (the accountant) of the Central Committee of the Austrian Communist Party in Great Britain. She was in touch with a number of prominent Austrians, some of whom were interned at this time, and was living in the flat of Bruce BINFORD-HOLE — a legal advisor to the Austrian Centre and the Czech Refugee Trust Fund.

Intercepted telephone calls of August and September 1944 showed that Edith was in touch with Bob STEWART and Jimmy SHIELDS at Communist Party Headquarters for reasons which are not clear. Information from the same source disclosed in August 1945 that she was also known, at least in a professional capacity, to Nancy BERGER and Joan MAIZELS, two members of the so-called BERGER group of the Communist Party, which was during 1945 engaged in a so far unidentified form of undercover activity.

From 1945 she was said to have gathered an interesting circle of intellectuals around her and to have organised discussion groups. The circle, which contained such persons as D.N. PRITT, Lizzy FEAVRE, Arthur WYNN, and prominent Austrian Communists in the United Kingdom, flourished throughout 1945 and up to mid-1946, when it appears to have declined.

In recent years the reports received about TUDOR-HART's activities have mainly concerned her contacts with various British and alien Communists resident in the United Kingdom, including some members of her 1945/46 circle. Her activities, however, do not appear to have been of much significance, though it is clear that she has continued to hold Communist views, while she is known to hold a 1951 Party registration card. The latter is completed in the name of an alias — Betty GREY — possibly to protect her professional standing.

Finally, it is perhaps worth mentioning a number of largely inconsequential connections between TUDOR-HART and the Soviet Embassy in London. In July 1937 her name mentioned was non-committally in connection with a lecture. Two years later her back statement showed a payment to Walter NUKI, a dentist occasionally used by members of the Soviet embassy. [REDACTED] in 1945 she had been in touch with Dr SKOLNIKOFF, another dentist whose services are periodically in demand by the Soviet Embassy officials. SKOLNIKOFF'S wife, however, was reported to have been a photographer, which may explain the contact. According to the telephone check recently instituted on TUDOR-HART, she is in touch with Miriam RISNER, wife of Mark RISNER, Communist tailor whose clients include Harry POLLITT and

ZARUBIN, the Soviet Ambassador. The same check has indicated that TUDOR-HART probably knows Saine LOEFFLER, one of Jurgen KUCZYNSKI's sisters.

4. Connection with the PHILBYs

Edith TUDOR-HART was first reported to be in touch with Lizzy FEAVRE in the United Kingdom in September 1945, when Lizzy was described as a member of the TUDOR-HART circle. They may, however, conceivably have been known to each other before that date, having both previously lived in Vienna. Certainly both were in Vienna together between 1931 and 1933.

From the reports received [REDACTED]in 1945 and 1946, Lizzy FEAVRE and Georg HONIGMANN (with whom FEAVRE was then living) were members of the TUDOR-HART circle, and together with other Austrian and British intellectuals used to meet regularly for political discussion.

At the end of August 1951, [REDACTED] TUDOR-HART expressed anxiety lest her flat be raided by the police. She said that she had therefore been going through some old photographic negatives, selecting for destruction those which might harm her were they found by the police. Amongst the latter, she had selected

those of D.N. PRITT, Paul ROBESON and PHILBY.
TUDOR-HART mentioned [REDACTED] that Philby
was "an ace man in M.I.5" and described his
family background. [REDACTED] certain that
TUDOR-HART had not been in touch with PHILBY
during [REDACTED] association with her, and
assumed that the PHILBY's photograph must
date from the 1930s.

[REDACTED] further stated that TUDOR-HART
after 1946, has been accustomed to sending
food parcels to Lizzy HONIGMANN in Berlin,
but ceased doing so at Lizzy's request some
time ago. [REDACTED] thought that the reason
for this may have been Lizzy's fear that
the Russians might take exception to this
kind of connection with the West.

5. Conclusions

  a) There is no form of evidence, beyond
     her own admissions to [REDACTED], of
     Edith TUDOR-HART's work for the Russian
     Intelligence Service, either in Austria
     or in the United Kingdom. The diversity
     and character of her contacts in this
     country, however, only serve to raise
     her above the mask of unimportant rank-
     and-file alien Communists and to set
     her into a special category. Exactly
     what her work in the United Kingdom
     for the Communist cause has amounted

to is difficult to assess, but there is a possibility that she has been a Russian intelligence service contact, possibly a talent-spotter, or a cut-out and means of communication between the British Communist Party and Austrian Communist Party in exile during the war years. At all events, she has been a convinced Communist in touch with top-ranking Communists and known Russian spies for the past twenty-five years.

b) The parallels between her marriage to Alexander TUDOR-HART and Lizzy FRIEDMANN's to PHILBY is worth some consideration. In both cases the husband, a British national, went to Vienna to marry a woman with a known Communist, and possibly R.I.S. or Comintern, background. These marriages were contracted at the time of political turmoil in Austria, when the R.I.S. and Comintern might well have sought such means to protect their agents.

c) Edith TUDOR-HART clearly knows PHILBY. There is no direct evidence that they have ever met, unless it can be assumed from her having a photograph of him. Kim PHILBY and Edith TUDOR-HART were clearly in Vienna at the same time

for several months during the latter
half of 1933. It is also clear that
Edith had post-1940 information about
PHILBY since she was able to describe
him (albeit somewhat inaccurately) as
an ace man in M.I.5. This information
may, of course, have come from Lizzy.
It is also worth speculating whether
Alexander knew PHILBY either in London
or Cambridge in the period 1930/34.
TUDOR-HART himself took his B.A. at
King's College, Cambridge in 1926, but
is believed to have returned there
for postgraduate medical study some
time in the 1930s.

B2a
1.12.51